After the fall of Queen Mab, DJ Suzuki res
of entertaining, drinking, and hooking up
twenty ageless years, she knows she can't
the fact that her brother still searches for h
her that her parents might have had a
orientation.

When a young woman named Talia shows up at DJ's workplace desperate for help, DJ sees a way to rid herself of the guilt of staying away: she'll take Talia where she needs to go if Talia rids DJ's family of all memory of her. Talia will be safe and DJ will be free to live in the Faerie Realm with a clear conscious. Everyone wins.

Except there's more to Talia and her situation than she's letting on. Her pursuers want more than just her. They want the Faerie Court, and Talia is the key to getting it. If DJ can't get Talia to safety before they catch up, a guilty conscious will be the least of her worries. She just might have a faerie civil war on her hands.

A NineStar Press Publication

Published by NineStar Press
P.O. Box 91792,
Albuquerque, New Mexico, 87199 USA.
www.ninestarpress.com

The Tale of a Faerie Knight

ISBN: 978-1-947904-75-0

Printed in the USA
First Edition
December, 2017

Also available in eBook

ISBN: 978-1-947904-69-9

THE TALE OF A FAERIE KNIGHT

The Faerie Court Chronicles,

Book Two

Tay LaRoi

Dedication

To Sophia—this book wouldn't have grown without your thoughts and insights. Thank you.
To Roz and Ashley—you're the best publicity coordinators I could have asked for. Thank you.
To Roz—Thank you for teaching me to be brave.

Chapter One

THE SOFT GLARE from the street lamp outside wakes me up. The soft drone of my box fan tempts me back to sleep, but the knocking at my door makes that impossible. I swear under my breath, but I should be grateful. I need to get up and get ready to go to work.

It turns into pounding as I roll out of bed and hunt for pants.

"Keep your wings attached," I bark, wiggling into a pair. "I'm coming."

The tiny little man at the door looks me over and scowls at my stained T-shirt, dirty jeans, and bedhead. Given that he's wearing leaves, vines, and moss shoes, I don't think he has room to judge. Thankfully, there's no one coming in or out of the apartments to see him.

"Delivery for Ms. DJ Suzuki," he grunts, holding out a large wooden crate. At least he's calling me DJ instead of Daisy Jane now.

I take it and perch it on my hip. With my free hand, I take a handful of pinecones and acorns from the bucket by the door and dump them into the man's hands. As he counts out his payment, I survey the contents of the crate. It's filled with fruits, vegetables, breads, a gallon of milk—*hey, wait a minute.*

With a tip of his dusty cap, the little man says, "A pleasure as always."

"Hey, whoa, hold on," I snap. "There should be a bottle of wine in here."

The man blinks up at me, then twiddles his thumbs. "Pardon me, miss, but I only make your deliveries. I don't pack them."

I study the large satchel hanging from his shoulder. It looks pretty weighed down, if you ask me. "What's in the bag?"

He shoves it behind his back. "Is Miss accusing me of lying?" With his squeaky voice, it's more like a small shriek. "Faeries can't lie. You ought to know that."

"Yeah, but you bastards steal anything and everything. Hand it over."

"Miss can't have my delivery bag. You didn't pay for it."

I glance at the clock on the stove and it nearly gives me a heart attack. It's 8:45 and I need to be at work at nine. I forgot to set an alarm. Curse my love of sleep.

"All right, here." I dig in the bucket by the door again and pull out a small plastic baggie. "You give me my wine and I'll give you this dirt from a witch's grave. Deal?"

His eyes get as big as harvest moons, and I know I've got him hooked like a goblin on gold. He digs around in his bag and, lo and behold, pulls out my bottle of Pixie Dust Sparkling Wine. "You drive a hard bargain, Miss."

We make the exchange, and he studies the dirt in the bag like an elated mad scientist, then tips his hat again. "Have a lovely evening, Miss." With a series of pops and a wisp of smoke, he disappears, leaving behind the smell of burnt herbs. His evening probably won't be so lovely once he realizes I got that dirt from a playground.

Oh, well.

I kick the door shut behind me and sort my groceries like a mad woman, tossing the things that need it in the fridge and leaving the rest of the counter. Glass jars filled with herbs for tea line the bottom of the crate, even though I assured my boss I still had plenty. If the faerie food didn't give me longevity, then surely the amount of herbal tea they make me drink would.

Being cursed to only eat faerie food from here to eternity isn't so bad, given how much healthier they eat than humans. The only things I ever miss are my mom's homemade lasagna and my dad's barbecue. Faeries don't cook much of either, unfortunately.

Thankfully, they like chocolate almost as much as I do. There's three bars sitting between the teas. Heedless of the time, I squeal for joy and rip the paper off of one, chomping off a huge bite and letting the beautiful blend of bitter and sweet cocoa melt on my tongue as slowly as possible, because, in addition to tasting like heaven, it tastes like home.

It tastes like chocolate chip cookies, fresh out the oven after making snowmen in the moonlight with my brother. It tastes like Halloween candy and staying up late to watch scary movies. It tastes like cake at countless birthday parties.

Just like the chocolate, the aftertaste of the memories is more bitter than sweet. I wrap it up and reach for an apple instead.

I throw on a black tank top and take a few bites. The shirt reveals the rivers of Japanese wood-block style images interwoven with Gaelic knots tattooed down my muscular arms. As I one-handedly rake a brush through my hair, a tuff of dark brown on top of my head and pixie-short sides, I finish the apple with the other. There's nothing but the core as I put on some basic makeup: foundation, mascara, and some smoky eye shadow to frame my round monolid eyes like my dad's. A bit of tinted lip balm is enough for my full lips, which match my mother's.

The clock on the stove reads 8:55 by the time I grab my equipment bag and head out the door for the night. A few of the building tenants smile as they pass me on the stairs, and I return the gesture, even though I've never learned a single name. It's too risky. People would notice too many strange things after a while, like strange little men delivering my groceries for example. Besides, my nightly work schedule doesn't leave a lot of room for a normal social life, even if I did still know how to socialize with humans. I'm not sure I do.

On hot June nights like this, I drive with my windows down. The wind off Lake Michigan feels fresh and alive. It fuels the hustle and bustle of downtown Grand Harbor and helps wake me up for the long night ahead.

While the city hums with activity—tourist families shopping, local artists selling their works, independent musicians trying to make it on the bar scene—the area where I work is as dead as the old factory buildings that surround it. At least, it is for now. In a few hours, it'll come alive.

Not that the humans will ever know.

When I first left the Faerie Court all those months ago, I thought it would be hard to walk the fine line of existing in the two worlds, but it's actually quite simple. When I work, I'm a part of the Faerie Realm: magic and strange creatures intermingling in a world just out of humanity's line of sight. At home, I'm as human as I was before I stumbled into my mistress's lair those twenty years ago. It's all TV, eating out, and paying my bills. The two don't mix. Faeries want nothing to do with the Human Realm and most humans don't believe in faeries enough to go looking for them.

Not that they should.

I park and slip in the nightclub's back door. The vacant dance floor and dark empty chairs look eerier while unoccupied than when they're overflowing with mystical creatures. I hate being alone in this place. Luckily, I hardly ever am. I find my boss, Iver, in his natural habitat behind the bar whistling as he takes inventory. He doesn't notice me come in, so I take the opportunity to mess with him.

As he kneels below the counter, I silently plop down on a barstool and wait. He sets a nearly empty bottle of vodka on the bar, which I hide behind my back the second his hand disappears again. He reaches back up for it, gropes around, then stands back up with a cross look on his face.

"Evening, Iver," I greet with a wide, unassuming grin. "How's it going?"

He shakes his head, but smirks, and holds out his hand for the bottle. "It was going great before my imp of an employee showed up. You're late, by the way."

"In my defense, the delivery faerie tried to cheat me out of my alcohol. I couldn't just let that slide." I hand him the bottle and hop off the stool. "Which reminds me..."

As he puts the bottle in its original spot, I flip the door latch and let myself behind the counter. He's tall, even for an elf, so I have to stand on my toes and pull on his shoulder to plant a kiss on his cheek. It's completely innocent. He made it clear on day one he didn't date employees. It's kind of a bummer. He's a looker and that's been my only standard for a while now.

"Thank you for the chocolate."

"I figured you deserved it." He wipes my kiss off with the back of his hand. "You've been working particularly hard lately, despite your tardiness."

"That's because I don't have any more online classes to worry about, thank God." Since I wound up trapped in Faerie at sixteen, I never finished high school. There's a lot I don't understand about the twenty-first century, but being able to get a GED online has been an absolute blessing, especially since dial-up is a thing of the past. Having friends in Faerie that were willing to help me write up some fake transcripts certainly helped too.

I can't tell you why I got the dumb thing. The Faerie Realm isn't exactly renowned for its stellar universities, so it's not like I'm going to be continuing my education any time soon, seeing as I'm not going anywhere. I've got all the time, booze, fun, and entertainment in the world, so why would I? A little voice in the back of my head, which sounded a lot like my brother, just told me it was a good idea. My brother tended to have a lot of those. I get pissed at myself for getting it if I think about it too long. It's almost like I still want my family to be proud of me or some shit, which is nonsense.

I kneel behind the bar and hunt for something to drink. It's all here for faerie consumption, so I have plenty to pick from. I think I'll go with a rum and Coke.

"If you're so grateful to me, maybe you'll ease my nerves and drink a little less?" Iver raises an eyebrow as he watches me drop ice into a glass.

"I don't know what you're talking about," I reply, precariously measuring out the rum. "I don't drink that much. And I always make sure to sober up before I leave. Can't enjoy eternity if I'm dead."

Iver sighs. "What if a human were to come in here and see you?"

"Humans don't come in here," I remind him, swirling my drink before taking a sip. Needs more rum. Maybe a little vodka to dilute the sweetness. "The one time they did, Calista got rid of them."

She accidentally got rid of me too. Some dweeb asked her to bewitch a group of human girls, who had wandered in here, to make them leave. Since I didn't come here that often back then, she thought I was one of them. It was quite startling to be dancing one minute only to wake up on James-Child College's campus the next. We've become pretty good...well, I'm not sure what you'd call us.

"I just don't like taking risks. That's all," Iver says.

I roll my eyes and lean on the counter. "Right. Mr. Let's-Stage-A-Coup doesn't like taking risks."

Iver gives me a dirty look. He doesn't like it when I bring up the coup last October in which he and a bunch of his buddies took back the Faerie Court. He's too humble. Given that he helped take out Queen Mab, whom I served for the better half of twenty years, I'm eternally grateful to him and everyone else for it.

"That was a completely different situation," he huffs. "You're comparing pixies to trolls."

"If you say so. How's the court doing, anyway? Other than sending us more enjoyable customers, that is."

Iver wipes the whole counter down before he answers. "It's fine."

"Uh-oh. Trouble in paradise?"

My boss glances around the club to make sure we're still alone. Leaning close, he mutters, "You know the string of human disappearances lately?"

"Yeah. It's all over the news around here." I down the rest of my drink and reach for the bottle again.

"The queen is starting to suspect it has something to do with Faerie. More specifically, the Mab supporters who broke out last November."

I give an impressed whistle. "Queen Titania inherited quite a mess, huh?"

I really feel for the woman. First, her sister, Mab, took the throne and trashed the place for about a hundred years, then as soon as she gets it back, several of her sister's supporters manage to escape. Now she's got human disappearances on her plate? Who would want to be Queen of Faerie?

"I thought faeries only snatched children," I muse, mixing my second drink. "Every missing person I've seen so far is either in their late teens or early twenties."

"We're not supposed to anymore. She dismissed the connection at first, but apparently, she's picking up a pattern. They're all loners. They disappear at night with their doors locked and live in secluded, wooded areas."

"What does Queen Shaylee think?"

These days, the Faerie Court is split in two. Queen Titania rules the Seelie Court, the area around here. Her daughter, Shaylee, rules the Unseelie Court farther to the south. I've never met Queen Shaylee, but if the stories I've heard about her are true, I wouldn't be surprised if she was behind it. After pretending to be Queen Mab's long-lost daughter and tricking a human girl into sacrificing herself so that the coup could happen, she doesn't seem like the most trustworthy individual.

"Her Majesty Shaylee is currently away, dealing with some rowdy solitary fae," Iver says. "Though her champion, Dominic, assures Queen Titania that there hasn't been any suspicious activity in the Unseelie Court."

"Of course, he said there isn't," I scoff. I scowl down at my glass. I jacked up the rum-cola ratio again.

"Dominic's loyalty still lies more with Titania. If he thought Shaylee was doing something wrong, he'd be sure to say so." Iver snatches the rum bottle out of my reach and sets it on the counter behind him. "And you have a job to do, missy. Don't get out of control."

"I'm not," I huff, swirling my drink. "I've worked in far more inebriated states than this."

Iver sighs. "Don't you have equipment to set up?"

I throw back the rest of my drink and wipe my mouth. "All right, all right. I'm going. Thanks for the gossip update."

Iver takes my glass. "You're an honorary faerie. You ought to be in the know."

Honorary faerie. That has a nice ring to it.

A few regulars trickle into the club as I set up my music equipment. Luckily, all the speakers, mics, and most of the wires were here when I took the job back in November. I just had to provide my own laptop and controller. Neither of them are very fancy, and I had to learn on the fly. Truth be told, I'm okay at best. I can do basic effects, put together a decent playlist, and weave it together seamlessly, but that's about it. I'm more of an acoustic guitar girl, honestly.

At least, I was before I got trapped in Faerie. I haven't touched a guitar in forever.

Lucky for me, faeries aren't very picky when it comes to human music. As long as they can dance, they're happy, so by eleven, the dance floor is filling up with people and creatures who look like they walked straight out of storybooks and nightmares. Bright glistening wings shimmer in the flashing lights while hollow eyes beckon into the shadows those too naive to know any better. Wispy ghostlike women twirl around men made of sticks and stones, promising them all the stars in the sky in exchange for a drink at the bar. They might give them the stars with or without the drinks since they're all so high on this place. I feel it too. The rhythm, the magic-infused atmosphere, the secrets and mysteries growing in the shadows. It's all more intoxicating than the alcohol I've already consumed.

So are some of the people who dance in the crowd.

The woman who slips behind my workstation is the perfect example. She runs a finger up my spine as the overwhelming smell of cloves hits me, then she wraps her arms around my waist, swaying in time to the music with me.

"Evening, Calista," I greet, craning my neck to meet her sparkling green eyes.

She removes one of my headphones to whisper, "Have you missed me?" That smooth, sultry voice sends a chill through me. Her cool body sends another one.

"Of course," I reply. "Where've you been? I haven't seen you around lately."

"Out and about," she giggles. "You know how it is."

I sure do. I have no idea how or where Calista spends most of her time, and I guess it's not really any of my business. What I do know is that whenever we happen to bump into each other here at the club, we have a good time together, no strings attached. Some of the other patrons are pretty good substitutes, male and female alike, but I'd be lying if I said Calista wasn't something special.

"Looks like you're working hard," she mutters, lowering her lips to my jaw. "You deserve a break."

I swallow hard and try to think straight, which is nearly impossible since her hands have started to roam. "Enticing as always, but I've got another two hours before my break. Iver'd have my hide if I slipped off now."

Calista huffs and lays her head on my shoulder. "Who am I supposed to play with until then?"

"Go dance," I suggest, lowering the volume on one song as another starts. "I'm sure you'll find somebody."

"I wanna dance with *you*, though," Calista insists, slipping one hand down to the lining of my jeans. "You're my favorite."

I try to ignore the way my heart jumps and how my skin heats up and attempt to focus on fading to the next song instead. Paying attention to those reactions could mean I might be developing feelings for her, and that's a no-go. She just meant that she has a better time fooling around with me than with other people here. That's it.

"How about this," I say. "My buzz is wearing off. Go get me a drink, and then we'll try to work something out, okay?"

"Sounds good." Calista kisses my neck and disappears. She shimmies through the dancing crowd, her loose translucent sleeves and bare midriff flowing with the beat while her low-hanging skirt sways.

I try to focus on the music and forget her words. I'm her favorite in the way we all have our favorite drinks to get wasted with. That's it. Even if she meant something more, it's not like I'd pry and risk ruining the fun we have. Trying to get close to people, opening up to them, that's the quickest way to let things go to shit, *especially* in the Faerie Realm. And I don't mean just bad breakups. She could get seriously hurt. Not everyone here likes that I'm human or that I used to work for Queen

Mab. They could use either of those facts to get...creative. Things are fine the way they are. Besides, nymphs aren't exactly famous for their ability to hold down a steady relationship.

Time passes, and then some more creeps by. I'm beginning to think Calista found someone else after all, but I survey the crowd just in case. I really did want that drink.

The Employees Only door flies open and catches my eye. It only leads to the back parking lot, but Iver usually keeps it cursed so no one can sneak in without paying. Since I'm human, I'm the only one who can go in and out without getting hurt.

A young woman sprawls in anyway, disheveled, bruised, and barefoot. She tries to straighten her ripped gown and breathes heavily as she looks around, in what appears to be an attempt to get patrons' attention, with shaking hands and wide eyes

Someone help me.

Chapter Two

I SET MY equipment to take care of itself for a while and go after the girl. If she needs help, this is the last place she'll find it. Iver might be able to do something, but there's no way to tell until I catch up to her. Thanks to her height, she's easy to pick out in the dancing crowd and shifting lights. She's probably average height for a human girl, five six or five seven, but tall around faeries (and me, sad to say). Once I catch up, I can make out her words.

"You've got to help me," she pleads, clinging to the nearest person, only to be pushed away. "Please. They can't find me."

A young man dressed in all black intercepts her. He's made of smoldering eyes, bedhead, trouble, and a devilish smile. "I might be able to help you, love." His sharp eyes look her up and down, resting briefly on her long legs and full chest. "For a price, of course."

What a creep.

I elbow my way between them and take a bit of smug satisfaction in knocking the wind out of him. "Buzz off, pal," I snap. "I'll handle this."

"I saw her first," the man snarls, snatching me by the arm and turning me around.

"And I help run this joint," I bark back, smacking his hand away. "You wanna get kicked out? Back. Off."

He glowers down at me with a glare that threatens to spark violence. Let his punk-ass glare. I've taken down faeries twice my size—which still isn't very big, but whatever. Like this dweeb is going to scare me. And is he *looking* at me? In what realm does picking fights with muscular people covered in tats seem like a good idea?

The loser straightens his jacket, flashes the girl one more mischievous smile, then melts into the crowd. With him gone, I turn to talk to her, only to lose my words at the sight of her face. I know those green eyes. Her full rosy mouth, slender nose, and high cheekbones send my mind whirling because I saw them every day for the past twenty years. Those green eyes lit up every time I slaughtered some poor innocent who accidentally insulted the crown. That mouth turned to a snarl any time I dared to argue or didn't do something exactly as I was told, never mind whether I was given the proper instructions. That nose turned up when I awoke with a start from a dream about my family.

I shake off the shock and the lingering buzz. That's why I'm seeing what I'm seeing. This girl isn't Queen Mab. They just have a few similar features. That's all. People look like each other all the time. I'm just a little tipsy. The longer I look at this girl, the less she looks like the woman I once served. Mab didn't have freckles or blonde hair. Mab's ears tapered to a point like every other faerie I've seen around here, and this girl's are rounded like mine. She must be human, which is exactly why she shouldn't be here.

She gently shakes me out of my thoughts. "Please, is there somewhere I can hide?"

I take her by her wrists. "Slow down. What are you doing here?"

The girl takes a deep breath. "I was kidnapped by a group of trolls and goblins. They're dragging me to only the gods know where, but they stopped nearby for the night. I managed to bewitch them and escape, but I'm sure it's worn off by now. My magic's terrible."

"Wait, what? Your magic? But you're..."

A light bulb flicks on.

"You're half human."

"Correct. Now can you help me or not?"

I don't think I can, but Iver might be able to. Queen Shaylee's half human, and he's pretty good friends with her. He'll know what to do with this girl, even if she's being kidnapped. I take her hand and lead her toward the bar.

The girl squeezes my hand and whispers, "Thank you."

She's warm like a human. I can't remember the last time I felt this sort of heat, the gentle warm pulse that radiates from within.

I shake my head again. Maybe Iver's right. I should quit drinking.

Nah. Just lighten up.

We wiggle through the crowd near the bar, so I can slip behind the counter. "Iver, we've got a situation."

He turns our way, still pouring a drink, and frowns. "What did you break this time?"

"Bite me. I didn't break anything. Look, this girl needs help." I pull her forward, so my boss can have a look at her. "She said a bunch of trolls and goblins kidnapped her." As he looks her over, I stand on my tiptoes to whisper in his ear, "And she's half human."

His eyes go wide and blink at me a few times, then at the girl. He studies her for a few minutes more and concludes, "So you are."

"What should we do?" I ask.

Iver looks over our heads toward the entrance. "Get down."

Sure enough, there's a troll lumbering through the doorway. He must be young because he only has to duck to get in. The dim and flashing lights don't do any favors for his ashen complexion and warts. The other patrons give him a wide berth. As if a troll's bulk isn't enough to scare people off, it looks like he hasn't washed that brown tunic in years. It can't smell pleasant.

The three goblins that tag along aren't much better. Their big ears flap and their long noses bounce with their crouched steps. They can't be that old either. Two hundred years old, maybe. Two hundred fifty, tops.

I turn to tell the girl to get beneath the counter, but she already thought of that. She's curled up beside the mini-freezer, hugging her legs to her chest for dear life. Iver glances around the bar, giving everyone a warning look to keep their mouths shut. Judging by the way everyone goes quiet and stiff at the group's approach, there shouldn't be an issue.

Even if we weren't hiding a possible fugitive, I doubt anyone would give these guys a warm welcome. Ever since the Faerie Courts split back up, faeries in Seelie Court lands haven't been too fond of faeries that willingly served Queen Mab, like trolls and goblins. One hundred years of oppression will do that to people. There are exceptions to every rule of course, but this crew doesn't look like one of them.

The goblins hop up on a couple of barstools and lean over the counter. "Evening, Iver," one says with a snaggle-toothed grin. "How's business?"

"It *was* going well until your sorry lot showed up," Iver grumbles, drying a martini glass.

"How's that sorry traitor cousin of ours, Hob, doing these days?" asks the other, tugging at his ripped ear.

"He's well." Iver sighs. "Happy to be away from cretins like you, I'm sure."

The three hooligans scowl at my boss.

"Enough niceties," Snaggle-Tooth spits. "We're looking for a half-human girl. Tall, blonde, green eyes, freckles. She came in through your back door. See anyone like that?"

Iver thinks it over as he stabs a cherry with a tiny plastic sword. "I've been here at the bar all night, so I would have seen her. Seen anyone with that description, DJ?"

"She sounds cute, so I'd definitely have noticed her if she came in," I answer.

The troll squares his massive shoulders. "You didn't really answer, elf," he growls. "And we can smell the stench of iron from her."

"That would be me," I say, pointing to myself. "Full-blooded human right here. And screw you. I don't smell that bad."

"She must have left already," Iver suggests.

"Wouldn't hurt to have a look around then," Snaggle-Tooth says, sliding off his stool.

Iver glares at them. "It would indeed, seeing as you haven't told me what this girl has done." His voice lowers to a dangerous quiet, and I snicker. Oh boy, these guys are going to get it.

"Ain't none of your business what she did," snaps Ripped-Ear.

Aw yeah, here we go.

Iver hands one of the patrons his drink with a sickly sweet grin and asks him if he needs anything else. When he says no, Iver turns the grin toward the troublemaker and turns to step out from the bar. The other patrons begin to whisper and back up from the bar. Some are placing bets.

Nobody tells Iver what is and isn't his business in his club. I don't even think the Faerie Queens would have the gall to try. I'm glad these guys do, though, because this is about to get interesting. I crack my knuckles in preparation.

"You clearly don't come around here much, so I'll explain to you how this is going to go," Iver says. "You're going to tell me why you want this girl and under whose authority you're looking for her, then I may or may not let you search my club. If I don't, you're going to turn around and walk out. Understood?"

The goblins shrink back. Even the troll seems caught off guard by the ice in my boss's voice, despite the fact that his grin hasn't budged. The troll tries to bounce back and pops his neck. "The little wench knocked us unconscious and stole something from us. We're here on our own damn authority. Can we go now?"

Iver's smile widens and I'm even starting to get a little freaked out. "Afraid you'll have to wait until she leaves my club, gentlemen, if she's even here. Now get out—"

Snaggle-Tooth stabs a serrated dagger at Iver's stomach.

Iver steps to the side as if he were dodging a child. The goblin swipes again, but Iver catches his arm and twists it at an angle that makes a pretzel look comfortable. As Snaggle-Tooth howls and drops his dagger, Ripped-Ear takes a dive at him, but his nose collides with my fist. I cringe at the touch of his oily, squishy flesh, but I'm sure that's nothing compared to the pain that followed the sickening *crack* I just heard.

The troll roars, giving away his attack, and I tumble out of the way.

"What the hell are you doing?" Iver calls. He has Snaggle-Tooth in a headlock.

"Helping," I reply. The troll snatches at me, catches me by my shirt, and tosses me across the club like I don't weigh anything.

So much for helping.

I crash and break a table in a flash of pain, a lack of breath, and a spinning nightclub. Stumbling to my feet and spitting blood, I grab a table leg and charge the troll again in spite of my inability to think straight. He pries Iver off his friend who gasps for air and feels around for his knife. Once he finds it, a nasty sneer comes to his lips.

Luckily the troll's back is turned to me as he lifts Iver to his feet.

"You could have made this easy," Snaggle-Tooth snickers. "Now we're going to find that girl *and* take your little club for our friends. There are more of us, you see. More than you could—"

Chair.

Table.

Whack.

I bring the table leg down as hard as I can on the troll's skull. It might be thick, but it's not very resilient. The troll sways and his knees buckle as he goes down. Iver breaks out of his slackened grip and jumps out of the way as the troll falls. Snaggle-Tooth isn't so lucky. He lets out a startled cry for help, then disappears under his giant friend. Ripped-Ear tries to pull his cousin or brother or whatever out from under the troll, blood still streaking down his face, neck, and shirt.

Meanwhile, I limp over to Iver and lift my left hand. My right wrist is too sore for someone to be smacking that hand. "Nice teamwork, boss man," I say. "Gimme five."

Iver scowls down at me.

"C'mon, don't leave me hanging."

"You should not have gotten involved," he scolds, leaning down to pick up Snaggle-Tooth's dagger. "You could have gotten hurt."

"Um, hello, I *did* get hurt and I lived. It's no big deal."

"Still, you need to be more careful. You're not a faerie knight anymore."

"So? I still got all the badass skills that come with it."

Snaggle-Tooth finally comes free. He and Ripped-Ear strain and grunt in their effort to drag the troll toward the door.

"You'll be sorry," Snaggle-Tooth snarls.

"More will come for that girl next time, and then you'll pay," growls Ripped-Ear.

"Yeah, yeah, and we'll wish we never messed with you," I call after them, rolling my eyes. "Now beat it."

Once they're gone, the club goes back to normal. Patrons come back to the bar, some exchange money and others pout at me. Apparently, I threw off a few wagers by jumping in. Whatever. It's not like I was getting a cut of the bets.

The girl pokes her head over the bar to check if the coast is clear, then slowly gets to her feet. "Are they really gone?"

"Probably not," Iver answers, joining her behind the bar. "They're waiting outside, no doubt. It would be best if you waited here for a while." Turning to me, he mutters, "Take her to my office and figure out what on earth is going on. I'll make sure the music is under control."

"Please don't break anything," I plead. "That stuff was expensive."

He gently nudges me toward the girl. "Just go."

She blinks at us, her face blank. I jerk my head toward Iver's office, and she follows behind so close that she manages to step on my heels. Once inside, she takes a seat in front of Iver's surprisingly ordinary wooden desk.

It always trips me out how incredibly normal this room looks. When Iver first offered me the job, right around the time of the coup, I expected his office to look like a mini-forest: the floor covered in leaves, trees lining the walls, even a little stream running through it. But, no. It's a plain-looking office. The only strange thing is that he doesn't have a computer. He hates technology.

I lean on the desk and cross my legs, glad to be taller than the girl, at least for a little while. "Okay, start talking," I say. "Who are you and what the hell did my boss and I just get ourselves into?"

The girl sighs and slouches, folding her hands between her knees. "My name is Talia, but I don't completely understand what's going on."

"You mean you don't know why they kidnapped you?"

Talia looks me square in the eye and says, "No. All I know is, one moment I'm minding my business, walking home from the lake, and the next I'm pinned to the ground, bound, gagged, and hauled off."

"What lake are we talking about here?"

"Lake Superior. I live near Blue Fish Point with my three aunts."

That's in the Upper Peninsula. I've never been, but it's a popular enough tourist destination that I've heard of it. Apparently, it's a town a lot like Grand Harbor. The whole UP belongs to solitary fae, faeries that don't swear allegiance to any court. They don't have many ties to any faeries here in the courts, so I'm rather curious as to why anyone went all the way up there to snatch someone.

"Did they say why they took you?" I ask.

"They just said, 'We caught ourselves a half-breed. We're going to be rich.'"

Who would want to kidnap a half-human girl? They're rare, but not unheard of or particularly powerful. Queen Shaylee of the Unseelie Court is half, but no one's ever given her trouble for it, which leads me to believe I'm not getting the whole story.

"What did you steal from those guys?"

Talia glowers. Despite her apparent innocence, it's an intimidating look. "Myself."

That part is believable enough.

Now to decide what to do. No doubt she just wants to go home. I suppose I could take her. Even if she's not telling the whole truth, it won't be my problem for long. Driving to Blue Fish Point would probably take a full day, but it's mostly a straight shot on I-75. No big deal. We can't leave right now, though, and I certainly don't want to drive in the morning without any sleep. I don't want to saddle Iver with her either.

"Here's the game plan," I say. "By morning, when I get off of work, hopefully those creeps will be gone. If not, we lose them with my car and hide out at my place. You can contact your aunts and let them know you're safe. We crash for a few hours, then I'll take you home. Sound good?"

Talia's eyes come alight, and she beams up at me. "That sounds wonderful. Thank you ever so much."

My heart catches in my chest. How the hell did I mistake her for Mab? This girl is clearly too pure.

"Yeah, well—" I cough, heading for the door. "—it's not like I can just leave you. Just, stay here until I come get you. Take a nap or read one of Iver's books or something. Just don't leave."

"Yes, ma'am."

I cringe. "For the love of God, don't call me ma'am. My name is DJ."

"Okay, DJ." Talia giggles. "Heh. It rhymes."

What the hell did I just get myself into?

I pop back behind the bar to explain to Iver what's going on. He seems on board enough with the plan, and just a little too smug for my liking.

"What are you smirking about?" I demand.

"Oh, nothing," he muses. "It's just interesting how you declined to join the knights of both the Unseelie and Seelie Courts after Queen Mab's death, yet here you are protecting a damsel in distress."

"Their Majesties wouldn't have me saving damsels."

"Do you *want* to save damsels?"

I purse my lips before I say something else incriminating. There's no point in telling him that he's getting it twisted without explaining everything and I'm not about to explain a damn thing. The new queens are better than Mab—there's no denying that—but they would still have the power to make me do whatever they wanted. Let's just say Mab abused that, so I'm not keen on giving it out any time soon. That's the simple line I feed myself to get me through the day, but I know it wouldn't be good enough for Iver. Best just to flip him off and move on.

The rest of the night goes by without incident. I keep an eye on the entrance, Iver's office, and the Employees Only door, but nothing stranger than normal comes about. Calista also never gets back to me with my drink, but I'm inclined to let that slide tonight.

Once everyone clears out and Iver begins to lock up, I go get Talia from the office. She's curled up in Iver's chair behind the desk like a sleeping mouse. Her hands are folded between her legs, her chin tucked into her chest, and her bare feet nestled between the armrest and seat cushion. Now that I get the chance to really look at her, she's more fae than I first realized. There are leaves and twigs entwined in her blonde hair, her dress is equal parts worn-out fabric, vines, flowers, and leaves, and the bottoms of her feet are dark with dirt.

She's a child of two worlds.

I nudge her awake, but she snuggles deeper into the leather chair. "C'mon," I say softly. "You can sleep back at my place, but we gotta go."

"Hmm? Oh." Talia finally sits up, stretches, rubs her eyes, and follows me without another word. She thanks Iver as we cross the club, and he flashes me a knowing smirk again, which I respond to by sticking out my tongue. He just laughs and finishes cleaning up.

Talia turns and asks, "What's so funny?"

"Nothing," I answer, peeking outside the Employees Only door. The coast looks clear, and thankfully, it's only about fifty feet to my car. The two of us make a mad dash and dive in. Still nothing. The car doesn't seem to bother Talia either. She doesn't look the slightest bit nauseous as I peel out of the parking lot and speed down the road.

"Iron doesn't bother you?" I ask.

She shakes her head. "Nope. It must be a half-human thing. My aunts can't touch it, but it doesn't affect me."

"Something tells me you're not related to these aunts by blood."

"I'm not," she answers. "They found me in their woods when I was a baby. My mother just left me there."

Holy shit. My parents at least *told* me why they were kicking me out—my liking boys and girls was a bullshit reason but, hey, the final choice not to choose between the two was mine. To just be left out in the woods like that as a baby? That's jacked up.

My thoughts must show on my face because Talia grins. "It's okay, though. Not only was I half-human, apparently I was quite ill too. Faeries are always abandoning their sick babies."

Yeah, but they leave them with human families. They take the human child and leave their own if they're too sick or weak. That's how you get changelings. Even if the child survives, they've got a better shot at survival in the human world. The Faerie Realm isn't very kind to those who can't take care of or defend themselves. I've never heard of a faerie mother just leaving her baby in the woods to die, though. Makes my folks look like Parents of the Year. At least, they kicked me out when I was old enough to take care of myself.

We make it to the apartment complex and check for anyone or anything suspicious. Crickets and frogs conversing in the nearby pond are all I hear, and the only things under the amber streetlights are mosquitoes and fireflies. Nothing stirs the muggy June air. We still sprint for the door. Safe inside my apartment, we take deep breaths.

"Do you have a pool of some kind I can use?" Talia asks. "I need water to contact my aunts."

My experience with solitary faeries is limited, so I've never heard of asrai. I sure as hell hope they don't need a real pool to be contacted. If so, Talia's gonna have shit reception.

"Uh, there's a sink here, one in the bathroom along with a bath," I answer, reaching in the fridge for the bottle of wine.

Talia steps into the bathroom and pokes her head out for a moment to say, "This will do lovely. Thank you," then shuts the door.

I'm on my third glass and mapping out our route to Blue Fish Point by the time she comes out. Not only did she use the bath to call her aunts, she apparently took one as well, seeing as she comes out wrapped in a towel, hair still damp.

The towel doesn't cover much.

"You wouldn't happen to have spare clothes, would you?" she asks.

I choke on my wine and scrabble to my feet. Averting my eyes, I step into my bedroom and hunt for something for her to wear. Since her legs are so long and she actually has hips, unlike me, none of my pants will fit her. Guess she'll have to settle for a gigantic T-shirt. We're both probably about to crash anyway, so that should work well enough.

She takes the T-shirt and smiles. "Thank you."

Just as she begins to drop the towel, I look up at the ceiling and exclaim, "Change in the bathroom, please!"

"Oh, sorry," Talia giggles, stepping back inside. "I forgot how modest humans can be."

That's one way to say it.

With my heart attack averted, I grab a pillow and some blankets to make a bed on the sofa. Talia gives the layout a curious look when she comes out with T-shirt barely covering what it needs to. God, this girl's got some legs.

I do my best to ignore that fact. "We should get some rest before heading out," I say. "You can take my bed. I'll sleep out here. Did you get ahold of your aunts?"

"They weren't home," Talia answers. "No doubt they're out looking for me. I was able to get ahold of one of our neighbors, though. She said she'll pass my whereabouts on to them. I left the bath full in case they try to contact me. I hope you don't mind."

"That's fine," I say, stretching out on the sofa. "If they do, I'll hear them out here."

Talia takes a few steps toward my bedroom. "Thank you, DJ, for helping me."

"Yeah, yeah." I yawn. "Go get some sleep."

I listen as she settles in, and then I listen for any strange noises outside the door or in the bathroom. Nothing. As I let the three glasses of wine do their work and drift off to sleep, I can't help but wonder again—what have I gotten myself into?

Chapter Three

A QUICK TRIP through the air and blunt pain wake me up. Before I can gasp for air, a hand slams my face into the carpet while two more twist my arms behind my back. Struggling just makes the pressure on my back worse and tears at my shoulder joints.

"Where's our niece, you human cretin?" a voice demands.

I crane my neck and meet the eyes of a stern-looking blonde woman dressed in bright yellow and orange. Her angry expression looks out of place with her big golden eyes, dainty nose, and tiny mouth. She looks more like a mildly annoyed doll than a dangerous home invader.

She slaps me nonetheless.

"Ow! Who the hell are you people?" I wheeze.

"Talia's aunts," snarls whoever has me pinned. "We received a message that she's being held captive here. Now, I'll ask you one more time. Where. Is. She?" This one sounds like she means business.

"She's in the bedroom," I gasp. Straining to turn my head, I call, "Talia! Talia, come call off your crazy family."

No response.

"Damn it, Talia, if you're still asleep—"

The front door opens, followed by the rustling of a grocery bag that plops to the ground. Talia stands stunned in a blue T-shirt and a red skirt I don't recognize. She's still barefoot. "Aunt Vervain, get off her. She's not the one that kidnapped me."

The woman doesn't have to be told twice, thank God. She jumps off me and the blonde scrambles to her feet with an elated squeal. By the time I get to my feet, they've nearly tackled Talia with hugs and their effort to make sure she isn't hurt. A third woman in a drab worn-out green dress gets up from the couch and joins the group hug. Was she seriously just lounging on my sofa this whole time?

"Oh, no, it's okay." I massage my shoulders. "I'm fine. No harm done."

The one who sat on me, dressed in blue from the flowers in her hair to her sapphire slippers, chuckles and breaks away from Talia. "We truly are sorry, dear girl," she says, taking my hands in one of hers and patting it with the other. "We shouldn't have jumped to conclusions, seeing as Nettle was the one who delivered Talia's message."

"Nettle's a pixie, you see," pipes up the blonde. "She probably didn't mean to mix up the message. She's just scatterbrained." She pauses a moment. "Then again, I suppose she could be scatterbrained and mix up the message on purpose for a good laugh. That's probably what happened, actually."

The one in green nods in agreement.

Talia's already starting to make a lot more sense.

Patting my hands again, the blue woman says, "I suppose we should at least introduce ourselves. I'm Vervain. That is my sister Eleadora." The blonde waves and bounces on her toes. "And that's our sister Juniper." The one in green meets my eyes and nods. "She doesn't say much."

Talia *tsks* and begins to pick up crude leather coats, gloves, and hats strewn on the floor. "What a mess you've made, aunties," she mutters, starting a neat pile by the sofa.

"Is the Upper Peninsula that cold?" I ask, studying the heavy clothing.

"Not this time of year, no," Vervain explains. "We're asrai."

Asrai? I've heard of them but didn't think they ever left the lakes and rivers they guarded. But then again, I didn't think they adopted random half-humans either. Whether they're beautiful enough to make human men instantly try to capture them still remains to be seen, but breaking into my apartment and attacking me is probably clouding my judgment.

"Direct sunlight turns us into puddles of water," Eleadora adds, studying her reflection in the microwave's window. "I hear it's no fun at all."

Juniper drops onto the couch, apparently doing her best to take up the whole thing, and shakes her head.

It's probably best not to question exactly where they heard that.

Vervain leaves me and taps her niece on the shoulder. "Talia, dear, make us some tea, will you? We've business to discuss. It's improper to discuss business without tea."

"Wait, business?" I repeat. Never mind the fact that they're helping themselves to my kitchen. I was under the impression this "business" would be over once these whackos showed up and took Talia home.

"Of course," Vervain says, raising an eyebrow. "Seeing as you were the woman who saved our dear Talia, I think you're perfect for the job we have in mind."

Eleadora and Juniper both nod.

"Yeah, but my boss helped."

"Maybe, but you were the one who took care of her," Eleadora says. "That's more important to us. And I'm sure the pay would be important to you."

I shouldn't take the bait. I should just kick all of them out and go back to bed and then go to work and mind my own business, maybe call up Calista and see if she's busy this afternoon.

But I've always been a glutton for punishment.

"What's the job?"

A smug, knowing smirk spreads across Vervain's thin lips. "Help Talia put the tea on and we'll tell you."

I tell myself again that I really should just kick them all out. Let them curse the place if they want. I'm sure Iver has something to get rid of that.

But instead, I do as I'm told.

"Sorry about all this," Talia mutters with a sheepish smile. She turns on the faucet and fills the kettle. "They can be a little much."

"A *little*?" I repeat, rummaging through my tea collection. I could definitely use some chamomile. Maybe a little lavender. And wine, but that doesn't mix well with tea.

"As if it's our fault," Eleadora calls. "We warned her time and again to stop sneaking off to the human camping grounds, even tried to keep a bell on her, but did she listen? Of course not. What do aunties know?"

Talia sets the kettle on the stove's eye with more force than necessary, but doesn't say a word.

Been there, sister.

The aunts might not be able to discuss "business" without tea, but I also can't drink tea without something to eat with it, so I open a bag of cookies and arrange them neatly on a serving plate. With all the grains, seeds, and dried fruits, they taste more like granola bars than cookies, but I'll take what I can get.

With the tea distributed and the cookies on the coffee table in front of the sofa, Talia and I sit on the floor while the aunts perch on the couch. Well, Vervain and Eleadora perch. Juniper lounges as if she's on vacation rather than a rescue mission.

"Before you even start talking about this so-called 'business,'" I say, "I want to know why anyone would take Talia in the first place. If you were just going to take her and leave, I'd mind my business and wash my hands of all this, but if I'm going to be involved, you need to tell me exactly what's going on."

The aunts and their niece all look at each other, communicating in looks and glances I don't understand, seeing as I'm not one of them. I'm not sure whether that means I should be worried or if it's just a family thing.

Talia finally clues me in. "There are some in the Faerie Realm that believe half humans have special powers, abilities belonging to neither faeries nor humans."

"Is that true?" I ask, taking a cookie.

Talia lets out a bitter laugh. "Of course not. My magic is mediocre at best. My only real asset is that I can withstand iron. It's not as if stupid louts like the ones who stole me know that, though."

"So, they wanted you for your supposed magic," I conclude. "Any idea where they were taking you?"

"I heard them say something about heading near the Unseelie Court, which is south of here, I believe. They got rather skittish once we entered the Seelie lands around here."

That makes sense, I guess. The more distant the solitary fae, the less they like being around the courts usually. Too many rules for their tastes. But then why was the Unseelie Court their final destination?

"Did they mention Queen Shaylee?" I ask. Then again, Her Majesty would be the last person that would kidnap Talia. If anyone knew about their lack of magic abilities, it would be her, seeing as she's half human herself. Maybe she wants to wipe out competition? Given the stunts she pulled to get the crown, I wouldn't be surprised.

Talia shakes her head. "They only ever mentioned a 'he.' They never used his name. When they contacted him, he always stayed hidden. I never saw his face."

I think I know less about what's going on than when I started asking questions. I wonder if 'he's' one of those escaped Mab supporters that Iver warned me about? It stands to reason, at least a little bit. Mab was originally the Queen of the Unseelie Court before she overthrew Titania and united the Faerie Courts. Then, thanks to Titania's forces and Shaylee's plotting, they took back the courts and split them up again.

Whoever wants Talia might want to take out Queen Shaylee with a half human of their own and reclaim Mab's original throne.

It's impossible to tell if mere suspicion is enough to make me take this supposed job. I guess I'll have to find out what the job is first.

I relay my suspicions to Talia and her aunts. They all nod along, expressions grim. They must have been onto a similar theory or don't like the sound of mine. None of them argue, though, and no one speaks until I'm done.

"If you're right," Vervain begins, folding her hands, "then our worst fears have been realized." Her gaze shifts to Talia. "We cannot take you home, my dear. They'll just keep coming for you."

Talia goes tense. "What are you saying? You're abandoning me?"

"Of course not, silly girl," Vervain insists. "We could never abandon you, but none of us will be able to return to Blue Fish Point for some time. We'll have to go live with our other sisters near Triple Lake. I'm sure they'll let us stay until this blows over. Shouldn't take more than a century or two."

Judging by the way Talia droops, that sounds a lot longer to her than it does to her aunt.

"Cheer up, Talia," Eleadora says, patting her on the head. "I hear Triple Lake is beautiful. Apparently, it's like Blue Fish Point, only with mountains."

Vervain turns to me. "That's where you come in, human—"

"My name is DJ."

"—DJ. Both you and Talia can survive in the Human Realm with no issue. It'll slow down whoever might come after Talia again." Vervain wrinkles her nose. "Not to mention you have one of those accursed iron death traps on wheels."

"You mean a car?"

"I thought it was called a horseless carriage," Eleadora interjects.

Juniper nods in agreement.

"They changed the name a while back," I say, trying not to snicker.

"Whatever you call it," Vervain continues, "it's made of iron, so it's safe and will be difficult for our kind to follow since it goes straight through the Human Realm. Your roads and cities just look like madhouses to us. Not to mention, Talia won't draw any attention in the Human Realm since she looks like a human. We'll go by faerie paths and meet you there."

"You're forgetting two important things," I say. "You still haven't told me where exactly this Triple Lake is, and there's the matter of what I get out of it."

Wherever Triple Lake is, it can't be in Michigan, seeing as there aren't any mountains. Not in the Lower Peninsula anyway. The closest thing we have to mountains are sand dunes. And last time I checked, faeries don't have a notion of chipping in for gas money, so whatever they want to compensate me better be pretty good.

"It's in one of those territories out west," Eleadora answers. She makes a rectangle with her fingers. "One of those square ones. It's called the Color Place or something like that."

My stomach drops and my blood turns to icy slush.

"You mean Colorado?" I suggest, my mouth dry.

Eleadora snaps her fingers and grins. "That's it!"

Talia's eyebrows pull together as she frowns. "Is there something wrong with Colorado?"

"Yeah," I answer. "It's a long-ass trip. My family's out there. I remember the hours being stuck in the car to get pretty much anywhere on this side of the mountains. Probably not worth my while."

The aunts give each other worried glances, then look back to me

"We'll reward you," Vervain says. "And provide you with whatever resources necessary."

"I'm quite happy with my setup, thank you."

"We'll lift the curse that forbids you from eating human food," Eleadora blurts. "You can finally go home to your family. We'll even make you as old as you're supposed to be. You can have your old life back."

"Why would I want that after twenty years in Faerie?" I argue. "Even if you age me up, people are going to have questions, none of which I want to answer."

"Tell us what you want then," Vervain begs, taking my hands in hers again. "We'll give you anything. Please, just take Talia where she'll be safe." There's desperation behind those big blue eyes on behalf of her niece. I can feel it in the way she squeezes my hands. She's not trying to trick or manipulate me, like most of the faeries I encounter.

She just wants what's best for the child she and her sisters raised.

Ugh. I'm such a pushover.

And a wimp. Colorado is a huge state. The likelihood of my family seeing me is slim to none. Especially if I'm just dropping Talia off and coming right back. I won't be in the state for more than twenty-four hours, hopefully. I need to pull myself together and take advantage of this opportunity. Besides, maybe I'm looking at this all wrong. Maybe there's a way to work this to my advantage. Maybe this is all God's way of giving a chance to take care of things back home and make things right.

Well, sort of.

"Fine." I sigh. "I'll take Talia to Triple Lake." Before the aunts can celebrate, I add, "Under one circumstance: when we get there, you make my family forget I ever existed."

Chapter Four

AS THE AUNTS discuss the deal behind my closed bedroom door, Talia paces the floor while I fiddle on my phone. Every once in a while, I glance up to watch her wringing her hands and gently pulling at her blond locks. Once she feels my eyes on her, she meets my gaze with unspoken words behind her eyes, but goes back to pacing without saying them. We go through the cycle four or five times before it starts to get on my nerves.

"If you have something to say, spit it out already," I snap.

Talia finally stops and blurts, "How can you want something like that? It's cruel."

"No, it's mercy."

Before she can argue with me, I pull up several missing persons pages that I know my brother hops on from time to time. Official ones, support pages, he's everywhere. I know because I've been watching him, waiting for him to quit. He hasn't. I stand and show the digital flyers with my face on them. One has how old I should be, and it makes me grateful I haven't aged. Whatever computer program they used on my face wasn't very kind.

"What's cruel is letting my brother continue to torture himself like this when I'm never going back. It would be kinder to let him just go on with his life like I never existed. My parents too, even though they probably already pretend like I never existed."

Talia studies the pictures, then my face. "Don't you want to go back? They're your family."

"A family is a group of people who want you and treasure you. I don't need blood for that."

"So, you have a family in the Faerie Realm then?"

I clear the phone screen instead of answering the question. She'd just use my words against me. Not to mention I'm not about to let her know she's got a point. I've got Iver, who's my boss, and Calista, who I guess you could call a friend with benefits. We're hardly even that. We mainly just focus on the benefits. That's still more than I have back in the Human Realm.

Isn't it?

I can't think about it too long. It'll lead to me thinking about things better left locked away, like how being queer would be the most minor offense I've racked up in twenty years.

Instead of running that risk, I head over to the Time Between, leaving Talia my cell phone and Iver's number in case anything happens. The drive will get my mind back on track and I need to tell Iver what's going on anyway. He's exactly where I left him this morning, wiping off the counter of the bar.

"Do you have a house? Or hobbies? Or *anything* outside of this place?" I ask.

"Of course," he answers, "but I do my best thinking here, so I came in early."

"What are you thinking about?"

Iver pours himself a drink. "That girl, Talia. There's something eerie about her."

"Like what?"

"I can't put my finger on it." My boss swirls his glass, studying the amber liquor as if it's a crystal ball filled with answers. "Maybe I'm just suspicious of half-humans."

"Because Queen Shaylee is a backstabbing sociopath?"

"Mind your tongue," Iver snaps with a glare. "Though I have to wonder just how universal Her Majesty's...tactics are to her kind."

"Well, I'll have plenty of time to figure that out, because I volunteered to drive her across the country," I explain. Iver listens attentively as I explain how Talia's aunts showed up at my apartment, leaving out the fact that they jumped me, and asked me to take her to Colorado where she'll be safe. His expression perks up at the mention of my old home, but his face turns to terror when I tell him what I want in exchange.

"Why on earth would you wish for such a thing?" he demands. "That's horrible."

I groan and roll my eyes. "Not you too."

"*Yes*, me too. To do that to your family, as well as yourself...by the gods, DJ..."

"Hey, I'm not doing anything to myself. I'm getting myself off the hook. My brother stops looking for me, I stop feeling bad about my brother looking for me, and I can get on with my life in the Faerie Realm."

Iver raises an eyebrow. "And what sort of life is that exactly?"

"Don't give me that shit." I bristle. "*You* gave me the job, remember?"

"Yes, because I saw that you could be so much more. You just needed something steady until you planned your next move. This place isn't supposed to be permanent for you."

"Oh, so I'm a charity case now?"

Iver sighs. "I didn't say that, DJ, and I didn't hire you as an act of charity. It's just..." He gulps down the last of his drink and studies the melting ice. "You can erase all signs that you ever existed in the Human Realm, and you can hide here in the Faerie Realm for hundreds of years, but that ache you carry isn't going to go away just by burying it. It won't dissolve with time. Believe me. I'm a bartender. I've seen people try to bury their pain pretty deep."

My stomach tightens, and that little door creaks open, letting out all sorts of nasty whispers.

You're not welcome in this house anymore. Not until you remember the values this family was built on.

You know me. You know this family. Don't do this. I beg you.

Have mercy on us.

Please, spare my son. He's the most innocent of all of us.

I snatch both the bottle and the glass from Iver, fill it halfway, and throw it back. The whiskey's burn and overwhelming bite wash the voices back behind the door and put my head on straight. "Strange." I cough, studying the bottle. "You always struck me as a rum guy."

Iver glowers down at me but gives up the fight by simply taking the bottle back and pouring himself another drink. "I'm more partial to vodka, actually. I choose whiskey when I'm particularly stressed." He side-eyes me for that last part, but I pretend not to know what he's talking about.

His phone rings from his pocket and he frowns down at the screen once he pulls it out. "Odd. It's your number."

"It must be Talia," I explain. "I gave her my phone in case of an emergency."

Iver nods and answers the call. "Hello? Yes, she's right here." He hands the phone over and whispers, "Take advantage of this road trip. Talia's bubbly personality would offset your stone-cold cynicism quite nicely."

I mouth, "Shut up," making Iver chuckle, then lift the phone to my ear. "What's up?"

"DJ? Will you be home soon? My aunts are saying we need to leave. There's something very strange going on around your building."

"Define *strange*."

"Faerie keep coming up to your door, but they're not Unseelie like the ones last night. They look like Seelie Court fae. They're prowling around outside too."

"Why would Seelie fae be after you?" I ask.

"I have no idea," Talia answers. "They could just be glamours, but they must be rather incredible. None of us are picking up any strong signs of magic."

"They could have once been Seelie fae who switched sides at some point," Iver suggests. "There are people who change their alliances depending on the queens' policies, marriages, their birthplaces, and so on. You can't always assume a faerie's alliance by their physical appearance, especially after having the courts blended for a hundred years."

"Did you catch that, Talia?" I ask.

"I did," she answers. "Whoever they are and whatever court they're aligned with, we need to get away from them. My aunts figured out how to hold up their end of the bargain. You just have to strike the deal with them and we can go."

"Sounds like a plan," I reply. "Be there soon as possible." I hang up the phone and hand it back to Iver.

"Do you want me to come with you?" he asks, slipping it back in his pocket.

"Nah, I'll be fine so long as we can get to the car. They can't touch us in there, thanks to the iron. Think you can hold down the fort while I'm gone?"

"I'll work out something. Be careful out there, DJ."

"I always am."

"And do something for me? Stop by your parents' place while you're out there."

I scoff as I head for the door. "And why would I do that?"

"I'll give you a raise."

"How much we talking?"

"It depends how long your nerve holds out."

I pause at the door and think it over. Depending on what it takes to wipe my family's memory, we might end up there anyway. Might as well get paid for it. I could use the extra cash. Besides, it would be nice to see my brother again.

"I'll think it over," I call. "See you in about a week."

Nothing looks particularly out of order outside the apartment building. Everything seems quiet. A young man stands at the edge of the parking lot talking on a phone. He glances at me as I get out of the car, but doesn't seem interested in what I'm doing. Still, I watch him out of the corner of my eye as I head to the door. As I walk up the stairs, I start to figure Talia and her aunts are just being paranoid, but then a woman rounds the corner, nearly knocking me back down the staircase.

"Hello," she greets with a perfect smile. "I'm Becky. I just moved upstairs, and the movers haven't shown up yet, so I don't have any of my baking supplies." She rolls her dazzling blue eyes, making me want to roll mine. Between her perfect straight brown hair and Barbie-like body, she reminds me of Suzie-Ann Davidson, a girl in high school that I played volleyball with. She told our whole team that I like girls.

I mean, she wasn't wrong, but you don't do that to people.

"Could I borrow a measuring cup and a cookie sheet?" Becky asks.

I try to slip past her. "Sorry. I'm not much of a cook. Plus, I'm in a bit of a hurry."

She blocks my path. "A bowl then?" she insists, standing a bit taller and squaring her shoulders. "I promise to bring it back. I only need it for the afternoon."

The stairway swirls a bit, and I suddenly feel off balance. Through the haze, I realize I'm being incredibly rude. I could lend Becky some stuff. Talia can wait for a few minutes more. It wouldn't take long, and I'd probably get cookies out of the deal.

At least I would if Becky wasn't actually a faerie neighbor-bewitching bitch.

It's an old trick but a good one. Use magic to compel someone to see things your way, to force them to do what you want. I'm all too familiar with it, and this Becky has nothing on Queen Mab.

I shake off the magic and smile. "Sure," I say, reaching into my purse. "Just let me find my keys...oh, here we go!"

I swing at Becky with a fury-filled left hook. No one fucking bewitches me. Not anymore.

She dodges and slices at my stomach with a small crystal dagger. It nearly cuts through my shirt, but I slip out of the way and nail her in the jaw with my other fist. She growls and manages to catch my right side just below my ribs. I yelp and slide into the hallway before she can do any more damage.

"Give us the girl," she hisses.

"What do I get if I do?" I ask.

"You get to live."

"Sorry, Becky," I snicker, "but I got a better offer."

She swipes at me again, but I aim low with a fist to her gut and avoid another swipe of her knife, ending up with the staircase behind me. Becky attacks again, but instead throwing another punch, I drop to the floor and dive for her legs. She tumbles over me and crashes down the stairs.

I stand and look just as the series of thuds ends. Becky lies in a contorted mess at the bottom of the stairs, moaning and wheezing as she tries to get back the breath the tumble knocked out of her. I can't help but call, "See you next fall," and head for my apartment.

Was the lame joke necessary? No. Was it worth it? Hell, yeah.

She'll be fine, unfortunately. It takes more than that to kill a faerie. If nothing else, their pride combined with their need for vengeance will keep them from dying from something so embarrassing.

The aunts leap from the sofa as I burst through the door. Vervain holds a kitchen knife, Eleadora a frying pan, and Juniper my only potted plant. All three of them are covered head to toe with the long jackets, gloves, and hats that Talia folded earlier. They relax once they realize it's me, but still hold tight to their weapons.

"I don't know what Talia was so worried about if she's got you three to defend her." I chuckle, locking the door behind me.

"This is no laughing matter, DJ," Vervain chastises. Her expression shifts to worry at the sight of blood on my shirt. "What happened to you?"

"Found one of the people after Talia," I say.

"You should let one of us heal it," Eleadora chimes in, putting down the pan.

"It's just a scratch," I insist, grabbing my duffel bag from the hallway closet. "Talia was right. We need to get out of here. She said you can wipe my family's memories?"

"That is correct," Vervain says. She reaches in her pocket and takes out marble-sized glass orb deep ocean-blue in color. "You must bury this behind your childhood home, Talia has to say the spell to break it beneath the earth, and all signs that it was ever yours will melt away."

I take a moment to study the answer to all my problems. How can something that changes so much be so small? It's almost too good to be true, but the words came from Vervain and faeries can't lie.

I finally manage to peel my gaze away. "Give me a second to pack."

Talia nearly gives me a heart attack when I find her hiding behind my bed with a deadly looking cued-up arrow in a bow. "Where the hell did you get that?" I demand, throwing a pile of reasonably clean clothes in the bag.

"My aunts brought it for me." She places the arrow back in its sheath and gets to her feet. "They knew I'd have to defend myself, and this is the only weapon I'm any good at."

"That would have been nice to know a while ago." I dig under my bed and pull out my long and short swords from my days of being a knight. "Do you need to put anything in here, Tal?"

"I bought some human clothes this morning," she says, tossing me the plastic bag she came home with earlier, and climbs off the bed. "Is it true you saw one of my pursuers? Could you tell what court they're from?"

I zip up the bag and throw it over my shoulder. "Yes and no. You're right that she looked more like a Seelie fae, but she didn't say who she worked for, just that she wanted me to hand you over."

Talia grabs hold of my arm and looks me dead in the eye. "And you didn't, right?"

"Of course not." I scoff, yanking away, and join her aunts in the living room. "I'm a lot of questionable things, but double-crossing is not one of them."

A violent bang comes at the door, followed by a muffled, "We know you're in there. Give us the half-human brat!"

"Well, there goes our way out," I grumble.

"We'll take care of them," Vervain says. "You and Talia go out the window."

It's a second-story drop, but if I can dangle from the balcony, I should be able to land without any serious injury.

"Okay, so how do we do this whole deal thing?" I ask, setting my bag by the balcony door.

Talia stands beside Vervain while the other two sisters stand behind them.

"Take my hand," Vervain orders, holding out her right palm.

I take it, slightly weirded out as always at how cool faeries feel.

"We sisters three do solemnly swear to grant you, DJ, the power to rid the Human Realm of all memory of you, should you see our Talia to the safety of Triple Lake and reunite her with us there," Vervain says solemnly.

Talia cups her mouth and whispers, "Now you have to say what you'll do."

"I, DJ Suzuki, do solemnly swear to see Talia to the safety of Triple Lake and reunite her with you there in exchange for the power to rid the Human Realm of all memory of me," I say.

Vervain frowns down at our hands. "There should have been a spark," she says. "DJ isn't your real name, is it? The contract won't work without it."

My blood turns to ice and I begin to question whether this is worth it. I don't need four more faeries running around with my name. Unfortunately, I don't have any other options at this point.

"Daisy Jane Ann Suzuki," I grumble under my breath.

"Speak up, girl. I couldn't hear you, and we have no time to dawdle."

"My name is Daisy Jane Ann Suzuki," I say louder, locking eyes with Vervain. "Use it for anything other than this deal and I'll make you regret ever learning it."

Vervain blinks as if I've just slapped her. "My dear girl, I would never."

"It's such an adorable name, though." Talia giggles.

I glare at her for patronizing me, but judging by the grin on her face, she really does think it's adorable. That's even worse. Vervain and I repeat the process, this time with the horribly embarrassing name that I constantly try to forget. This time, I feel a slight spark fly between our hands and Vervain shoves the orb at me

"You're giving this to me already?" I exclaim. "What's to stop me from running off with it?" I wouldn't, but they have no way to know that.

"You were a knight, weren't you?" Vervain asks with a raised eyebrow. "Where's the honor in going back on your word?"

I decide not to remind her that I served Queen Mab. The notion had been gone for a hundred years by the time I showed up.

She and the others give Talia quick hugs and shoo the two of us in the direction of the balcony. "We'll see you soon," Vervain calls in a whisper as the three of them head to the door. "Take care of our girl."

I peek beyond the balcony curtains and see that the coast is clear, at least for now. After inching the door open, I slip outside and look down between the floorboards. There's no one camping out at my neighbor's place either, it looks like. Talia joins me with no problem, so she must not sense anything wrong out here.

"I'll go first and catch you," she insists. "You don't look that heavy."

"What? No," I snap. "I can get down myself." It's bad enough she knows what DJ stands for. I'm not about to let her catch me like some sort of damsel. If anything, she's supposed to be the damsel.

She shrugs and crawls over the banister. "Suit yourself, but hurry up."

With one graceful leap, she lands on her feet like a cat. I expect some sort of smug smirk as I climb over the metal bar, shimmy down the rails, and drop, landing on my butt. Instead, she hoists me up and dusts me off.

"I'm fine." I squirm away from her and head around the building.

We don't get far before an arrow slices my right arm and embeds itself in a nearby tree. Before I can even swear in response to the pain, Talia spins and releases an arrow of her own in retaliation. I look up just in time to see the other archer tumble from the roof with an arrow in his neck. Talia keeps running as if it was no big deal.

Holy shit, who is this girl?

I don't get to ask aloud. Another would-be kidnapper leaps from the nearby brush with his sword swinging. Finally, my element.

I have to admit, he's good. His lack of accuracy is made up for with speed, putting me at a slight disadvantage, but it's still nothing I can't handle. Whoever these guys are, they're nothing like the goons that attacked Talia last night, which begs the question: are they working for the same person, or someone different?

"Give us the girl, and we'll let you live," the stranger orders as our blades grind together. "We might even be able to find a space for a sword wielder such as yourself among our ranks."

"I've got a prior engagement," I huff. "Thanks for the offer, though."

"She hasn't told you, has she?" he grunts, pushing hard against my sword. I have to grip it with both hands, which my injured arm doesn't like. "She hasn't told you who she is—" An arrow to his chest cuts his words short. Talia stands behind me, bow still raised.

"Will you stop that?" I snap, sheathing my sword, and once again head for the car where I dig my keys from my pocket.

"Stop what?" Talia replies, rounding the passenger side of the car. From what we can see, there aren't any more kidnappers or, more importantly, witnesses.

"Stealing my victories," I gripe, sliding in and revving up the car. "I'm getting paid to protect you, not the other way around."

"I'll keep that in mind next time," Talia replies with a roll of her eyes.

I imitate the gesture and peel out of the parking lot. Every few seconds, I check the rearview mirror to make sure no one followed us. The aunts were right. So long as we stay on main roads and drive like a bat out of hell, we should be safe.

"We need to take care of your wounds," Talia says as I merge onto I-196.

"They're not that bad. Let's put some distance between us and them," I say.

Talia's quiet for a moment. "Do you think my aunts made it out okay?"

I certainly hope so, but that's probably not the answer Talia wants.

"Oh, totally," I reply. "I mean, they gotta be as tough as you, right? I'm sure they're fine."

That puts a smile on Talia's face. It's a smile that makes my heart race for a reason completely separate from our current predicament.

Chapter Five

ONCE WE CROSS over into Indiana, I finally give in to Talia's nagging and pull into a gas station so that I can get patched up. I pick a parking spot near the back beside the wire fence that lines the highway exit so that we won't draw too much attention. Then I send her in with some cash and instructions on what to buy: bandages, antiseptic, and some wipes. While she walks off to the station, I roll the windows down in the hopes that the summer breeze will help clear my head. Unfortunately, it's a humid, still, muggy day, so all my mind does is stew.

Talia has not one but two sets of people after her. At least, that's what it looks like. I know Iver said it's possible that they all work for the same person, but the people who attacked were trained fighters, probably even knights. If they worked for the same guy, wouldn't he want to lead with the highly skilled henchmen rather than basic goons? That seems like an easier way to avoid interference from troublemakers like me.

And then there were that one guy's final words. "She hasn't told you what she is."

That probably just means the fact that Talia's half human, right? What else could it be? Like she said, faeries apparently think people like them have some sort of special powers, which I still don't know if I buy. Then again, so long as the little blue orb in my pocket does its job, I suppose it doesn't matter that much what Talia is. Once I drop her off with the other asrai and get my payment, it won't be my problem.

A plane glides through the sky, low on the horizon. Too bad I don't have a real license, or we could have flown. Talia doesn't have one either, and I'm not keen on trying to bewitch a TSA agent to get us through security. Too many things could go wrong, and I don't need any more enemies than I've already made today. Not to mention I have no idea how the full-body scanner would read Talia. Would her magic jam it? Probably best to play it safe and not find out. Besides, despite the circumstances, I like driving. Long trips like this were always the most relaxing part of my childhood. I wonder if the highways have changed at all.

My phone buzzes, bringing me back to earth. It's from Calista.

Heeey. You busy? I'm bored. ;)

I type back. *A little. Took a job out of town for a week. Be back soon.*

*Aw. Don't have too much fun, now. You know how jealous I can be.
>:(*

Yeah, because you're the poster child for faithfulness.

I'm a nymph, love. It's my job not to be.

That's her favorite line.

She continues. *Besides, I just said not to have too much fun. Not to have none at all.*

I'll do my best.

Talia slides back into the car with a small plastic bag and I put my phone away. "Got the stuff. And the person who worked there was incredibly nice."

What poor guy wouldn't be nice to a bombshell like Talia?

I refrain from asking that question aloud and rummage through the bag instead. "You forgot the bandages."

"We don't need them." She hands me the change and points to herself. "You've got a faerie with you, remember?" Shifting in her seat, Talia reaches out and gingerly rolls up my sleeve. "Well, half faerie anyway."

"I can take care of it myself," I say, wiggling away from her.

She sighs and sits back. "I know that, but it'll just go faster if I do it. Hand me the bag." Much to my annoyance, she has a point, so I give it to her and try to hold still as she dabs at the dried blood. "You were lucky," she says, yanking a clean wipe from the pouch. "If that archer had been better, you'd be dead."

"Better like you?" I chuckle.

Talia smirks. "Exactly like me."

"Where did you learn archery like that?"

Talia blows on the clean cut, sending a chill down my arm. "Aunt Juniper. She always took me hunting while growing up. When I was little, she would even strap me to her chest."

"Damn. That's pretty impressive."

"She is," Talia answers, putting the bloody wipes in the plastic bag. Her eyes get distant for a moment, but then she shakes it off and comes back. "What about you? Where did you learn to use a sword like that?"

"Eh. I was a faerie knight for nearly twenty years," I explain.

As expected, Talia's eyes go wide with awe. "Were you really? That's incredible."

"It really isn't," I say with a shrug. "Especially since I served under Queen Mab."

Talia tenses for a moment. "That must have been very difficult. I've heard that she was not a very kind person. Now, hold still."

She wraps her hands around the cut and closes her eyes. There's a small jolt of energy from her touch, and I try to tell myself it's the magic, not Talia herself. A warm tingling sensation spreads out from the cut and flows through the entire length of my arm. I wonder if this is what it feels like having magic. The warmth fades and Talia lets me go with a smile. A small pink scar stretches across my arm where the cut once was.

"There. All done," she says. "Now, let's get that one on your side. Lift up your shirt."

My heart jolts and my face gets hot, which is stupid. Who gets nervous when a cute girl asks you to only partially lift up your shirt? I've done a helluva lot more than that with Calista.

Talia rolls her eyes and takes initiative herself. "For heaven's sake, DJ, stop being modest." With one hand holding up my shirt just above the second gash, she dabs at the cut to clean it. "Honestly, how have you made it in Faerie for twenty years being so shy?"

"Mostly with my eyes closed," I joke. "I knew most of the queen's keep by memory by the time I left. It was pretty impressive, if you ask me." The more I talk, the less I picture those slender fingers roaming over the rest of my waist.

Talia chuckles. "I imagine it was rather difficult to be a knight with your eyes closed all the time." She tosses away the bloody wipes and presses both her hands to the cut, sending my heart racing wild. "Is that why you didn't want me to help you back at your apartment? You still have a faerie-knight-sized ego?"

"Something like that," I affirm. "I became a knight to protect people. It would be nice if I actually got to do that for once."

"You didn't get to protect people serving the queen?"

I scoff. "Of course not. You've heard the stories."

"Is that why you left?"

"It's some of it."

"What's the rest of it?"

"I didn't feel like exchanging one puppet master for another."

"The new queens are nice, though, aren't they? They wouldn't have treated you like that."

"They could have if they wanted to, though. That was the problem."

"How?"

Both of our stomachs growl, saving me from answering, thankfully. Even if I didn't tell Talia what happened to me, any story about Mab forcing a knight to do something against their will would throw a wet blanket on our little road trip. Dark magic, bodies tearing apart from the inside, blood. It's all grim stuff.

Talia laughs and lets me go, leaving behind a completely healed scar. "I guess in the heat of all this action, we forgot to eat, huh? Think we should stop at one of these places around here before heading out again?"

"I'd love to." I sigh. "But unless you know of any restaurants selling faerie food, I'm going to have to wait a while."

"No worries," Talia says, tossing the plastic bag in the back. "There's a spell that turns any food into faerie food."

"You mean to tell me," I say, looking her square in the eye, "all this time, I could have had Iver deliver me normal human food and ingredients with that spell on it and I could have eaten it?"

"Well, he would have had to find it in a human market, which would have been a hassle."

"But I could have bought it and taken it to him?"

"I suppose so, yes. You honestly didn't know?" Talia asks skeptically.

"No, I didn't. No one ever told me. I thought everything had to be grown with magic seeds in fields with magic soil and watered with magic or something like that."

Talia nods. "I suppose that makes sense. It's far easier to manipulate humans trapped within the realm if they don't know that little tidbit."

Son of a bitch. Those jokers are *still* playing me.

"Still, it's not as if you could get too far, seeing as a faerie has to cast the spell," Talia continues.

I turn on the car and put it in reverse. "Well, good thing I've got just that, then."

Talia lurches back in her seat as I fly out of our parking place and zoom toward the road. "Where are we going, exactly?" she asks, scrambling to put her belt on.

The signature red and yellow insignia for Pizza House stands tall in the row of restaurant signs, catching my eye. "I'm going to introduce you to the epitome of American cuisine," I say. "Chased by kidnapping faeries or not, it's an experience worth having, I assure you."

We pull into the parking lot, and I almost jump out of the car without shutting off the engine. I nearly drag Talia inside in my excitement. As we wait to be seated, I grab a free US map from a rack of brochures about local attractions and road-trip destinations. My phone has GPS, but I still prefer a map for the big-picture stuff. It feels more solid.

Once seated, I proceed to drool over the menu. Talia's nice enough to let me pick the toppings, so I go with pepperoni, sausage, bacon, and pineapple. Given some of the weird stuff I've seen faeries eat, I imagine pineapple isn't much of a stretch for her. With our order in, we spread out the map and power up the GPS to plot our course.

"Here's where we are now," I say, pointing to the northern side of Springfield, Indiana. I find Triple Lake nestled in the Rockies of Colorado a few hours away from Aspen. "Here's where we're going."

"That's such a long way." Talia slouches a bit as she scans the route.

"It's only about eighteen or nineteen hours, without traffic," I reply, studying the GPS on my phone. "And once you get into Missouri, you've got pretty scenery. What about your aunts, though? How long do you think it'll take them to meet us?"

Talia nibbles on the straw in her water as she thinks it over. "A bit longer than us, I'd imagine, seeing as they can only travel at night and can only travel via paths in Faerie."

"So, we'll beat them there," I concur. "Do you think we'll be safe waiting?"

"I don't see why not. Especially since no one knows where we're going."

I nod in agreement and continue to study the map. A small dot south of Denver catches my eye. It's labeled Red Well. Reading it silently makes my stomach churn, but we've got to go if I want my existence erased from my family's mind. Not to mention I'll get a raise out of the deal. We'll swing by, break the orb, and go on our way. Easy enough.

"Here's where my family lives," I explain, pointing at the dot. "Should only add a few hours onto our trip."

"And you're sure this is what you want out of this deal? My aunts could give you just about anything."

"Oh, trust me. I'm sure. It's for the best."

Talia frowns but shrugs her shoulders instead of arguing. "We've got a long way to go. Maybe you'll change your mind on the way."

Luckily, the pizza comes just then, so I don't have to think up reasons why she's wrong. I'm too distracted by the smell of cheese, meat, and bread to do so anyway. Judging by the wide-eyed look on Talia's face, so is she. The waitress sets the twelve inches of perfect, hot, gooey goodness between us and leaves us to it. Before I can dig in, Talia places her hands on both sides of the pizza and closes her eyes. It looks like she's praying.

When she opens her eyes again, she smiles and says, "Let's eat."

It's not like she has to tell me twice.

The salty, savory, sweet blend of sauce, cheese, and toppings turns me into a blissful puddle in my seat. The airy crust lifts me up onto a cloud of joy I don't know if I'll ever come down from. I devour two pieces before speaking again.

"That's seriously all it takes to make food edible for humans trapped in Faerie?" I ask, helping myself to a third slice.

Talia still nibbles on her first. "Yes. You just have to infuse it with a little bit of magic."

"I'm gonna kick Iver's ass when I get home," I gripe around a mouthful of cheesy wonder. "After he gives me that raise, of course. We could have been getting pizza and takeout and all the wonders of the human world, but instead, every time I have him order me a shipment of food from Faerie, it's always fruits, vegetables, and whatnot. I thought that was my only option."

"It sounds like I have Iver to thank for keeping you alive this long." Talia giggles. "I can't imagine pizza is healthy in large quantities." What could possibly be a flirtatious smirk crosses her face. "And I'd hate to see you lose that physique."

Now, I say *possibly* because as she speaks, I realize I have cheese still attaching me to a slice. Not exactly the most flirt-inducing look. It must have been a fluke. Talia doesn't seem like the type to do a lot of flirting anyway.

Once I chew my food like a proper adult, I say, "I think I've been in Faerie long enough that I'd be fine."

"I don't know. Would you want to risk it?"

"For pizza? Definitely."

Talia laughs and goes back to eating and lets me do the same, allowing my mind a chance to wander again.

The last time I ate pizza was my older brother, Shunsuke's, twentieth birthday. It was a Friday and he was planning to go on a camping trip with some of his college buddies the next morning to celebrate, so we had a quiet family evening, filled with pizza, ice cream, and movies we used to watch as kids. He always was incredibly low-key. He never really liked parties or big get-togethers. Maybe that's where I got it from.

Over glasses of wine for my parents and cups of soda for my brother and me—because twenty and eighteen weren't twenty-one and that was that—Mom and Dad talked about how proud they were of Shun and all the hopes they had for his future. They talked about how good a big brother he was and how they were so happy that we got along so well.

Then they mentioned how proud they were of me, too. Straight As, a promising career in software programming ahead of me in the coming fall, and producing award-winning short stories in my free time. Why wouldn't they be proud of me?

A few months later, I'd find out the hard way.

Talia's voice breaks through. "—right, DJ?"

"Huh? What?"

She frowns as she dabs her mouth with a napkin. "I asked if you were all right."

I shrug and finish the last piece of pizza my stomach can comfortably hold. "I'm fine."

"You look upset."

"Nah. I just have resting bitch-face syndrome. My face always looks like this when I'm thinking."

Talia gives me a puzzled look. "You must not think very often because I haven't seen you like that before."

The comment is so far out of left field that I can't help but laugh at it. "Hey, you want to walk all the way to Colorado?"

Talia glows bright red, which I have to admit is adorable. "I-I didn't mean it like that," she stutters. "I was merely worried about you."

"I figured. I'm just messing with you." I snicker. The pizza's gone, so I look around for our waitress. "And don't worry. I won't make you walk to Colorado."

Once I've paid the bill and left the tip—a custom Talia finds rather strange—we head down the road again. There's still plenty of daylight ahead of us, and I have no problem with driving through the night. Eighteen hours isn't that long of a time.

And regardless of what Talia says, it's not long enough to make me change my mind.

Chapter Six

MOST OF THE highways in Illinois are straight continuous roads for miles upon miles. The scenery on either side of the road varies between stretches of farmland that are lush and green in the summer heat, patches of dense woods, and exits that serve as quaint little spots that let you catch your breath. Add a beautiful setting sun, the sky ablaze in vibrant pinks and oranges, and you have quite a peaceful view.

Maybe a little too peaceful.

The rough stretch of road at its edge blares at me to pay attention, and I jolt awake. Talia bolts up from her curled-up position in the passenger seat and looks around with wide eyes.

"Did we hit something?" she exclaims, leaning forward to look over the hood of the car. "A monster of some sort?"

"It's a feature of the road to keep people alert," I explain. A sign flies by stating that Champaign, Illinois is coming up. I think we'll turn in there for the night. It's only going to get darker and quieter as the night goes on, which doesn't bode well for someone who's already falling asleep at eight fifteen. Driving through the night isn't such a great idea after all. I didn't take into account how much this trip was going to mess with my sleep schedule.

"Are you getting tired?" Talia asks. "Would you like me to drive?"

"Have you ever driven a car before?"

"I borrowed a cart that a campgrounds worker was using once."

"That counts as a no," I reply. As I pull off the exit, I ask, "How did the joyride with the cart end?"

"In Lake Superior," Talia answers meekly. "I was young and wanted to know what was on the other side of the lake. My aunts had made the mistake of leaving me unsupervised."

I can't help but crack up. "So, it's a big no, then. I have to say, I'm impressed, though. I wouldn't have imagined it could have even made it down to the water."

"That's why faerie children aren't supposed to be unattended until they're at least twelve. Magic is too great a power for a child to know how to control on their own."

"Given my past experiences with faeries," I reply, "I think you might want to up that age restriction to, like, ever."

Talia opens her mouth, then shuts it again to ponder the idea as we pull onto the main road near the exit and look for an inn with vacancies. The Wine Glass Motel looks promising and reasonably clean, but disappointingly empty of wine. We reserve a room for the night, unload what little we've brought with us, and I order Chinese takeout. Talia's gracious enough to let me pick again. Given that takeout doesn't taste as good cold, I'm careful to only order food for tonight, which is damn near impossible with how good everything on the menu looks. I forgot how much I loved sesame chicken, Hunan beef, crabmeat cheese rangoons, and eggrolls back when I could eat it all.

After I order, I flip on the TV. I don't have one in my apartment and don't spend that much time on the internet, so I'm still pretty far out of the loop about what's popular in this day and age. As the TV blinks to life and a news anchor starts talking, I realize the room's too quiet.

The light from the bathroom spills into the entrance way, so I poke my head in, expecting Talia to be playing with the complimentary bottles of shampoo or something, but it's empty. So is the closet.

Shit. I've lost Talia. I had one job and I'm blowing it.

I grab my sword and dash out into the parking lot with my heart pounding against my ribs. "Talia," I shout. "Tal, where are you?"

I hear a series of splashes and giggles followed by a cheerful, "Over here."

Jeez. If her kidnappers don't kill me, she just might give me a heart attack that will. I place my sword back in the room, then head over to the open-air pool.

"You can't run off like that." I sigh, letting myself through the gate. "I thought someone had snatched you."

Talia rolls her eyes as she swims closer. "No one's going to snatch me in the middle of a human city. Besides, you were on the phone. I didn't want to interrupt you."

"Leave a note next time, at least," I argue. "I'm responsible for you."

"No, you're just responsible for getting me to Triple Lake."

"That's pretty much the same thing, Tal."

Talia tries to splash me. "Fine."

I jump out of the way. "Don't be too long. Dinner should be here pretty soon."

"'Kay. I'm pretty much done anyway. It's been a while since I could swim, so I just needed to take a quick dip." She paddles over to the edge and reaches for me. "Pull me out?"

Pfft. Like I'd be that stupid. "Take the stairs," I say, heading back for the gate.

"Oh, no fun," Talia calls, hoisting herself out of the pool. "Can't you swim?"

"Of course, I can, but—"

A sudden *patpatpatpat* races up behind me, and I dodge out of Talia's way. She still manages to grab my hand and pull me toward the pool as she jumps in. I wiggle out of her grip as she hits the water, but it's too late. My balance is gone, and I fall in.

I surface and gasp for air to the sound of Talia's laughter. I whip a splash toward the sound of her voice before wiping my eyes. "What the hell, Tal?"

"Sorry." She chuckles, wiping the water from her face. "You were just so tense all day, and I couldn't help driving, so I figured I'd try to help you unwind. Doesn't the water feel nice?"

I want to stay cross with her, but I have to admit that after the heat of the day, the cold water does feel good, even if my clothes are now soaked. "Is this an asrai thing?" I ask. "Pulling poor unsuspecting humans into bodies of water?"

"Nah, this is a me thing," she says, floating on her back. "My aunts avoided humans. Of course, they told me to, but I liked to visit their campgrounds sometimes, just to see what they were about. There was a pool like this and children would often pull each other in."

"I'm gonna take a guess and say they were wearing swimsuits," I grumble, hoisting myself out of the pool and sitting on the edge.

Talia studies my clothes, then her own. "I do suppose they were dressed quite differently." She shifts to tread water again. "What was it like being around humans all the time?"

I slick back my hair and think it over. "Easier in some ways. Harder in others. I never had to worry about people bewitching me or trying to steal from me as some sort of joke. At the same time, high school was a bitch and human families can be...complicated."

"Was your family complicated?"

A chill runs through me, but it's not from the water. It's from my very bones.

"Yeah, it was." I get to my feet and do my best to wring out my shirt. "But that was mostly my fault. If I had just stuck with the program and did what I was told, there wouldn't have ever been an issue."

"You don't seem like the kind of person to just do what you're told," Talia comments, leaning on the wall of the pool.

"It's not one of my fortes, no," I joke. "What about you? What was it like being raised by three faeries?"

Talia lazily kicks her legs and tilts her head as she thinks. "Simple. I learned magic, learned how to breathe in time with the trees and the lake. There was a lot of dancing and celebrations for the smallest reasons."

"Sounds nice."

"It was, but..." Talia studies the tiny beads of water on her skin. "It didn't always feel like enough. When I spent all my time around faeries, being a faerie, it felt like some part of me was missing. Going to the human campgrounds helped for a little while, but that never felt like enough either." She looks up at me with a deep sincerity I never expected from a girl like her. "Does that make me bad or greedy?"

That's a question I've asked myself a lot over the years.

"I don't think so," I answer. "You were trying to figure out who you are and where you fit. I think everyone strives to find that. It just takes some people a longer time. Being a part of multiple worlds certainly doesn't help, especially when it's literal in your case."

Talia nods along with my words. "That makes sense. How do you understand this so well?"

I shrug and sit on a plastic beach chair. "I've had to do the same thing. My dad's family is Japanese. My mom's is white—Scottish to be exact. Growing up, I *definitely* didn't fit in with my Japanese cousins—I barely spoke the language, wasn't into the same celebrities or hobbies. We were just different. But, I didn't completely fit in with mom's side either. My perspective was different: I ate things that were strange to them and watched shows and movies they thought were weird. I had to form my own identity within each, yet separate from both. We all had a pretty good relationship as we got older, which helped I guess, but there was still never really a space for all of me, in hindsight."

"Do you have space for all of you in Faerie?" Talia asks quietly.

I can't help but chuckle. "When I'm left alone, I guess."

"Don't you get tired of being alone?"

I shrug.

"Do you miss your human family?"

My heart tightens in my chest. I haven't thought about that answer in a long time. "I do."

"Then why would you make them forget you?"

"It's just better this way."

"Better or easier?"

I get to my feet and try to wring my clothes out a bit more. "Food's gonna be here soon. We should head back to the room and get dried off."

Talia pouts, probably disappointed at my lack of a real answer, but lets it go. She hoists herself out of the pool with each inch of soaked cloth clinging to her curvaceous body. Thank God no one else is out here, because the sight would *definitely* throw off our low profile. I turn away and head toward the gate. Talia catches up, squeezing out her hair as we walk.

"Do you remember any Japanese?" she asks.

"A bit. I can hold a pretty basic conversation."

"Will you say something for me?"

I switch languages and tell her how much I hated that question growing up.

Talia, the girl who grew up dancing with faeries and learning magic, stares down at me with wide-eyed wonder. "What did you say?"

I smirk back. "A translation's gonna cost you extra."

She lightly punches me in the arm. "No fair. You never said this was going to be a business transaction."

"You're a faerie," I tease. "You should be used to surprises like that."

Talia punches me again as we let ourselves into the room. I let her take a shower first and begin to flip through the TV channels, landing on *The Fifth Sight*. Nice. I remember seeing ads for it right before it came out, but never actually got to go see it.

Man. These special effects did not age well.

Talia joins me just as the delivery boy shows up, and, thankfully, she remembered to change into one of her spare outfits before coming out of the bathroom. Over a movie I should have gotten to watch with my brother, I introduce Talia into the wonders of Chinese food. Judging by the look of joy on her face as she eats, this is going a long way for all the human experiences she's missed out on.

I don't want to say it out loud, but I feel it's doing the same for me.

Chapter Seven

AFTER A CONTINENTAL breakfast of coffee and Belgian waffles soaked in butter and syrup, we get back on the road without any incident. No word from the aunts, but Talia doesn't seem too worried. At least she doesn't when I'm looking. From where I'm sitting, she's enjoying the way the Midwestern fields turn into hillier farms in Iowa. As the trees thin out, the sky grows bigger and bluer above us, dotted with colossal marshmallow clouds. Talia leans against the door with the window open, her hair whipping behind her as she squints against the wind up into the sky. It hasn't gotten too hot just yet.

Just as it gets hot enough to turn on the AC, something underneath the hood of the car explodes, nearly scaring me out of my skin and sending me into oncoming traffic. Talia dives in the back and reaches forward for her bow.

"Relax," I order, easing into the left lane again as best I can. "We're not under attack." The car doesn't want to turn or go faster than thirty miles an hour. With the way it's handling, that's probably for the best. I scan the horizon for hope and spot an old red sign that reads Gas. Below it sits an equally worn-out building facing the road just beyond the exit.

"Did your vehicle devour a terrible monster then?" Talia asks, setting her bow back down.

I snort and pull the car onto the exit ramp. "I don't know what the hell it just did, honestly." Though judging by the sharp, rancid smell coming through the air vents, Talia might be onto something.

The tiny-horrible-car-that-couldn't inches around the stop sign, pulls into the gas station, and lets out a final pained sigh before going deathly silent. I try to start it up again only to get a few pathetic coughs in response.

"What does that sign say, DJ?"

I look up and see a faded sign in the dusty window that says: We've Moved! Come See Us at our New Location! I lay my head on the steering wheel and groan instead of reading the address we don't have any way to get to.

"You need that many characters on paper to make that noise?" Talia asks.

I glare over at her, but judging by her curious face, she's serious. "Wait...can you not read?"

Talia shakes her head. "No. Relatively few solitary faeries can even read fae script, let alone English. It's usually something only court fae have the chance or the reason to learn."

"Oh...well...good to know," I say, pulling out my phone. There's got to be a towing service nearby. "I'll keep that in mind next time we—son of a bitch."

Talia reaches for her bow again. "What? What happened?"

"Put the bow down," I order. "We just don't have cell service out here." Of course, we break down out in the sticks without service. Because the universe doesn't want anything to be easy. With another groan, I reach in the back and grab my purse. "Grab whatever you need—*not* the bow."

As I climb out the car, I catch Talia giving me a dirty look as she hides her bow under the back seat before getting out as well. Wincing in the bright light, I scan our options. All two of them: the exit we just came from and a quaint little farmhouse down the road. Seeing as I'd rather ask someone to use their phone while they're working in a field rather than speeding on the highway at 70 miles per hour, the farmhouse is our best bet.

"Let's go," I say, locking the car. "The sooner we get there, the sooner we get out of this sun."

"Maybe I could fix it," Talia offers, rounding the front of the car.

I scoff and adjust my purse on my shoulder. "No offense, Tal, but you've never even ridden in a car before now. How do you expect to fix it?"

"With magic, of course," she answers, crossing her arms and shifting her weight to her right leg. "If I can see what's wrong, maybe there's something I could do. We could carry on our way at least until we find a facility that could probably repair it."

I suppose she's right. Even if she can't help, it won't take long to figure out and get walking, so I sigh and pop open the hood. We're met with the hot stench of gasoline and scalding steam, which makes me think it's worse than it looks. With our arms covering our faces, we search for the problem.

After a moment, Talia coughs, "Um, well, maybe I could just send a current of magic through it and direct it to fix whatever's broken."

"Does magic work like that?" I ask.

She shrugs and places a hand on either side of the front of the car. "That's what happens when magic is used for healing, more or less." Taking a deep breath, she closes her eyes and concentrates.

The world around us quiets. The nearby highway turns to a whispering hush as if it wants the singing birds and swishing crops to be still and witness what's about to happen. Even the clouds above seem to pause to see what will happen next. It's only then I realize I'm holding my breath.

Maybe Talia's captors are onto something. Maybe there is something different about her magi—

The radiator cap shoots into the sky, making Talia scream and duck for cover. Her cry sends me stumbling backward in shock. My heart doesn't start beating again until the cap lands on the ground, rolls, and nudges Talia's foot. She peeks out from beneath her arms to find that it's harmless. The world turns on the volume again, this time with the addition of my laughter. By the time Talia gets back to her feet, I'm bent over with my arms wrapped around my waist.

"I've never seen someone so afraid of a radiator cap in my life," I gasp, wiping tears from my eyes. The fact that it shouldn't be this funny makes me laugh until I can't breathe. "Did you think it was going to bite you?"

Talia shoots to her feet, face bright red and mouth crinkled in her attempt not to laugh. "It could have," she replies, accidentally releasing a few giggles. "What if it shot *at* me? Some bodyguard you are, standing all the way back there."

"If you can't defend yourself from a cap, you need more help than I can provide." I sigh, standing up straight again. "What went wrong?"

Scooping up the cap, Talia replies, "I'm not sure. I found a lot of problems—"

"No surprise there. The thing's old as dirt."

"—but I guess the magic just didn't know what to do since its inorganic material. I guess that's why it built up and backfired." She screws the top back on, shuts the hood, and grabs her bag.

"You talk about magic like it's alive," I observe, adjusting the purse on my shoulder.

"It is in a way," Talia joins me by the road. "I don't know how to explain it, but magic has this sort of...spirit, if you will. Its energy feels positive and negative, joyful and sad, frustrated. It's like it can sense what its user is feeling and amplifies it."

"Weird. Using magic sounds a lot more complicated than I thought it would be."

"Most things in Faerie are."

"True that."

With one final glance at the car, we head off toward the farmhouse in the distance, praying that someone's home. Every once and a while, I snicker at the mental image of Talia cowering in front of the car, and she elbows me, despite the smirk it brings to her face. All and all, I guess this whole mess isn't so bad after all. The scenery is just as pretty here as it was from the highway, and there's a breeze today, thankfully.

Giant willow trees give us some shade as we turn onto the farm's driveway. Nestled within them stands a large beige farmhouse with a wide front porch and bright clean windows. Two giant silver silos tower over a bright red barn with quaint white paneling on the windows. Next to it sits a wider white barn and a cozy white shed. The strong, musty smell of animals wafts toward us as the wind blows past them.

"What a curious place," Talia whispers. "What are all those buildings for?"

"Storing equipment, storing animals, storing grain, storing whatever it is they grow. Stuff like that," I assume. Despite living twenty years in Faerie, I'm still a city girl at heart, so my only source of farm knowledge comes from movies and my fourth-grade social studies class.

I hop up the front steps and knock on the open screen door with Talia close behind me. She cranes her neck to get a better look at the baby blue entrance way. Just as I'm ready to call out, footsteps stop me, and a woman emerges from a side room, wiping her hands on her jeans. She brushes a stray blonde curl from her face as she opens the door and grins at us.

"Can I help you girls?" she asks with a faint accent. Her smile seems genuine enough, but there's a curious glint in her brown eyes. Can't say I blame her. She probably doesn't get a lot of tall hippie-looking girls like Talia knocking on her door. Short muscular girls are probably even rarer.

"Yes, well, you see, ma'am," I say, trying to put her as much at ease as possible, "our car broke down over at that old gas station, and I don't get cell service out here. We were wondering if we could use your phone."

The woman opens the door even wider. "Well, of course. Come on in. Landline's in the kitchen."

We follow her and the scent of food into a wide eggshell-colored kitchen. The worn wooden table and chairs, faded cabinets, and dented and stained linoleum show that this is a well-loved space. The sight of grilled-cheese sandwiches stacked high and a giant pot of tomato soup makes my stomach growl. I *knew* we should have stopped in Des Moines for food. Curse my faith in that stupid hunk of metal I call a car.

"That smells awesome," I say.

The woman chuckles and sets a laptop on the table. "Thank you," she says as the computer wakes up. "It's nothing much. Just something I whipped up for lunch." She types for a moment, then asks, "Where you girls heading?"

"Colorado," I answer.

"By yourselves? You seem awfully young."

I shrug. "We do it every summer. Our sisters are best friends too and live out there, so we go and have a girls' week hiking, camping, stuff like that." Talia raises an eyebrow at me. Once the woman turns her back to work on the food, I put a finger to my lips to signal for Talia to keep quiet.

The lady nods along with the story. "That sounds fun. Sorry you broke down." She faces the laptop toward us. "Here's the number for the closest tow truck. If you can't get ahold of them, there's a few farther ones you could try. If you'll excuse me, I need to go call my kids for lunch."

I nod as she heads back toward the front door. "Thank you, ma'am." With her out of earshot, I study the screen and take the phone receiver from the wall.

"She seems nice," Talia comments, studying the American flag-themed clock on the wall. "I don't see why we need to lie, though. At least, lie so much."

"Trust me, the less truth these people know, the less trouble we'll have later on. By the way, while we're here, call me Sarah."

"Then I'll be Daisy."

I glare at Talia as the receiver rings, and she sticks out her tongue.

"It's payback for laughing at me back at the car."

A gruff masculine voice answers on the other end, and I begin to navigate the tangled mess that is my car insurance policy. The good news is that I can get a tow truck, but the bad news is that the nearest garage that could take my car is a good forty-five-minute drive from here. As is the towing service itself, which is currently helping clean up several accidents farther down the highway. The earliest they can get to us is three thirty.

"We're going to get to Triple Lake early anyway, right?" Talia points out.

She's right, but I hate waiting.

The rushed patter of children's feet announce the woman and her kids. Three slightly burnt faces pop through the doorway with wide brown-eyed wonder and sweat-dampened blond hair. The oldest, the only girl, looks to be fourteen or fifteen, the second is probably around twelve, and I imagine the youngest is eight.

"Don't be rude," the mother says, shooing them into the kitchen. "Say hello."

Talia takes initiative and smiles at them with a wave. "Hi there. I'm Daisy."

I resist the urge to flash her a dirty look and grin at the kids as well. "I'm Sarah. Nice to meet you."

The children take turns introducing themselves as they set the table for lunch. Maddie's the oldest, followed by Jackson, and Samuel's the baby, a fact he greatly protests.

"I can't believe I didn't introduce myself," the mother says, setting plates in front of Talia and me. "What sort of example is that? You can call me Deb. My husband, Jack, is up in Des Moines, unfortunately."

"Oh, you don't have to feed us, Deb," I say, hanging up the phone. "We were just on our way out."

"Nonsense," she replies with a wave of her hand. "That tow truck'll take forever, won't it? Everything does out here. I can't let you girls go hungry seeing how we always have plenty."

"We really couldn't," I insist. "It'll only take a couple of hours." Talia droops a bit in her chair and eyes the plate of sandwiches Deb sets on the table.

"Can you stay for just a little while?" Samuel pipes up, reaching for a sandwich. "I wanna ask you why you've got boy hair."

Jackson kicks his brother under the table while Deb hisses, "Samuel Thomas Porter."

"What?" Samuel whines, rubbing his shin. "Davey Smith's older brother's got hair like that, so I just wanna know."

Deb shoots me a nervous glance. I can't tell if it's because she's worried I'm offended or because the next words out of my mouth might be considered offensive in this house. I'm not about to say anything to upset the hand that's *literally* about to feed me, so maybe we should just go.

Talia apparently has other plans. She pulls up her chair and puts her elbows on the table as she leans forward. Meeting Samuel's eyes, she says quietly, "You see, Samuel, Sarah's a secret agent. Sometimes she pretends to be a boy to trick the bad guys."

Maddie rolls her eyes and Jackson scoffs, but Samuel gasps and looks up at me with unadulterated wonder. I notice Deb's shoulders relax. Again, I can't tell exactly why. I probably don't want to know.

Samuel looks over to his mother and exclaims, "Can you make them stay, Mom? Can you? Can you?"

Deb gives me a sympathetic smile. "It really is up to Sarah and Daisy, but I'm sure they've got some fun stories to tell if they'd like to stay."

Both Talia and Samuel look up at me with giant puppy-dog eyes. I've never been able to say no to puppy-dog eyes.

With a sigh, I pull out my chair and sit down. Leaning toward Samuel, I warn him, "If I tell you any secret agent stories, you have to promise not to tell any of them. It's super important that you keep them secret."

Samuel takes a giant bite out of a sandwich. "Only if you tell me all of them."

Good thing we've got a few hours until that tow truck comes, because this might be a long lunch.

Chapter Eight

THANKS TO TALIA'S quick thinking, lunch actually proves to be rather enjoyable. Lucky for me, my dad was a huge James Bond nut while I was growing up, so I have a ton of "special agent" stories to draw from. God knows I can't share any of my real adventures with this nice farm family in the middle of Iowa. Ho, boy. If Samuel's boy-hair comment put Deb on edge, I don't want to know what she'd do if we told her the truth.

After lunch, Talia and I insist on doing the dishes as payment for letting us use her phone and feeding us. Seeing as it's usually Maddie and Samuel's job, they don't see a problem with it, but Deb insists we have a cup of ice coffee with her on the porch while the kids clean up.

"You've done plenty for us already," I say, easing myself onto the porch swing. "I'd hate to inconvenience you any more."

"Nonsense," Deb says. She takes a seat in the old rocking chair in the corner and stirs the milk into her coffee. "We so rarely have company and it was fun to watch Samuel listen to your 'special agent' stories." She adds a wink and laughs. "I'm sorry if his question offended you."

She was worried that *he* offended *me*?

"It's fine," I reply after a sip of coffee. "He was just being curious. It's what kids do."

Deb smiles fondly. "I suppose it is.... do either of you have any siblings other than your sisters?"

Talia and I look at each other. Tal shakes her head and says, "I was raised by my aunts and never knew my mother, so I don't know."

Deb's smile turns to sympathy. "I'm sorry. I didn't mean to—"

Talia waves away the apology. "It's okay. I don't mind talking about it." As she stirs her coffee, or coffee-flavored sugar-milk at this point, she looks out over the lush green field with distant eyes. "They were— are wonderful parents. A little eccentric at times—"

I choke back a scoff.

"—but wonderful." As she speaks, her eyes gloss over, but she's quick to blink it away.

Maybe we should change the subject.

"I've got an older brother," I chime in. "Shun—I mean Sean. He's..." I do a little mental math to figure out how old he'd be. "He's forty. He lives in Colorado, too."

Holy shit. Shunsuke's forty. The realization nearly knocks me off the porch swing.

"That's quite the age difference."

"Yeah, well...I was kind of an *oops* baby."

It's not exactly a lie. I just turned out to be a different sort of *oops*.

Deb chuckles. "I know the feeling. So was I. Funny how God works sometimes, isn't it? Putting unexpected turns in our way, putting us where we never imagined we'd be."

I squirm at the possibility of this becoming a sermon. This could go from fine to hella awkward in about two seconds, so I'd rather not even run the risk.

"Is that God?" Talia pipes up. "Do the Forces That Be let Him do that, or did He just decide to on his own? Doesn't seem to be His place."

Turns out it takes one-point-five seconds. Thanks so much, Tal.

As Deb blinks at us, possibly trying to figure out what sort of crazy cultist she's let into her home, all three kids pile out the front door.

"Dishes are all done, Mom," Maddie says.

"Can we have some ice cream? Please?" Samuel begs.

Deb shakes her head. "You know the rule: after dinner only." Before any of the kids can protest, she adds, "You'll get an extra scoop if you get your chores done extra early."

Samuel's eyes go wide, and he looks to Talia and me. "Are Sarah and Daisy going to stay?"

I gulp down the rest of my coffee and get to my feet. "Actually, we should head back to the car. The tow truck will be along in an hour or so. They might get there early." Talia continues to sip her drink, so I elbow her to make sure she gets the message.

"I could drive you girls if you like," Deb offers. "It's getting awfully hot out there."

"It's not that far. Thanks for everything."

We hand her the cups—Talia does so rather reluctantly—say goodbye to the kids, then head back out into the summer sun. Samuel waves at us until we lose sight of the family behind the trees. Only then do I feel like I can breathe properly again.

"I don't think we needed to leave so early," Talia comments. "Besides, couldn't they call Deb's house?"

"That conversation was just getting really uncomfortable," I reply, shaking off the unease. "You don't talk religion with strangers. Hell, I'd rather not talk religion with anybody. It always ends in fighting."

"Is that what we were doing?" Talia asks. "I thought we were just chatting."

"Of course, you did," I mumble. "Just don't bring up the Powers That Be around random humans, okay? Humans look at the supernatural a lot differently than faeries. They can get a bit nasty if you disagree with them about it."

"Well, that seems a little silly," Talia huffs. "Unless I was about to turn them to stone with magic or something, it shouldn't be a big deal."

"Yeah," I scoff. "You would think."

We fall into a comfortable quiet as we walk back to the car and sit up on the hood of the car to wait. Thanks to its light color, it's just cool enough to lay back on, so I lean back, fold my arms behind my head, and close my eyes for a while. The heat feels nice, even if it is a bit too hot for comfort. The Faerie Queen's keep was always so cold in comparison that I never mind heat any more.

"Hey, Tal? Why are faeries so cold all the time?"

She quietly drums her fingers on the hood of the car for a moment before speaking. "No one's really sure, but Aunt Vervain used to tell me that it was because faeries are actually reincarnated humans."

My eyes pop open, and I sit up straight. "You're messing with me."

Talia shakes her head. "According to legend, thousands of years ago, a human clan leader died, but he wasn't ready to move on to the afterlife. He begged for the Powers That Be to let him stay on Earth to watch over his people. The Powers considered it and offered the clan leader a deal: if he took care of the forest, he could stay on Earth and watch his people from afar, but it was impossible for him to stay in the Land of the Living. That's why faeries can't touch iron. It prevents them from staying within the human world for long periods of time.

"The more humans moved into the clan leader's land, the more stressed he became in his efforts to take care of the forests. He came to the Powers again and asked if it could allow more souls to join him. It agreed, deciding to extend the offer to every member of the leader's clan that passed away."

I stare up at the sky, mind reeling as Talia speaks. "So, why are there so many different kinds of faeries? I doubt the clansmen looked like goblins to start with."

"It depended on their human lives. If they lived good, virtuous lives, they're born as court or benign solitary fae. Malicious people are born as more malicious fae."

Well, shit. Being an "honorary faerie" like Iver said doesn't sound so great anymore. Not if I get roped into their afterlife when I die. Would I? I made the choice to be baptized when I was twelve and called myself a Christian for a long time, so would God get first dibs or would He duke it out with the Powers That Be for my soul? Would he send Jesus to duke it out? He seems to take the whole individual soul thing pretty seriously. Which would be more merciful? The Powers That Be, most likely. They know about magic. They know what's up. Everyone seems pretty split on whether God likes people like me, but the Powers That Be don't seem to give a shit, so there's that angle too.

Talia chuckles. "What do you look so worried for?"

"Just questioning every single life choice I've ever made. No big deal."

She gently elbows me and says, "It's just a legend, DJ. Besides, I'm sure you'll be fine. You're a good person."

"Are running away from home, stealing from grocery stores, serving a crazy, masochistic queen, and bumming around Grand Haven the definition of a good person?" I ask.

Talia frowns. "You stole from grocery stores?"

"Someone jacked my wallet while I was running away to live with my aunt in New York. You get hungry hitchhiking across the country."

Talia goes quiet. Not just verbally, but in the way she's looking at me. There's a stillness in the way she sits and studies my face. "You never made it to New York, did you?"

I shake my head and shift under Talia's gaze. "Nope. The Faerie Realm got to me first."

I wish she'd stop looking at me like that. Her gaze is too intense for me to meet, and I hate it. It makes me feel small and powerless as if she could simply pull any explanation she wants out of me. Mab made me feel like that all the time and she took full advantage of it.

In a soft voice, Talia asks, "What happened to you, DJ?"

Her question opens the door in the back of my mind just enough for the whispers to creep out.

You've got to fight it, DJ.

Please spare our son.

Don't do this. We beg you.

"Hey, when the hell is that tow truck gonna get here, am I right?" I sputter, sliding off the hood of the car. I walk over to the edge of the road and scan the horizon in either direction. It's completely empty. Seeing as it's only 3:15, it's probably going to stay that way for a while. Great. That means at least fifteen more minutes of awkward question dodging. At least I think it does until I hear distant cries from a grove of trees on the edge of a nearby field.

They sound like they belong to a child no older than Samuel. While they don't sound pained or frightened, they definitely sound like something's wrong. The sound makes my muscles tense as I study every potential hiding place with suspicion.

Talia slides off the car and stands beside me. "You hear it too?" she asks quietly, shielding her eyes as she looks toward the thicket.

"Yep." I scan the road again in search of the tow truck. As I do, the crying gets louder and more urgent.

"We should go check it out," Talia says, walking back toward the car. "I'll get my bow, just in case."

"Because a random lady with a bow is definitely going to calm a panicked kid," I reply. Still, I follow her to the car and unlock the door. "I'll take my dagger. It's easy enough to hide and, at most, the kid's cornered by a freaked-out animal. They probably fell and twisted their ankle playing or something."

Talia raises an eyebrow. "You actually want to help?"

"Of course," I retort, slightly offended by her tone. "I'm not about to leave a kid out there by themselves. Besides, I doubt it'll take long, and we'll be able to see the car from there in case the tow truck shows up."

Talia smirks and nudges me as I lock the car back up. "And you don't think you're a good person?"

"Oh, shut up," I grumble. I just know what it's like to be scared and alone. A kid shouldn't have to feel that, even if they actually are perfectly safe.

Not like I'm going to tell Talia that, though.

We set out across the neat, organized field, careful not to step on any crops, and reach the thicket in a matter of minutes. Much like Deb's yard, the temperature plummets in the shade so that it's nearly comfortable now and the sunlight turns to glowing patches as it streams down through the trees. While we can still hear the kid, they're nowhere to be found. The thicket isn't any longer than a football field. They've got to be in here somewhere.

"Hello?" I call, treading lightly as we move deeper into the woods. "Kid? You okay? We heard you crying and thought you needed help."

The crying gets louder, but there's no movement or reply. We can see through to the other side of the thicket from where we stand and there's not much more to search. A chill runs down my spine as I realize that something's very wrong.

"Talia, we need to get out of here."

The air fizzes with static and grows heavy—signatures of magic.

I shove Talia back toward the field. "Tal, go! Now!"

We turn and nearly run into a troll emerging from a nearby tree. He swipes at us but gets a hand full of dagger. He howls as it slices through his leathery palm, and swings his other fist in fury. The wind rushes across my face as he just misses his target. It distracts me from the figure to our left, which hits me and knocks me to the ground. I don't have enough breath left to shout for Talia to keep going. It wouldn't matter. My face is shoved in the dirt as a tall gangly man snatches her by the shirt and slams her into the tree.

"Get off her, you bastard," I wheeze.

He ignores me and binds Talia's hands behind her back. My captor does the same, keeping me pinned to the ground with one knee. Talia's assailant spins her around, revealing scrapes along her cheek from where she hit the bark. The expression of terror on her face makes my blood boil, and I struggle against my bindings.

There's a quick flash of metal and a thin bite against my neck. That makes me stop.

"Knock it off," my captor growls. "We only need your friend, so you'd best not give us any more trouble than you're worth."

Snickers rise from the brush as goblins, trolls, and several other varieties of nasty fae emerge from the greenery. With a knife to my throat, I force myself to calm down and take in the situation, which helps me realize some of our attackers are not like the others. They're human like me.

The man who holds Talia has close-shaven hair, making his rounded ears visible. Judging by the weight and warmth on my back, this man is probably human as well. There's also the way he speaks. To my right, a woman with red hair sneers down at me. She's missing her top right tooth and her bottom front teeth are crooked, not a look faeries usually go for.

What the hell are other humans doing working with faeries?

"Just kill her and let's go," Redhead says, snapping her bubblegum. That sound is like nails on a chalkboard for me, so I've got one more reason to hate her. "She's just going to fight the whole way."

"No," Talia screams, trying to break away.

Her captor gives her a violent shake and winds up to hit her across the face. Before I can shout all sorts of threats, several faeries close in on him with weapons of their own at the ready.

"Easy now, lad," one of the goblins growls. "If you want what's promised, you'd best not go hurting Her Majesty."

Her What? They can't be talking about Talia.

But, nonetheless, the man backs down with a harsh glare at the goblin who threatened him.

"And if any of you want my favor, you'll let my friend live," Talia barks, though her voice trembles. She holds her head up and glowers down at the goblins, making them cower. "And you'll let her go."

"No can do, Your Majesty," one of them dares to say. "She's too much of a threat."

"She's been protecting me," Talia snaps.

"She stole you away from your people, as did your so-called aunts," argues the goblin. "You've been away from us too long to understand. Once you speak to Master Lyle, it'll all become clear."

Master Lyle? Wasn't that Queen Mab's champion? Then that would mean...

No. No, no, no, it can't be. There's no way, and yet the sudden block of ice in my gut tells me the truth. The rushing blood in my ears whispers it past all the doubt and silent pleas running through my head. This sweet, innocent, naive girl can't be related to that heartless monster. The universe isn't that cruel.

Who am I kidding? Of course it is.

"Talia," I gasp. She looks down at me, her face pale and eyes wide. "They're wrong. Please tell me they've made a mistake. Tell *them* they've made a mistake."

Talia opens her mouth to speak, but nothing comes out.

That's all the answer I need to color my vision red and turn my blood to boiling froth.

That woman tormented me. Every day for twenty years, she found new ways to make my life a living hell. I stripped people of all they owned for her. I threw innocent people in dungeons for looking at her wrong. She made me watch as she laughed while people begged for their loved ones' lives. She made me take lives. Whole families—families I knew—lest my body tore itself apart from the inside out for disobeying the woman I had sold my soul to. She made me choose: slaughter children or die a slow, painful bloody death. I'm still standing here, so guess which one I chose.

She turned me into a cowardly monster, just like her.

And I've been protecting her daughter all this time.

I was even starting to...

Bile rises in my throat at the very thought.

My burning shoulder blades distract me a bit.

"If we show up with the bodyguard, Lyle's gonna be pissed," says the guy on top of me. "He gave us direct orders to off her."

"Would you rather anger him or your future queen?" Talia snaps.

Judging by the looks everyone gives each other, they're not quite sure.

"I'll make you a deal," Talia says. "Leave her here, unarmed, and I won't tell Lyle. I'll cooperate, and after all this has been settled, I'll reward you for your loyalty."

Everyone exchanges more uncertain looks, but judging by the way they're looking between me and Talia, her offer is sounding pretty good.

"She's just going to follow us," Redhead says. "We gotta make sure we lose her."

My captor hauls me to my feet with a nasty sneer. "I think I have an idea."

Before I can fight or argue, pain erupts in the back of my head.

The world spins and goes dim. The man lets me go and I go down. I hardly feel the ground as I hit it, and everything finally fades to black. The only thing I can make out is Talia's voice in the darkness.

"DJ, I'm sorry."

I wish that was enough and I hate myself for it.

Chapter Nine

THIS IS THE second time since Talia came into my life that I've woken up on the floor with a headache without alcohol being involved. The world spins as I ease myself up and try to remember exactly what happened and where I am. As dark shapes sharpen against the night, it all comes back to me in a flash and my heart jolts.

"Talia."

Worry is quickly overshadowed by rage.

She's Mab's daughter. Their shared appearance and Iver's uneasy feeling about her weren't a coincidence. What's worse, I can't just leave her in Lyle's clutches like I want to. Vervain said I need her to say a spell to make the blue orb in my pocket work. I've got no choice but to go after her somehow. I want to scream at the universe about what a total dick it is, but screaming would make my head hurt worse.

Instead, I grab hold of a nearby tree, so I don't fall over again, refusing to sit back down. I don't have time to recover while Talia is out there held captive by a bunch of wacko faeries and humans, but my apparent concussion has other plans. Three steps away from the tree and I'm on the ground.

Looks like I don't have a choice in the matter.

As my body tries to catch up to my mind, I try to figure out exactly what I need to do. First, I need to grab our stuff from the car. I'm not saving anyone without weapons, and we won't be getting anywhere without my wallet. Something tells me we won't have time to come back for the car, seeing as it's dead and the tow truck never showed up.

Nearby whispers convince me to try to stand up again. They're nervous and rushed, the voices of people who don't want to be discovered, but not nearly harsh enough to be anyone who attacked us earlier.

"Lift it higher," hisses one, male by the sound of it. "It's not out of the hole yet."

"It probably wouldn't even be in the hole if you weren't driving," grumbles another.

Whoever it is sounds busy, but if they've been out here for any length of time, maybe they saw Talia and her captors. Better yet, if I can help them out, maybe they'd like to return the favor, so I follow the voices.

After twenty years in the Faerie Realm, I could swear I'd seen everything, but here I stand, watching five gnomes, all wearing crude leather gloves to protect against the iron, trying their damndest to get the front wheel of a large red ATV out of a deep dip in the ground. They must have hit an animal burrow of some kind.

The oldest sits in the driver's seat, his short legs dangling and tiny hands just barely reaching the handles. His long gray beard wraps around his neck like a thick wool scarf and his beady blue eyes glare down at his fellow gnomes as they strain and puff, trying to free the wheel. None of them are spring chickens, but their beards are shorter, their clothes slightly less worn, and their faces aren't quite as wrinkled.

"Excuse me?" I call. They all freeze at the sight of me. "Hi, hate to bother you, but I've run into some trouble. You see—"

"Human," screeches the oldest. "A human has seen us." The four drop the ATV wheel, nearly knocking the oldest out of his seat, and run for me, teeth and stubby claws bared.

"What? It's not like that," I shout, backing away as they close in.

"Don't let her get away," the eldest orders, standing on his seat to bark orders.

I grab a nearby branch and hold my ground. "Listen. I'm not a regular human. I'm a—"

"Get her! Get her! Get her!"

One of the gnomes dives for me and I step out of his way. When another tries to chomp down on my leg, I bonk him in the head just hard enough to dissuade him from trying again, but he's persistent, just like the rest of them. I have to knock it into them repeatedly that this is not how it's going to go.

I don't have time for this bullshit.

"I am a knight of the Unseelie Court," I finally shout, raising the stick above my head. "Anyone who wants to assault my person again will be met with swift and lethal force under the queen's authority. Do I make myself clear?"

Wow. I haven't had to use my knight voice in a long time. It doesn't even really sound like me. It works, though. The gnomes back off and retreat to the ATV while the eldest glares at me from atop the seat.

"Your queen has no power here, missy," he scoffs. "Consider yourself lucky that tales of her cunning and ferocity spread far enough to keep you safe. The last thing we nisse need is a woman like you investigating an attack on one of her own."

"You're not gnomes?"

The little man glares at me. "Bite your tongue lest you want me to sic them on you again! Gnomes do a tenth of the work we do, protecting their quaint little gardens. We take care of entire farms!"

Nisse. Not gnomes. Got it.

The old nisse begins stroking his beard. "Though that begs the question of what you're doing all the way out here. You're quite a ways from your queen's domain."

Finally, I get a chance to speak. "I was escorting a young woman across the country when we were attacked by a group of goblins, trolls, and humans. Did you happen to see a group fitting that description pass through here?"

After a few more moments of stroking his beard, the nisse hops down from the ATV. "Get this blasted human contraption unstuck for us and I'll tell you where they went, Lady Knight."

Well, that was easy enough, minus the branch swinging. Despite the pounding in my head it brings on, I hoist the wheel out of its trap and make sure the ATV is completely on solid ground. The surrounding nisse cheer and pile back on top of the vehicle behind their apparent leader.

"On our way to the Akerman farm, we spotted a troop like the one you described. On our way back, we saw lights on at the old Holst place. Nobody has lived there in the longest time."

"Where's the old Holst place then?" I ask.

The leader narrows his eyes. "That'll cost you extra."

I resist the urge to roll my eyes and take a deep breath. "What do you want?"

One of the nisse pipes up, "The nisse at the Falk farm stole our horse, Satin, a few months back. We still haven't repaid them for that."

"We got Satin back the next day," another nisse argues.

"Yes, and the Akermans will get this tiny automobile back tomorrow once our humans realize it's there, no doubt, but it's the principle of the matter," argues the first. "It's about tradition."

I'm about start racking up extra demands for all this bullshit, both the truth of who Talia is and these yahoos.

"How about this," I interject. "I'm actually big enough to drive that ATV, so I'll help you get it back to your place. Then, I'll help you steal the Falk's ATV if they have one—"

"Oh, they have one," says the leader. "Their farm is twice as big as ours. It would be horribly inconvenient to walk everywhere on their land."

"Okay, so I'll help you steal that one too, if I can use it to save my friend first. Deal?"

The leader goes back to stroking his chin while the others look on nervously. The idea of stealing not one, but two ATVs in a night has them wiggling with anticipation.

"What's your name, human knight?" the leader asks.

"People call me DJ," I answer, praying I won't have to use my full name.

"Well, DJ of the Unseelie Court, my name is Borg." He holds out his hand for me to shake. "And we have a deal."

I take his hand and the other nisse cheer. There's no spark between our palms the way there was with the aunts, and it looks like my nickname works well enough. I guess a promise to steal an ATV isn't quite as dire as one to protect one's adopted niece who's secretly a princess, which makes enough sense. It also means they could turn on me if I'm not careful.

With the deal struck, I settle into the ATV surrounded by nisse. Their leader sits in my lap and gives me directions back to their farm, but allows me to swing by the car and grab what I need to take with us. With it hidden in the grove behind their silo and a few more nisse in tow—apparently this horse thing was a pretty big deal—we head out to the Falk farm.

The nisse weren't kidding. Their place is huge, with fields stretching out in every direction. Lucky for us, they keep their ATV in a shed separate from the barn, where their nisse apparently live. The keys are on a small hook by the door too. With a little magic, a bit of patience, and a lot of elbow grease, we manage to disarm the Falk's nisse's charms, break in, and wheel the ATV down the road with no problem. Of course, the one thing that goes right on this trip is robbery. Typical.

"Which way is the old Holst place?" I ask. "Is it far?"

"We'll just come with you," Borg says. "The Holst nisse stole a cow of ours back in the day and we never got them back for it. Sabotaging a kidnapping operation on their land will have to do."

"You mean they don't even live there anymore and you want to get back at them?" I ask.

Borg shrugs. "It's the principle of the matter."

The "principle of the matter" is getting me my distraction, so I guess that works for me.

Borg sits on my lap again and his friends hold on as we take off down the road. The old Holst place is a good ten miles away. Not quite ideal, but with the ATV at my disposal, at least for a while, we should get a good head start. We park the ATV behind a nearby thicket. I leave our stuff with it and then crawl through a patch of trees to get a good look at the old Holst place.

The surrounding fields are lush and green with corn just past my knees. It looks like someone bought the land years ago and hasn't bothered to tear down the condemned farmhouse just yet. Two humans stand outside, armed only with faerie crystal daggers. It's the woman and the man who knocked me out. Everyone else must be inside. The first floor is dark, but light flickers from a broken second-story window. That must be where Talia is.

"Judging by the magic I'm picking up," Borg whispers, "there's three goblins and a troll inside on the first floor with another two goblins upstairs. I don't think the second story could withstand a troll's weight."

"The two humans should be easy enough to take out," I mutter back. "A few of you can lure them away from the house and knock them out. I can handle goblins, but I'll need some help with the troll."

"Say no more," Borg says. "While you're taking care of the goblins, we'll keep it distracted and confused. Can you take it out then?"

"Should be able to, yeah," I answer. "And the two upstairs won't be a problem."

With what we know and what we have, that's as good as our plan is going to get, so we all go to work. Borg sends four of his nisse to take care of the human guards. They let out a squawk from the corn, which lures the woman into the field. With a muffled cry, she disappears under the sea of long glossy leaves. The man takes off running after her, only to meet the same fate.

Stellar human recruiting effort, Lyle.

The four nisse pile out of the cornfield as the front door opens, revealing the goblins and the troll. The rest of us spring into action. Like we decided, the nisse attack the troll, aiming to badger and annoy rather than to do any real damage, while I take on the goblins.

They're no better than the ones that came to Iver's club. Sloppy technique, lazy footwork, and completely unaware of how to take advantage of the fact that there's two of them. One of them does manage to nick me under the eye, but I repay him with my sword through his gut. When the other tries to run me through the back, he gets a knife in his chest instead.

I ignore the sinking sensation in my gut and focus on my racing heart and the adrenaline racing through my veins. Fighting again, really fighting, feels incredible. I'd be lying if I said I didn't enjoy that part of being a faerie knight. The killing, however, has never sat well with me, no matter how necessary it turns out to be.

With the goblins taken care of, I turn my attention to the troll. He's perfectly positioned underneath a nearby tree as the nisse weave in and out of his grasp, sending him into a furious frustrated tizzy. I put the knife back in my belt, slip behind him with ease, and shimmy up the tree. If I can just get on his back...One, two, three—shit!

My foot slips on the branch, and while I still manage to crawl onto the troll's back, my sword falls out of my hand and lands on the ground. Guess I'm doing this the hard way. With my arms tight around the troll's neck, I hold on for dear life as he thrashes around. Between his stench, the force needed to hang on, and his heavy, jerky movements, it feels like it takes forever for him to pass out. Finally, he stills, sways, and falls forward. I tumble out of the way and snatch my sword as I go.

"Everyone okay?" I ask, taking deep gulps of fresh air. "Everyone accounted for?"

"Yes, and yes, Lady DJ," Borg says, brushing himself off. There's a slight tear in his shirt, but other than that, everyone looks unscathed.

"Go get the ATV so we can jump on and go," I order. "Think you can handle driving it that far?"

"We got the other one all the way to that grove where we found you, didn't we?" Borg scoffs. "We'll be fine."

As they scurry back to the thicket, I hear one of the others mutter, "But it took us nearly two hours." Borg knocks him upside the head and insists it's the principle of the matter.

Shaking my head, I bolt up the stairs and into the house. The first floor is completely gutted. Black scorch marks are all that's left of what must have been a lovely home. They're so extensive and deep that I'm surprised that there's a second story left at all.

As expected, one of the goblins jumps me at the top of the stairs. His higher ground gives him an edge, but not enough of one. He leans too far forward, and it just takes a slice to his right thigh to send him tumbling down the stairs. That seems to be a signature move of mine lately.

I find Talia in the second room on the right along with the last goblin.

She sits up straight in her corner and pulls at the ropes binding her. "DJ." She laughs. "You came."

I can't bring myself to look at her.

The goblin pales at the sight of me, drops his blade, and lifts his hands. "I yield," he cries, dropping to his knees. "I was only told to be on the lookout for a human girl. Not a demon."

"No demons here," I say, keeping my sword at the ready as I gingerly walk toward Talia. "Just a former faerie knight."

The goblin glares up at me with burning hatred. "No difference in my book, really. Besides, you won't get far. The one I serve shall be here any moment."

"Well, good thing we're leaving, then." I lower my sword to the goblin's neck. "Unless you want to try to stop us?"

The goblin gulps and eyes the blade. "I'd rather watch him run you through himself," he stutters.

What a coward.

"Tell him to bring it, then," I say, "If Lyle wants Talia, he's going to have to do better than this to best a knight of the Unseelie Court."

A smirk creeps onto the goblin's face. "You forget that Master Lyle is of the Unseelie Court himself. There's not a trick of yours he doesn't know. Not a place you can hide that he hasn't been, not a—" I clonk him on the head, and he crumples to the ground. I don't kill people who aren't attacking me, but he was getting on my nerves.

With that, I begin to saw at Talia's ropes.

"I was so worried about you." Talia sighs. "How did you find me?"

"I helped a band of nisse steal an ATV," I answer as the ropes snap.

"What's an ATV?" Talia asks as she gets to her feet.

"You'll see in a minute," I answer, dragging her toward the hall.

She resists the effort. "DJ, wait," she mutters.

I reach into the deepest crevice of my soul to scrape together some patience. "What is it, Talia?"

Talia bites her lip for a moment. "I'm sorry I lied. My aunts and I knew you wouldn't help me if we told you the truth, but I can't fall into Lyle's hands. The peace in the realm is shaky enough as it is. It could ruin everything."

I force myself to meet her green eyes. They're filled with remorse and guilt under furrowed brows, but they don't stir a single ounce of forgiveness. Those eyes match Mabs. Now that I know that, I don't know if they'll stir anything but resentment within me.

All I say as I grab her hand is "We need to go."

Talia slumps as she follows, but stays quiet.

I don't hear the ATV yet, but the nisse should be on their way. Unless…What if they just took off for home and left me here? So help me if they did, I'm walking all the way back and kicking their tiny asses. Using that thing was part of our deal.

It'll have to wait, because there's a bigger issue blocking our exit. This one makes my blood run cold.

I know that pale blond hair and those cold, steely blue eyes. This isn't the first time the thin mouth has sneered at me with that upturned, crooked nose. It is the first time, however, that I've been on the receiving end of his sword. It's a place I've never wanted to be. Very few people have been on this end of Lyle, Queen Mab's champion's, sword and lived to tell the tale.

"Daisy Jane, what a surprise," Lyle snickers, taking a few steps into the house. "When my men gave me your description, I thought that it surely couldn't be you. I thought you were smart enough to leave the Faerie Realm months ago."

"Well, you know me, Lyle," I reply, shoving Talia behind me. "I'm a bit hard-headed."

"Too true." He sighs. "I'm going to have to ask you put that nasty habit aside and get out of my way. Her Highness and I have a lot to discuss, and I'm afraid you'll just be a distraction."

"Well, actually, Tal and I talked it over and she's not really feeling up to it," I reply.

A look of sadistic glee spreads across Lyle's face. "Did you talk over who she is? Her birthright? Where she belongs? The destiny that awaits her?"

Why is he so melodramatic?

I tighten my grip on my sword. "Yes, jackass, we covered that already. Your henchmen can't keep a secret worth shit."

Talia takes ahold of my shoulder. "DJ, be careful. He's dangerous."

"So am I." Not exactly escaped-crazy-faerie-convict dangerous, but that's what bluffing is for. "Besides, finders, keepers. I call dibs."

Lyle throws his head back and cackles. It's a sound that's always filled me with terror. Nothing that follows it is ever good. "Unfortunately for you, Daisy Jane, you'll have to live through the night to keep her."

Chapter Ten

WITH JUST A blink, Lyle is only a hairsbreadth away from me, sword posed to run me through.

I barely raise blade in time to save my neck, literally. The effort knocks me into Talia, who falls up the stairs behind us. Lyle might be a better swordsman than me, but I'm physically stronger, so I manage to push him back just far enough for Talia to get past both of us.

"Get out of here," I order. "Out the back if you can. I'll find you again."

"I'm not leaving without you," Talia protests.

Lyle sneers and keeps me on the defensive with blows I practically have to run from. My blade blocks them with mere seconds to spare before they would've run me through.

"Damn it, Talia," I gasp. "I'm already not happy with you. Do you really want to make it worse?"

Instead of an argument, I hear rushed footsteps. Hopefully, she can find the nisse before any more of Lyle's lackeys show up. Pure spite pushes me through the fatigue. I've got to get out of here and catch up with Talia again. There's no way I'm letting Lyle win. He will *literally* have to step over my dead body to get her back.

Somehow, between all the attacks that I can just barely hold off, Lyle still has the breath for banter, one more thing I can't stand about him. "I have to say that I'm rather curious about what's come over you that you'd knowingly defend Queen Mab's daughter. Didn't you despise Her Majesty?"

"It's just a job."

"Whose? What's their payment?"

"Are you honestly stupid enough to think I'd tell you?" I huff.

"You misunderstand me. Whatever they're paying, I could pay you more. A place in the queen's daughter's court. Not as a common knight, but as her champion. Imagine the prestige. Imagine the glory."

I try to laugh, despite my lack of breath. Sweat threatens to drip into my eyes due to the summer heat. My shaking arms and wobbly legs can't take much more of this. I need an exit strategy.

"Why in the hell would I ever want to go back there? I *left*. I just want to live my life, not being bothered and not bothering anybody."

Lyle nearly slices me across the face and cackles. "You still believe that? That's never been the Daisy Jane I know, and despite our relationship, I do know you. You want to belong. You've always wanted to belong."

I recoil from his words. They distract me. I stumble over a hunk of charred wood and go down backward, landing wrong on my wrist as I try to catch myself. Before the world stops turning, Lyle's blade is at my chin. I lift my gaze to meet his and force myself to breathe slow. If I'm going to die like a loser, tripping over wood and spraining my wrist, I'm going to die like a somewhat dignified loser.

"Think about it, Daisy Jane," Lyle continues. "You'd be the woman who brought back the Unseelie princess. You'd be a hero. You'd be adored by the entire court, maybe even the Seelie Court once we bring it back under our rule. Who knows? If the princess shares your affinity for women, she'd have no choice but to make you her lover out of gratitude, once she sees who she truly is."

Yeah. Lover to the girl whose mother turned me into a killer. I should be so honored.

Stranger things happen, though.

Like how Lyle, a man I've never seen spare a single soul, lowers his weapon and extends his hand to me. His expression softens, which freaks me out more than him trying to kill me. "What say you?" he asks. "The princess will need people like you at her side, especially with what could be coming for the Faerie Realm."

How could anything be coming for the Faerie Realm? They've survived for thousands of years despite human destruction and growth. What could be threatening them now?

As much as I hate Lyle, the curiosity is more than I can stand, so I open my mouth to ask—

Except Talia flies out of *absolutely nowhere*, nailing Lyle in the back of the head with a branch as thick of my arm. His face goes blank. He sways for a moment, then falls forward, causing me to scramble out of the way and onto my feet with my sword back in my hand. The sight of blood blooming beneath his pale hair is more satisfying than I'd like to admit.

Before I can stop and call myself out for being such a sick individual, Talia grabs my good hand and sprints out the door. Halfway across the yard, the rumble of an engine and the glow of distant headlights draw my attention as well as a sigh of relief.

The nisse didn't abandon us after all.

I wave to signal them and Borg waves back, nearly flying off the vehicle as they hit a bump. We have to jump out of the way while they figure out how to properly brake, but the ATV isn't still for long. I jump on and grab the handles with Talia's arms wrapped tight around my waist and nisse crawling all over us. After a quick stop to pick up the bags with our things, we fly down the road toward the nisse's home.

They're kind enough to change plans and drive us to the freeway entrance ramp and then go home. While their assurance that they can drive the ATV themselves doesn't completely convince me, I'm too exhausted, both mentally and physically, to argue with them. I helped them steal it; they let me use it to get Talia; we're even in my book.

As the slightest hint of pink slices across the eastern sky, we begin our trek to Des Moines on foot. Talia cast a spell on her bag so that we could hide our weapons from passersby. With the car still broken, I don't trust it, and if we go back to that nice family, they'll no doubt start asking more questions than I'd like about us. The fact that we both pass as minors wouldn't help either. It's better to just stay on the main human roads and find a bus station once we get to Des Moines. I'm sure Talia's aunts will figure something out once we meet up again.

All the strategies and plans keep the seething anger toward Talia at the edges of my mind instead of front and center where I'd like them to be. I don't mind the tense silence. It's not the worst I've ever traveled in. It's nothing compared to, oh, say, walking back to the keep after killing people who'd hardly even whispered discontent toward the Queen. Every step felt like agony since my body tried to destroy itself when I resisted. Walking next to the daughter of the woman who made me kill those people is nothing. At least that's what I'm going to tell myself to get me through the rest of this trip.

But that's too simple for Talia. Oh, no. She can't let well enough alone.

"DJ, please talk to me," she mutters as the sun peeks over a distant line of trees.

I'm just going to ignore her. She'll shut up eventually.

"DJ? Say something, I'm begging you. I know you're not just thinking. Your face is far more severe than just resting-birch-face syndrome."

I refuse to correct her, and I'm sure as hell not laughing at her mess-up.

"DJ, we can't travel to Triple Lakes like this. This silence is too uncomfortable."

I halt in my steps. My muscles are too tense to move any farther forward. "You think silence is uncomfortable?" I hiss. "How about being lied to? How about learning who you are from someone *other* than you? How do you think all that feels, Tal?"

Talia flinches and takes a few steps back. "I understand you're upset—"

"No, Talia, I don't think you do," I snap. "You *knew* I served your mother. You *knew* what a monster she was. And yet you had the audacity to ask for my help anyway. Not to mention the apparent political cluster-fuck you've dragged me into. I left the court for a reason, Tal. You can't even begin to understand—"

Talia's eyes well up with tears. "I understand how it feels to be Mab's daughter and I hate it. That should count for something, damn it,"

"She made me kill innocent people. *My friends.*"

"She left me in the woods *to die of exposure,*" Talia shouts, voice cracking.

The sound of something usually so joyful and kind shattering stuns me into silence.

"I was one of the people she wanted dead, one of the people you could have murdered, and she tried to kill me when she was supposed to be my first means of protection, so don't you *dare* act like you've got some sort of monopoly on the pain caused by that god-forsaken wench I have to call a mother, Daisy Jane."

As the breaks in Talia's voice turn to sobs, I have no choice but to stand in shock as if she's slapped me. All my rage, all my pain, all the screams begging to get out, so I can have *some* means to communicate the raw agony I can't seem to let go. It's all justified, but not when it's aimed at Talia.

The words start pouring from her mouth faster than the tears in her eyes. "Do you have any idea how scared I am every day of my life that I'm like her? That some of her maliciousness got passed onto me and that I could hurt someone because of it? That someone will someday have to kill me so that the madness that gripped her won't take me too? That it might have to be one of my aunts that does it?"

Talia begins to try her hardest to wipe away her tears with both hands and my stomach twists. Damn it. Mab's daughter or not, I hate it when girls cry. I feel like I have to fix whatever caused it, especially if it was my fault.

And man, was this ever my fault.

"I'm sorry I lied to you," Talia hiccups. "Truly, I am, but my aunts and I knew you wouldn't help me if you knew the truth. No one would. The shadow of my mother's cruelty is too big for me to ever outrun. I won't be part of that 'political cluster-fuck,' as you called it. I won't hurt people for Mab, especially now that she's dead. If I want even the illusion of someone caring about my well-being, I have no choice but to lie."

Those words hit me like a sucker punch. I might not know what being Mab's daughter feels like, but I definitely know what it feels like having the lie. The one time I told the truth, and I mean *really* told the truth, it cost me home, my family, and my future.

With a sigh, I reach out and pull Talia's hands away from her face, flinching as I move my sprained wrist. "You don't have to fight it," I say. "Just cry if you need to."

That seems to have the opposite reaction. Talia's tears cease, and she blinks down at me as if I grew another head.

"What?" I demand, suddenly self-conscious. "I'm just trying to apologize. I shouldn't have yelled at you like that. If I was in your shoes, I probably would have lied too. Just be honest with me from now on, okay?"

Talia gives me a weak smile and nods. "I think that's the nicest thing you've said yet." Even with her hair a mess and circles under her eyes, there's something dazzling about that smile.

Before I can shake myself out of it—clearly, I'm exhausted too—Talia eyes my sprained wrist and takes it in both her hands, studying the bruises starting to form. "Did this happen when you fell?"

"Yeah," I scoff. "How lame is that?"

"It wasn't lame at all," Talia argues, beginning to gently massage the muscles of my wrist. "You held your own rather well against Lyle. I was impressed."

"Ha. Thanks, I guess." Warmth spreads along the length of my arm, numbing the throbbing and reaching my fingertips. As Talia works, I watch her expressions instead of her hands.

I am such a jerk. Here this girl is healing me after I just yelled at her and gave her the silent treatment for the past several hours. If I were in her shoes, I don't know if I'd be as forgiving that quickly. Mab might have given birth to her, but Talia isn't her daughter. Not by a long shot.

"Who did she make you kill?" she asks softly. "Your friends?"

Their names dry my tongue and make it stick to the roof of my mouth, but she's told me so much. It wouldn't be fair to keep her shut out. I don't want her to think I'm still angry with her.

"One of the cooks in the keep, Amarantha. When I got there, she sort of took me under her wing and looked out for me. And then there was her husband, Oren. He looked after Her Majesty's garden. They were both young by faerie standards, probably only a hundred years old or so. Their son, Tamir, couldn't have been older than ten. I don't remember his exact age."

"What happened?"

"You just asked for their names. That's all I'm going to say."

My throat closes, and I slam the door in the back of my mind shut. Enough got out today. No reason to let any more escape. I've still got a job to do. We've got a long way to go. Still, I guess you could call that progress. I haven't uttered those names in years.

Talia nods and flexes my hand as the warmth of her magic fades. "How's that?" she asks with a small grin.

I don't want her to let go of my hand, which is stupid, so I quickly wiggle out of her grip and adjust my backpack. "Perfect. Thanks. We should get going. Omaha, Nebraska, is still a ways away. It's probably the closest city with a major bus station."

Talia falls into step beside me with a revived spring in her step. "So, are we friends again?"

I hadn't thought of us as friends to start with, but I don't see any reason to point that out after we just made up. "Yeah, we're friends again."

Tal drapes an arm around my shoulder, pulls me closer, and beams down at me with the goofiest grin I've ever seen. Even though it makes me laugh, I wiggle out from under her. "What the hell are you doing?"

"Humans friends do that, don't they?"

"Maybe in cheesy movies, yeah, but don't. It makes me feel short."

"But you *are* short."

I lightly punch her in the arm. "I like to forget, thank you very much. Besides, neither of us are exactly human. We don't have to do stupid stuff like that."

"So, you don't consider yourself human anymore?"

The question, as well as my initial words, catch me off guard. When had I stopped calling myself human? Did Iver calling me an "honorary faerie" trigger the change? What could have made me stop seeing myself that way? The prospect of spending eternity in the Faerie Realm? The ties to humanity I'm about to destroy forever? The way I see the world now? It doesn't feel much different. Darker, maybe, but I can't say how much that has to do with the Faerie Realm.

Before I can piece together an answer, a navy-blue minivan pulls to the shoulder of the freeway a few feet ahead of us. Talia reaches for her bow, but stops after I give her a look. If Lyle and his goons were going to come after us, he wouldn't come for us in a *minivan*. At least, I hope he wouldn't. That's just embarrassing.

A slender woman, maybe in her early forties, gets out, rounds the car, and approaches us, all the while keeping an eye on the morning traffic speeding by. "You girls look like you could use some help," she calls, tucking her long brown hair behind her ears. "Need a ride?"

Talia looks at me with a curious expression, probably wanting some explanation about this strange human ritual. I just shrug. I highly doubt Lyle has resorted to enlisting soccer moms for his little rebellion. We're fine.

"Sure," I reply, walking the short distance to the woman. "Are you heading toward Omaha?"

"I sure am," the woman says with a grin. "We're going to meet my husband there for his family's reunion. We're going in plenty of time, so I'm sure we could drop you off where ever you need to go."

"That would be awesome," I reply with my best innocent-passerby smile. "Thanks so much." Motioning to myself and Talia in turn, I say, "I'm Deidre; this is Tanya."

"Nice to meet you. I'm Karen." As we head back toward her car, she gives us a sympathetic look. "Hope you don't mind kids."

If it means not walking all the way to Omaha, I absolutely love kids.

I take shotgun while Talia crawls in the back with Karen's two rug rats, Marcy and Grace. With everyone buckled up and the little girls already running their doll brushes through Talia's hair, we get back on the road.

"So," Karen begins, "what are two girls like you doing walking all the way to Omaha?"

Oh, boy, Karen. Are you in for a story.

Chapter Eleven

HUMANS ARE SUCH an unassuming group. I hope they never change. I won't be able to get away with jack shit if they do.

Karen buys our story about being college students conducting a social experiment about hitchhiking hook, line, and sinker. She's confused as to why two girls would do such a thing, which is understandable enough, I suppose.

Mostly for comic relief, I roll up my right sleeve and flex to show that a random creep in a big white truck would definitely have a bad day.

"It's okay," I say. "We're packing a couple of guns."

Karen laughs at my terrible joke and lets the topic of our gender go, focusing instead on the details of our experiment. Thank God, I've taken a few sociology classes, both in high school and in the last few months on my own, just for the hell of it. Judging by the way Karen nods along with the story, my rambling about "social conditioning" and "regional variations" and "gender presentation" sounds legit.

I might have to try that college thing one day after all.

Around noon, Karen drops us off at the Omaha bus station, waves goodbye, and heads back toward the highway. We stand on the curb and wait until her minivan blends in with the rest of the city traffic.

"She was nice," Talia says as we head for the front doors. "And her daughters have quite the gift for styling hair."

"I noticed," I chuckle, batting at one of the loose braids the girls left in Talia's hair. "Now, let's finda bus to Denver."

Our options are slim, to say the least. There's a bus that leaves at 9:45 tonight, which would get us there at 6:50 in the morning tomorrow, or one that leaves at 5:30 tomorrow morning. Obviously, we go with the one leaving tonight, but that means we have over nine hours to kill in Omaha, Nebraska.

Great. Waiting. My favorite.

"It looks like there's a small theater down the street," Talia exclaims as we leave the station with our tickets. She studies the tourist brochure she grabbed inside and nearly gets smacked in the face as the door swings shut. I hadn't realized she wasn't looking. "They're playing *A Midautumn Day's Dream* today at one o'clock. Want to go?"

I've never really been one for classic literature. In school, I always wrote my own stories while we read the assigned text in class and then paid attention when the teacher explained it. Then, when I wound up in Faerie, every other person I met claimed to inspire the classics in one way or another. It kinda ruined all of it for me, especially the old water hag who claimed to lend inspiration for poets and bards across Europe.

But, given that we don't really have anything else to do, I don't see why not. The map says tickets are only three dollars for students and we pass for students easy enough. I'd rather pay three dollars to nap in a cool, comfortable auditorium than nap out on the ground in the sun.

Talia pretty much bounces the entire way to the theater four blocks away, which begs the question of how she even knows about the playwrite Shakesword. Her aunts don't exactly strike me as the classic literature types, and his works don't exactly make the best bedtime stories, so I ask.

"Oh, all faerie children know your old tales. They're like the equivalent to what you call fairy tales here in the Human Realm," she explains, proving me wrong. "Also, I would sometimes sneak into town to watch their high school productions. It was the only time my aunts wouldn't get mad at me if I got caught. All of your best writers are part fae like me, after all."

That's another story I've heard a lot, but I decide to just nod rather than scoff. I'd rather not go back to fighting with Talia, especially over something so harmless that makes her so happy.

Sure enough, the people working the front desk believe we're high school students without even asking for our IDs, though I think Talia might have something to do with that. I let Talia pick seats in the center of the auditorium and settle in for the two hour-ish show.

Turns out that I was wrong about that whole nap thing. Talia's whispering of lines and giggling at the smallest of things makes it impossible to fall asleep. But instead of being annoyed, I find that I'm actually having fun. Talia's imitation of the actors is hilarious, and her commentary is so ridiculous, that I have to laugh at it, if not at the show itself.

The fifteen-minute intermission is a good chance to catch my breath from the hilarity.

"If there's a theater company in or near Triple Lake, you need to join." I sigh, wiping a tear from my eye. "You could write and act retellings of this stuff. It would be hilarious."

Talia sighs and shakes her head. "I can't read, remember? Let alone write."

"I could write, you could dictate," I offer. "I'm a wicked fast writer. I was always the first one done with my essay tests in school and I wrote a lot in my free time."

Talia's eyes widen. "You're a writer?"

I shrug off the unspoken assumption that being a writer is something magical or glamorous. "I used to be. Once I became a knight, I didn't have much time, even though my poetry is what made Mab take me from my mistress in the first place."

Talia's expression goes somber. "Someone owned you?"

"Who *didn't* own me in the Faerie Court?" I scoff. "But yeah, that's how I ended up there in the first place. An old banshee tricked me into eating from her table when she found me trying to take a shortcut from the highway. So, not only was I trapped because I ate faerie food, the banshee kept me, saying I owed her my life since she saved me from starvation, which was bullshit, but that's how it goes in the Faerie Realm."

Talia nodded in agreement.

"Anyway, she liked my poetry, so I would write in the little spare time I had from chores. She even presented my poems as a gift to Queen Mab when we visited court once. Queen Mab took such a liking to me and my work that she wanted me for herself. When the banshee refused to hand me over, Mab killed her."

Talia winced and sank in her chair a bit. "I'm sorr—"

"Nope. Don't say it. I don't want you to say it. I don't want to be pitied."

"It's not about pity," Talia argues. "I would never be foolish enough to pity you. You went through something terrible that no child ever should have to. You were taken advantage of, and you're the only one who ever put a stop to it. It just hurts my heart that someone I care so much for had to go through all of that."

I fold my arms and mutter, "I'm not a child, remember? Don't let this face fool you."

"You were, though. In many ways, at least."

My heart tightens. I hold my arms tighter to my chest and try to ignore it. I've always just had to ignore it. Unpacking too much from the last twenty years really would make me look pitiful, which I can't afford, especially considering I'm still technically in the middle of a job. Hell, if I knew I'd have to unpack so much on this trip, I wouldn't have taken the job in the first place.

"I guess you can be a little sorry then," I grumble.

Talia chuckles and gently elbows me. "I'd like to read some of your poetry sometime."

"I'm really out of practice," I reply as the lights above dim again. "It would probably be terrible.... I could probably write you a half-decent story, though."

"I'd like that very much," Talia whispers in my ear.

A chill runs through my body. The AC's just cranked up too much That's it. It's probably best to ignore it.

The second half of the play isn't as funny as the first. Talia doesn't say the lines anymore and her commentary is more about the costumes and sets than the story itself. Even as we leave the theater, she doesn't have much to say. Her expression is thoughtful, and I can feel her eyes boring into the back of my head as we step into the blazing afternoon sun.

I can't take this for six more hours, *then* an all-night bus ride.

"Let's find something else to do," I suggest. Maybe if I can keep her distracted with the wonders of the human world, she won't ask any more questions, so I grab another tourism brochure near the front door of the theater. "There's a park with a lake a few stops away. Want to check that out?"

Talia rolls her eyes. "I grew up on Lake Superior," she says. "Unless it's that big, that clean, and that beautiful, I'll pass."

I can't help but snicker at her being snooty about something so odd. "All right then, Your Majesty—"

She winces. "Don't call me that."

"Sorry. Anyway, it looks like there's an art museum close by. Want to just walk instead of taking the bus? We'll be sitting for a while tonight."

Talia taps her foot, takes a look around, and concludes, "Sure. Why not?"

The buildings, traffic, and passersby distract Talia from her weird fixation on me. Walking was a good idea, the art museum even more so. Just walking in the door lights Talia's eyes up like Christmas lights. No sooner do we have our tickets—again, discounted since we look like students—than she speed-walks toward the first gallery.

I took Talia for even less of an art gallery girl than I did a Shakespeare girl, but it's a nice surprise. Instead of talking about artists' use of lighting and the style of the time and originality, she just hypothesizes which artists are part fae and how much. That or if they spent any time in the Faerie Realm. She refuses to take responsibility for any of the modern art.

"That's all on humans," she says with a turned-up nose. "A faerie would never allow for something so ghastly and tasteless." I guess she's more fae than I figured. Everyone in court was a bit of an art snob too. To each their own, I guess.

By the time we wrap up, it's just after six o'clock. Should be enough time to grab a bite to eat, head back, and ready ourselves to get on the bus. As we roam the path back to the station, Talia trails behind to stare at a chalk sign outside a small hole-in-the-wall burger joint.

"DJ, what's that glowing sign say?" she asks.

I double back to read. "Karaoke? It's when you get really drunk and embarrass yourself in front of a bunch of strangers by singing songs you barely know."

"Sounds fun. What's this below it?" she asks, pointing to a particular sentence.

I should just make my life easier by lying to her and finding somewhere else to eat, but I can't bring myself to lie to those big curious doe eyes. "Participants get a ten percent discount off their bill," I mutter.

"That's good, right?"

"Yeah, I guess, but I don't sing. Like, ever."

"I like singing, though."

I think it over for a minute. It's no doubt safe enough in there, and it's a small place. I can keep an eye on it easy enough. Not to mention I'm always down for a discount.

"If we do this, you have to bewitch our waiter let me buy a beer," I offer.

Talia smirks and holds out her hand. "Deal."

We shake on it and enter the restaurant.

It's a decent little place, I have to admit. Probably not that appealing in proper lighting, but in low light, the neon advertisements, worn tables, and clacking of pool balls has a rustic all-American feel to it.

Talia picks a table near the empty stage and holds up her end of the bargain when the waiter comes over. His eyes go a bit fuzzy when I request whatever pale microbrew they have on tap. Talia decides to have the same.

I'm a beer snob and I'm not sorry. There are too many carbs in beer to waste time drinking the bad stuff.

I order a burger while Talia sticks to a salad. Given that my meal is almost as big as my face, I don't really blame her. After twenty years of eating like faeries, there's no way I'm going to finish it all. Luckily Talia's willing to try it.

Judging by the disgusted look on her face, one bite is all she's willing to take.

"Excuse my manners, but how can you eat that? It's ghastly," she mutters, mindful of the waitress nearby.

"It's no different than pizza," I remind her, saving the chargrilled beef, pickles, cheddar, and red onions. The fries have the perfect amount of salt and pepper on them, which is a rare find. If I'd met Talia when I first returned to the Human Realm, I would have probably gained about twenty pounds by now. Or if someone had just told me I could eat human food using a spell. I'm still kicking Iver's ass when I get back. Raise or no raise.

"Pizza has a better ratio between vegetables and meat. Also, there was fruit," Talia argues, taking a bite of her salad.

I shrug and continue eating. "I can respect that."

Halfway through dinner, someone finally gets the gall to climb up on stage. He signals to the bartender that he's ready—though judging by the way he sways and has to lean on the microphone stand, I question that—and the bartender hits a few buttons on the small karaoke machine. An old country-western song comes on over the speakers and our three minutes of torture begins.

To be fair, classic country actually isn't that bad. I grew up listening to it on long road trips to see my maternal grandparents who lived in Oklahoma, which explains how my mom got into it, but this...this is a whole new monster.

While I'm glad this guy is clearly having fun, he sounds as if a banjo and a howler monkey got into a screaming match with a nail on a chalkboard as a referee. He takes his buddies' encouragement as a sign to get louder.

"Tal, I need another beer," I mutter. I'd order something harder, but we still have to get back to the bus station.

"I think I need one too." She sighs, waving over our waiter, who gladly obliges us. While Talia has him here, she whispers something to him while glancing and pointing at the stage. The waiter smiles and nods as he goes to get our drinks.

"What did you say to him?"

"Just if I could go next," she says. When our beers come, she chugs half of hers before I even take a sip. "I may not have thought this out," she said, scowling at the glass bottle. "The beer and our deal. If this is the sort of entertainment people look for when they come to karaoke night, I worry they might find me rather unbearable. And gods above, human beer is terrible and yet I'm on my second one. What means of magic is this?"

"You could have ordered something else." I chuckle. "And screw what these people think. You're not doing this for them. You're doing this because it's something you want to do, and because it gets us a discount."

The song finally ends, thank God, and the man stumbles off the stage. The bartender waves to Talia that it's her turn and she smiles back, despite the way her face goes pale.

I tap her on the hand to get her attention. "Hey," I mutter, "go knock 'em dead, and get us ten percent off our bill." Talia smiles at me, this time for real, sighs, chugs the rest of her beer, then gets to her feet.

One of the rowdier patrons whistles at her as she takes her spot behind the mic and I shoot him a glare that, surprisingly, actually shuts him up. Good. Last thing we need before getting on a bus is a bar fight.

Talia gives the crowd a sheepish grin and waves. "Um, hi. My name's Talia."

A bunch of people call back, "Hi, Talia!" in drunken slurs.

"This is a really old song, and it's in Scottish-Gaelic, so you might not know it, but I hope you like it."

I can't help but shake my head, wondering how Talia turned out this adorable and innocent. It's not like the Faerie Realm is anything like in the storybooks. Still, it's nice. As much as she's driven me crazy in the past few days and caused me numerous headaches, I'm glad she's the way she is. It's nice to have a ray of sunshine after being in the dark all these years.

And her voice...

As the first word leaves her mouth, the entire restaurant goes quiet. The rowdy customers settle, the waiters stop taking orders, and even the bartender stops what he's doing to listen. I can't understand the song, but I've definitely heard it before. It's a common tune among solitary fae, and it popped up at court every once in a while, much to Mab's disdain. She hated anything she deemed "common," which just made me like the song even more, but Talia's rendition is something completely different simply because of her voice.

It's like a mother's lullaby, sunlight and wind mixing with summer leaves and the flowing of a brook all wrapped up in one sound. It clenches my heart and threatens to close my throat with something neither sad nor forlorn. I'm not quite sure what it is, but it needs to knock it off. I gently shove my half-finished beer to the other side of the table. I think I've had enough for one night.

My phone buzzes, which is a welcome distraction. It's Calista.

Come back already. Iver won't tell me where you are or what's going on.

I'm working. That's all you need to know.

:(

Something's off. Usually I would eat up Calista's need for my attention, but tonight, it's just annoying. It's not the booze. Usually that gets us both off and running.

Talia's song comes to an end, leaving a stunned silence in its wake. The bartender is the first to applaud, causing the entire restaurant to follow with hoots, laughter, and calls for an encore.

Tal turns bright red and shrinks away from the mic, despite her smile.

We've still got time to kill, and she clearly enjoyed herself, so I lead the crowd in a chant of, "One more song. One more song." When Tal obliges, everyone goes wild. Luckily, she sings an Irish jig instead of another quiet emotional piece. She bounces in time with everyone's claps, and I find it impossible to keep from smiling along with her. Everyone will just have to find out how scary I can be the hard way if they mess with Talia.

My phone buzzes again. Still Calista.

If you're stressed, you probably need a break. Want some company? I'm sure we can work something out from this far away. Phones have cameras for a reason. ;)

My body freezes with panic. It's definitely not the first message Calista's sent me like this, nor the most suggestive, believe it or not, but what if Talia were to see it? Hell, why do I care if Talia sees it?

Stop. I can't do this anymore, Calista. It doesn't feel right.

It takes her a while to reply.

Uh-oh. You went and fell for someone, didn't you?

I swallow hard and type. *Don't be ridiculous. This just isn't working for me anymore.*

As if I haven't heard that one before. It's all right, though. I understand. Make sure they know how lucky they are to have you. If things don't work out, you know where to find me.

I'm not in love with anyone.

What's the point of being able to lie if you're this bad at it?

I don't dignify that with a response.

Instead, I close out my messages and check the time. We should probably head back toward the bus stop, so I motion for Talia to come down once her song ends so we can pay and head out, which gets me several boos.

Talia hops off the stage and glides toward me as if she's walking on air. "I guess karaoke can be fun after all." She giggles, taking a swig of my beer. I forgot that faeries are lightweights.

I gently pry it from her hands and motion for our waiter to bring us the check. "Take it easy." I chuckle. "If I have to carry you to the bus station, we're going to be late."

Talia runs a hand up my arm as she takes a seat, leaving a chill where she touched me. "We'd be fine," she says. Leaning forward and looking up at me through her long lashes, she adds, "You're plenty strong enough."

My heart stops. It doesn't start up again until the waiter hands me the bill. I quickly pass him my card, try to organize the table a bit, and gather our things. Anything to avoid looking at Talia. She doesn't mean it. She's drunk. That's all. She doesn't know what she's saying. All the air seems to leave the room as I realize something terrifying.

I desperately *want* her to mean it.

You've gone and fallen for someone.

No. I just find Talia attractive and we've both been drinking. That's it.

As we leave the bar, Talia waves to everyone and they wave back. When I hold the door open for her, she slips her hand into mine and drags me out onto the sidewalk.

"That was the most fun I've had in the Human Realm yet," she exclaims, skipping a few steps ahead. I let her go. She stops and looks back at me. "Is something wrong? Didn't you have fun?"

"Yeah," I answer with a shrug. "We should just try to keep on the alert. It's getting dark and we're not familiar with the area."

Talia slips both her hands into mine. "It's okay," she says, closing the space between us. "I've got you here."

I pull away and start walking back the way we came. "Tal, stop messing around. We gotta go."

She slips her arms around my waist and holds me tight. "What makes you think I'm messing around?" Her voice in my ear makes me melt inside. "And we've got plenty of time. Stay with me a moment."

"No more alcohol for you for the rest of the trip," I tease, weakly trying to get out of her grip. I'd be lying if I said I wanted her to let me go. "It makes you too loopy."

Talia lowers her lips to my neck, making me tremble. "This is the clearest I've thought this entire journey."

"Hey, you know what sounds fun? Reading. Reading sounds fun *and* it's a very important life skill, so let's focus on that for a while, shall we?"

I search high and low down the street for something, *anything,* to draw Talia's attention away from me before it gets to be too much. I can't promise that the next time she touches me like that I won't touch her back, no matter how wrong it might be. This is a job. Two, three more days tops and I'll never see her again. What's more, she's Mab's daughter. How can that be okay?

A coffee shop sits open across the street. Its warm windows glow like an exit sign, and I jog across the street toward it as if I can ignore the fire that Talia lit in my blood. Having her follow close behind doesn't help, but the robust earthy smell of coffee begins to put my mind at ease.

Just as I had hoped, there's a few racks filled with magazines. The closest fashion one should work well enough. Not too hard to read and plenty of pictures. Hopefully the bright colors will keep Talia distracted until she sobers up. Judging by her intense gaze on the back of my head while I pay, I might not be that lucky.

"DJ."

I shove it into her hand on my way out and head back toward the bus station with her trailing behind. "Not exactly grade-A material, but it'll do."

"DJ."

"I read somewhere that we're wired to read words, not letters, and I'm no teacher, so hopefully this won't blow up in my face—"

"Daisy Jane."

With the way Talia says my name, I have no choice but to stop and look at her. The magazine's still rolled up in her hand. She probably hasn't even glanced at the cover. She's too busy looking at me as if she's studying the very fabric of my soul.

"Why are you so scared all of a sudden?"

"I'm not scared," I scoff and keep walking. "You're just more intoxicated than me. It wouldn't be appropriate. You don't know what you're doing."

Talia's bright green eyes narrow into a sharp glare. "I know what I'm doing. I'm tipsy, not wasted."

"Still, I'm a knight. Gotta be honorable and all that jazz."

She studies me for a longer while, then opens the magazine. "I suppose my behavior has been a little inappropriate tonight. I'm sorry."

"It's cool."

After settling on a page, Talia catches up with me. "This looks like a good place to start. Not a ton of words, and they're about clothes. I like clothes." At least it feels like I got one thing right tonight. "Will we have time back at the bus station?"

I check my watch. "A little bit. Then we should probably sleep on the bus. We've had a long two days."

And given that we're going to wake up a few hours from my childhood home, tomorrow will probably be longer.

Chapter Twelve

THE EARLY MORNING sun rising over the plains wakes me up. They're so tranquil and empty that it feels like a dream. Strange what changes and what doesn't in twenty years. The dusty yellows and bright greens glow as bright in the sun as when I left, but there are more suburbs and cul-de-sacs than I remember. The roads are busier. Growing up, you could drive on these roads for quite a while before seeing another car. Mom used to say that it felt like being the only people left in the world.

Mom. I'm going to see my mom today. And my dad and my brother. That realization dissolves any sort of peace I felt faster than a sugar cube in boiling water. Maybe not. Maybe we could bury the orb in the yard, Talia could say the spell, and we could leave without them being the wiser. It would be less painful that way. They could all stay the same people they've always been in my mind.

No. I wouldn't hide. Not like that. I at least have to see how they're doing without me.

The starts and stops of driving through Denver wake Talia. She stretches and yawns, but keeps her head on my shoulder. Despite what happened last night, I let her stay there. I even let her keep hold of my hand. Her touch is comforting in the face of so much uncertainty packed into the next twenty-four hours. I just hope she doesn't read too much into it. I mean, she's Mab's *daughter*. Talia's sweet, but there can't be anything between us with that sort of history. It wouldn't be fair to her to be with someone who saw her mother behind those big green eyes.

And yet not a single thing she's done has reminded me of Mab.

But what if I did one day? What would I do?

We pull into the bus station. Everyone begins gathering their things with sleepy eyes and disheveled clothes. Once the bus comes to a stop, the driver stands up and says over the P.A. system, "Welcome to Denver. The local time is six fifteen a.m. Please be careful not to forget anything and watch your step as you exit the bus." With a smile, he adds, "Thank you for riding with us and have a wonderful Fourth of July."

I quickly look at my phone and see that he's right. How did I not notice that until now? My whole family is going to be home. Mom's probably already awake, making food for the party. Dad might be up too, seasoning the raw hamburger with a blend of spices he refuses to tell any of us. He probably already jokingly reached for a beer or two, only to have Mom slap his hand. I don't know what Shunsuke's doing. As kids, he'd sleep in until almost noon on holidays, but as a full-grown adult, I have no idea. Whenever he gets up, he'll be at the house in plenty of time for the food. There could be aunts, uncles, cousins, and even family friends there too.

Shit.

Talia nudges me, and I come back to reality. "DJ, are you alright?"

The bus is nearly empty except for us, so I scramble out of my seat with my bag and head for the exit. "Yeah," I lie. "I'm fine."

With a nod to the driver, I hop off the bus and head inside, hunting for the nearest bathroom. Cold water on my face wakes me up, but does nothing for my nerves. If anything, they're wound tighter now that I'm alert. As the water drips off my face, I list everything in my reflection that they'd disapprove of: the boyish undercut, the dark masculine clothes, all the tattoos. Even if I see them, they can't see me. I can't go through that again.

Talia sets a hand on my shoulder and I jump. I hadn't even realized she followed me in.

"We can wait if you want. Take a few days. We're ahead of schedule."

I shake my head and grab a handful of paper towels. "No. We're getting this done. It'll be quick. You'll be with your aunts' family by nightfall."

"Am I really that exhausting?" Talia teases. Judging by how tired her smile looks, she's only half joking.

I hold the door open for her as we leave. "It's not you. This trip has just been a lot more...emotionally exhausting than I thought it would be."

Talia gives a weak chuckle. "I have to agree with you there."

We buy tickets for the next bus to Red Well, which will leave in an hour. We take the time to eat at a nearby fast food joint, but neither of us is too hungry. I end up eating two bites of my pancakes, cut up the rest and push them around my syrup-soaked plate. It takes Talia five solid minutes to finish a spoonful of her parfait.

"You don't have to do this, you know," she says, studying the swirls of blueberry juice and vanilla yogurt. "You could ask my aunts for something else. They'd be more than happy to oblige you."

"I *need* to do this, Tal. It doesn't feel right leaving them in limbo like this."

"Then talk to them."

"Yeah, that'll go over real swell. 'Hi, everyone. I'm stuck being sixteen forever and I'm gonna be hanging out in a mystical realm for the rest of eternity. Just wanted to stop and let you know so you can stop wondering if I'm dead.'"

Talia scowls at me. "Do you have to be sarcastic about *everything?*"

I shrug and take a bit of sickly sweet pancake.

Leaning in and lowering her voice, Talia says, "You know what I think? I think you're just trying to bury your own feelings about what happened. You don't want to think about the hurt. You don't want to think about the rejection or the fact that they might reject you again if you go back, so you're burning this bridge once and for all. It's not about saving your brother the heartache of losing you at all. It's about you building that wall around your broken heart a little higher."

I choke on my coffee, spilling it down the front of my shirt. "I'm sorry, but did I ask you your thoughts about what I was doing with *my* family?" I rasp, dabbing at the stain forming down my front. "Or are you just mad that I told you to stop coming on to me last night?"

Yikes. That was a low blow, even for me.

Shit. Could Talia be right about me?

Her face turns bright red as she leans back in her chair and folds her arms. "Don't be ridiculous. I'm not that sensitive. I just figured a faerie knight would want to do the braver, more honorable thing."

I glare at her instead of responding. It sets a silence in motion that I can't decide whether to love or hate. Either way, it follows us all the way back to the bus station and the entire trip to Red Well.

The town's twice the size as what it used to be. There are entire neighborhoods and streets that didn't exist back when it was my home. Streets that were once slow and safe for kids to play in are now bustling paths to and from businesses that didn't exist before. Finally, with the help of a kind little old lady, we figure out the bus schedule and set about reaching the house I grew up in.

Part of me wants to "accidentally" get on the wrong bus and go downtown. Maybe I can distract Talia with all the Fourth of July festivities, but she's still carrying the quiet I caused with the argument. The banners and decorations lining the road don't hold her attention and the eccentric red, white, and blue outfits don't raise any questions, though she does look severely confused when we pass a couple with a dog dressed like the Statue of Liberty. Can't say I blame her.

My part of town looks the same. The same small fenced-in yards, the same wide two- and three-story houses, the same view of the mountains cloaked in dark green forests with streaks of pale and reddish stone. I don't recognize any of the cars in the driveways, though, and the children playing out in the yards are different for obvious reasons. I do, however, look to their parents and grandparents, searching for familiar faces. There are some that may have been my classmates and their parents, but my memory is so fuzzy that I just consider myself lucky to even remember the way to my house. A few streets down, I pull Talia behind a tree that was much smaller when my brother and I use to climb it.

"Can you make a glamour that will turn us invisible?" I ask.

She frowns and thinks it over. "Yes, but it's much harder than one that would simply alter our appearances. The easiest way would be if we stood together and I cloaked us both. It would take too much energy to alter the light around us both separately the whole time."

"Do whatever you need to do," I reply. "My family just can't see me when I go inside."

Talia's eyes grow twice their size. "You mean you're going to see them?"

I pull the orb from my pocket. "Just for a minute." I refuse to look like a coward, even if I still think wiping their memories is for the best. Hopefully, checking in on them will count for something. "Then we're burying this bitch in the backyard, you'll say the spell, and then we're off to Triple Lake."

Talia scowls at me for a moment, then sighs and takes my hand. "Fine. It's your family. I can't force you to talk to them, but I still think you should."

A tingling sensation washes over me, and the edges of my vision go fuzzy, like I'm viewing the world through some sort of tunnel. It's still clear enough for us to make our way to my childhood home.

It looks exactly the same. It's the same pale blue that my mother always complained about and swore she would paint one day, and the shutters are still white. In the yard sits the same gnomes and ceramic geese that we inherited from my grandparents when we moved in. My brother's basketball hoop still hangs over the garage and shows the only signs of change. It's worn and ragged with faded paint and graying netting.

"How do we get inside?" I ask, though my mouth suddenly feels dry.

Talia takes hold of the front door handle, closes her eyes for a moment, and we here a small click. She slips it open, pulls me in, and shuts it again in with one swift fluid motion.

Footsteps coming down the stairs freeze us in place.

"Shunsuke? Did you forget something?"

My mother stops and stands a few feet in front of us.

She's shorter than I remember. Since when wasn't she larger than life? She cut her hair into a neat bob at some point, and she's given up hiding the streaks of gray mixed in with the dark brown. Good choice. Gray actually looks pretty good on her. Something about the creases across her forehead, around her mouth, and at the corner of her eyes make her seem timeless and elegant instead of aging. I'm glad she still likes to wear bright colors. The jewelry Dad would buy her for their anniversaries is missing as always. I wonder if he gave up and started sticking to chocolate.

"It wasn't me, Mom. I thought that was you."

My brother rounds the corner from the kitchen, somehow taller than he was in college. I didn't think that was possible. He's thinner, though, and similar smile lines to Mom's have begun to etch themselves into his face. His jet-black hair starts farther back then I remember. And what the hell is he doing with a short, slicked-back adult haircut? What was all that talk about never cutting it as long as he lived?

They're both so close that I could reach out and touch them if I let go of Talia's hand. I could hold them and tell them I'm here and that I'm sorry that I made them worry. I shouldn't be sorry. Not to Mom anyway, but saying anything would probably loosen the knot in my chest.

"We can lift the glamour if you want," Talia whispers.

I shake my head.

Mom and Shun exchange quizzical looks, then study the door. Talia and I have to dodge out of the way before they run right into us as they walk toward it.

"It wasn't me," Mom mutters, opening the door. A frown etches more lines into her face. "It should be locked. Go ask your father."

"It's probably nothing, Mom," Shun says with a shrug. "It's an old door. Maybe you forgot to lock it last night and the wind blew it open?"

"What wind, Shunsuke?"

Shun walks back to the kitchen. "The kind that opens doors, I guess. Want me to stick the potato salad in the fridge?"

My mother looks around the living room in search of something out of place. Her gaze rests on us for a moment, and my blood runs cold. I wouldn't put it passed past my mother to have X-ray vision, or whatever gift would let you look through a glamour. She always did have a knack for knowing everything.

"I'm telling you, Shun, something opened that door."

"Well, until you figure out what did, tell me what to do with the potato salad."

With a roll of her eyes, Mom follows him into the kitchen. "I told you, put it on the bottom shelf. It's the only place there's room."

I drag Talia along, to following them to see if...aw, yeah. It's Japanese-style potato salad. Nothing but potatoes, cucumbers, ham, salt and pepper, and Cupie Kewpie brand mayo, and none of the egg nastiness of American potato salad. It may seem like a strange thing to be passionate about, but I could eat tubs of that stuff as a kid and never get sick of it.

The kitchen hasn't changed much. The artwork on the fridge belongs to someone else, though. I don't know who *"Hannah"* is, but she certainly likes pink and yellow. And race car stickers.

As they rearrange the fridge, I take the chance to look downstairs at the den. It's pretty much the same as I remember it. The TV's in the far corner, Mom's scrapbooks still line the walls, and Dad's *butsudan*, a small Buddhist shrine, still sits above the fireplace. He inherited it from his grandparents years ago. No doubt their names are included with all the other Suzukis by now. I'm sorry I missed their funeral, but can't bring myself to feel too heartbroken. I never knew them well.

"Go get your sister's picture and sit it outside on the porch," Mom says from behind us. "Food should be done soon."

I scramble to get out of the way of the stairs, but Talia panics, unsure where to go in our small dining room, and I run into her. Shun smacks into me hard enough to knock me off the top stair. I catch a glimpse of his confused, horrified face, then hit every sharp stair as I tumble down and smack my head on the wood floor. While my body stops moving, the world spins at full throttle.

"DJ!" Talia pushes passed past my stunned brother to get down the stairs and helps me sit up. "I'm so sorry. Let me see. Are you okay?" She gingerly turns my head to see where I bashed against the ground as the den swirls in a blur.

Shunsuke storms down the stairs and towers over us. "What the hell are you people doing in my mother's house?" Before we can explain, he adds, "Mom, call the cops."

"No, no, no, Mom, don't call anyone. Shun, wait. Listen," I exclaim as Talia pulls me to my feet. I quickly shove her behind me, despite the fact I have to hold onto her to stay standing. "It's me, DJ."

Shun's face pales, then turns back to rage. "Don't play with me, bitch, and don't you *dare* play with my family."

"Really, it's really me." I look around the room for something that could help my case. Next to the *butsudan* sits one of my senior pictures in a frame. I grab it and push back my hair. "Look. It's me, Shun."

Shun's fists unclench, but he still looks like he might beat us to a pulp before the cops show up. "What kind of sick game is this?" he hisses. "What do you know about my sister? What do you want from us?"

Rolling my eyes, I set the picture back down, lift my shirt up a little, and point at the semi-circle birthmark around my belly button. "Remember this? I used to think this meant I was a going to be a magical girl when I grew up. I'd dress up as Super Moon and chase you around the yard, chucking pine cones at you, remember?"

Shun snatches me by the front of my shirt, clearly unconvinced. "Where is my sister?" he snarls. "Tell me before the police have to take you away on a stretcher." My head pounds as he shakes me.

Talia grabs my brother by the wrist with fury in her eyes. She doesn't say a word, but Shun gives a yelp of pain and jumps away, cradling his glowing red wrist. "Touch her again and that stretcher will be for you, whatever a stretcher is."

Mom bounds down the stairs and jumps between us, holding her hands up to keep us separated. "Everyone just calm down for a minute. No one is leaving on a stretcher, whether you broke into my home or not." Studying us with narrow eyes, she asks, "What do you want with DJ? Why wait all these years to come forward about her?"

My family is making my concussion worse.

"I'm telling you I *am* DJ, Mom. What could anyone get from pretending to me? We're not exactly loaded and no one's even looking for me anymore."

"You're wrong," Mom snaps. "We're always looking for you— I mean her. After all this time, we're still looking." Her voice cracks as if my words struck a chord, whether I'm a criminal or not. She takes a deep breath and drops her arms. After studying me with a look that seems to be deconstructing my very soul, she approaches me and cups my face in her hands.

I almost break down then and there. It feels so nice to feel my mother hold me again, even if she doesn't believe it's really me. I take a deep breath and swallow to steady myself. "What do I have to do to prove to you it's me?"

My mother takes a shaky breath to hold back the tears forming in her eyes. "When you were little, you kept a book under your pillow. You called it your secret book and would only ever let me read it to you."

"Dad had to translate it for you. It was in Japanese."

Mom smiles from ear to ear and a few tears fall. The quickest way to make me start crying is to have my mother start crying too. "That's right," she says. "What was the book?"

"*Kaguya-Hime,* The Moon Princess, but I always called her the Bamboo Princess instead because that's where the old man in the story found her."

"That's right!" Mom laughs through her tears. "That's absolutely right!" She kisses me on the forehead and wraps her arms around me, holding me tight, transforming the last twenty years into a bad dream I'm finally waking up from. Moms have that kind of power. "You called her the Bamboo Princess." After a second, she lets me go just enough to face Shunsuke, who still looks a bit freaked out. "Shun, it's her," she sniffs. "It's your sister."

"Mom, she's messing with you. Deej should be, what, thirty-six? This kid can't even be out of high school." Nonetheless, Shun inches toward us.

"Funny story about that actually," I say, looking to Talia. "Do you have time because—"

"Shunsuke? Martha?" That voice freezes my stomach to a block of ice. It's my father. "Where are you two?" He looks down the stairs in search of them. "I'm getting ready to—" His eyes go wide when they fall on me. It's the kind of reaction I always strove for, whether it be through jokes or antics, but right now, it terrifies me because I don't know what's going to be left behind after it dissolves. Rage like Shunsuke? Confusion like my mother? What one do I even want?

Why do I even care?

Twenty years of absolutely *everything* breaks free, despite my best efforts as Dad comes down the stairs, pushing Shun out of the way and ignoring my mother's pleas not to get angry the way Shun did, begging him to believe that I'm real. He reaches for me with open hands, but I smack them away.

"*No.*" The voice that escapes my mouth is raw and strained. "No, no, no, you do *not* get to act like I just got back from a friend's house or some shit. You don't have the *fucking* right." My vision blurs, and I focus on keeping my hands up to create a barrier between us. I can't read my father's expression. He's sure as hell about to read mine. Now that they believe it's me, they all are. "You can't even begin to imagine where I've been these last twenty years because of you. Because of what you did and the fact that you didn't come after me."

Shunsuke lowers his gaze to the ground. Mom tears up. Dad still does nothing.

"I was a scared sixteen-year-old kid," I bark. "How fucking hard could I have been to find? Mom said you've always looked for me, but when did you start? When you realized me being missing was going to ruin your reputation? I was still in the Human Realm, I bet. I was here for weeks before it was too late to come back. You could have found me if you really wanted."

I don't care that I've called it the Human Realm. We appeared before their very eyes. Talia burned my brother to get him off of me. They already know something's strange about me now. Stranger. Hardly even human, maybe.

"I've done and seen things to survive that would shake you to your very core. Things your worst nightmares can't even compete with. And you know something? I'm still queer!" That makes me cackle. It's so small and stupid compared to everything else and *that's* what they couldn't stand. "I still like boys and girls and it's not about to change, so—"

"I know."

I don't know if it's my father's low, calm tone or the words themselves that catch me up short.

"I know," he says again. "And what we did to you because of it was wrong." His words taper off as he tries to breathe deep and keep his own emotions at bay. "God knows we were wrong."

I want to hate the way he looks at me, filled with sympathy and hurt and remorse, but I can't bring myself to. It's too unlike what I expected. It's too much like what I wanted. How long have I even wanted this?

Dad takes a step toward me. This time I let him. "We had no idea you'd get so far, DJ. You have to believe that. When you didn't come back that night, we panicked. We called all your friends, all our relatives. No one had any idea where you were going. The idea that you had ran for New York didn't even occur to us until we called the police and they started investigating at the bus stations. If a clerk hadn't heard you mention it, we never would have known."

"After that, we never stopped," my mother adds softly, afraid to disrupt my sudden calm. "We never stopped wanting you back. Never stopped wishing we could fix what we did wrong. Never stopped loving you, even when we didn't understand you."

Tears start to blind me again, but these ones are different. They fall down my face like soft spring rain rather than an angry torrent, so I quickly try to wipe them away in vain.

Damn it. This wasn't how it was supposed to be. They were supposed to hate me. They were supposed to be disgusted at what I've become. All those ugly, nasty feelings that have been festering for two decades were supposed to scare them away even quicker than the pure, innocent feelings of having a crush on one of my girl friends did. How am I supposed to keep going about my life knowing they want me back? What am I supposed to do now?

I'm so lost in my thoughts that I don't notice Dad until his arms are around me, holding me as gently as all the times I fell and scraped my knees. After all this time, he still uses the same aftershave. It smells just as sharp and safe as when I was a kid. His grip tightens until I can't breathe. It's okay, though. I'd fall apart otherwise.

"I'm so sorry, Daisy Jane," he sobs. "I made a terrible mistake. I forced this family to make a terrible mistake. Can you ever forgive me for what I did to you?"

Instead of answering, I wrap my arms around him and hold tight to his shirt as if he can carry me back to a time where none of this ever happened, back to a time when things were simple, and the world made sense. I don't belong to that time anymore. The world won't let me. Who I am now makes it impossible.

But maybe I can bring a little bit of that time back with me. Back then, I could forgive my parents for everything. Every bad thing that happened faded away as soon as they held me the way they are now because back then, I wasn't afraid.

Not of them, not of truth, and certainly not of love.

Chapter Thirteen

MY FAMILY TAKES me being forever sixteen and a faerie knight rather well. Dad downs two beers while I tell the story and my brother mixes himself three rum and Cokes--the last one didn't even have Coke--and my mother won't stop trembling, but all in all, I think it could have gone worse. At least they're not calling the cops or kicking me out again.

I think Talia bringing one of their house plants back to life really seals the deal on the whole belief-in-magic thing. Shun's pretty disappointed when she can't figure out how to fix his cracked smart phone screen, though. Can't say I blame him. The thing's totaled.

Careful of the cracks, he checks the time. "It's nearly noon," he announces. "Amanda and the kids are going to be here soon. What are we supposed to tell them?"

"Well, first of all," I pipe up, "Who are they?"

Shun beams with pride as he hits a few buttons on his phone. "My wife and kids, Hannah and Mark." He hands it to me so that I can see the picture he pulled up.

On the screen my brother stands beside a beautiful willowy black woman with braids piled in a bun. In front of them stand two children, both with wild brown curls and my brother's big dark eyes. They have their mother's smile. Our family is even more mixed now. Japanese, Scottish, Black, Faerie. Talk about a melting pot.

"Hannah will be six next month and Mark is going into sixth grade," Shun explains, taking back the phone. "Amanda's a nurse in the pediatric ward up at the hospital here in town."

"What do you do?" Talia asks, craning her neck to see the picture.

"I teach high school English and an evening creative writing class at the community college," Shun explains. He glances at our father. "*Some people* weren't thrilled when I changed majors, but I love it."

"I came around and you know it," Dad says with a smirk and a roll of his eyes.

"Why the change?" I ask, secretly floored by the news. My engineer brother teaching kids how to find metaphors and write research papers? I think I might have to see the degree to believe it.

Shun shrugs. "Once I got to college, I realized I missed being around stories and sharing them with people...I missed *you*, DJ."

The way he speaks and looks at me makes my throat clothes and my eyes tear up. Nope. I'm not crying again. Not twice in one day. Not ever again if I have any say about it.

"Well, good for you," I say, standing up and stretching. "So, what are we going to tell your family?"

"While you figure that out," Dad sighs, getting to his feet, "I should go start grilling." Before he leaves, he places both hands on my shoulders and looks me in the eyes. "You're not going to disappear on me, are you?" he asks.

I shake my head. "Nope. Never again."

My father smiles and pats my cheek. "Good. I don't want to chase you through the Faerie World or whereever it is you say you've been."

I just smile back and wait for him to leave. Once he does, I whisper to Mom and Shun, "What the hell have you been drugging him with for the past twenty years?"

Shun snickers, but Mom scowls up at me and hisses, "Daisy Jane."

"What? He threw me out for being bi. I have a right to be thrown off when he welcomes me back covered in tattoos, ageless, and running around with a faerie princess. And since when does he drink more than one beer at a time?"

Mom sighs and takes a sip of her wine. "Throwing you out almost destroyed him, DJ," she says softly. "Him and this family. I almost left him more than once." Shun sobers up at that. "I don't know how time flows where you've been, but it's been a very long, hard, trying time for us. It's only been in the last several years that we've begun to try and piece everything back together without you."

"Mom and Dad only met the kids two Christmases ago," Shun adds, "and they weren't invited to our wedding. And the family has stopped coming over for holidays."

Holy shit. The surprises keep coming today.

"Why didn't you leave?" I ask.

"Because of you, at first." Mom sighs. "If you ever came back, I wanted to be here, in this house, in your home. Slowly, your father started to change. He began to read everything he could get his hands on about your...lifestyle and what we believe. I read them too, and more when I could."

I resist the urge to ask, "The faerie one or the queer one?" Instead I ask, "And?"

"And we were wrong about you, DJ. We were wrong in what we did, and we were wrong in what we thought. Even if you're back to stay, I'll never stop being sorry and trying to make it up to you. I'm sure your father won't either."

That's probably the fifth time they've said that in the past hour. I'd be lying if I said it wasn't still good to hear.

"Are you staying?" Shun asks.

I slip my hands in my pockets and pace the living room. "Like I said, I gotta get Talia to Triple Lake."

"And after that?"

I honestly don't know anymore. My family wanting me back changes things. I need time to figure out *what* exactly it changes, though.

Son of a bitch. Talia was right. Why did Talia have to be right?

Instead of answering the question, I shrug. "That depends on a few things."

"What kind of things?" Talia asks, just as surprised as my brother and mother, judging by the look on her face.

"You know," I reply. "Faerie things."

Talia smirks and puffs up a bit in her seat. Looks like she knows that she was right. Great. Now I'm gonna have to deal with that the entire way to Triple Lake.

"My head hurts from all the 'faerie things' you've already told me about, so I'm not going to ask," Mom says. "But you'll stay for the Fourth at least, right?" Mom asks. "And the night? The bed in your own room is still made up and we could put Talia up in the guest room."

I can't say no to the pleading look on my mother's face, but it's really up to Talia, so I glance her way for an answer.

"We should stay," she says. "You haven't seen your family in so long and a celebration seems like the perfect time to spend time with them. Besides, we'll still arrive sooner than my aunts if go tomorrow." There's something in the way she looks around the room and wiggles in her seat that tells me there's more.

"You want to stay and see what the Fourth of July is like, don't you?" I sigh.

"What's wrong with that?" Talia huffs back.

I just shake my head and snicker at her.

Mom gets to her feet. "If you want to see the Fourth, then we'll have to go to the fireworks tonight. Usually we watch them in the backyard, but that's not good enough if you've never gone before." She hooks arms with Talia and leads her to the kitchen "Why don't you help me finish the food up while Shun and DJ cook up a story to tell his family?"

"Sounds fun," Talia says, patting my mother's hand as they round the corner.

"Don't let her actually cook anything," I say. "Her magic isn't good enough to rebuild the house if she burns it down."

Tal pokes her head back in the living room and sticks her tongue out at me. "I'm an excellent cook, thank you very much."

Shun laughs as she disappears again, then wraps an arm around my shoulders as I join him back on the couch. "So, I gotta know," he mutters with a sly smirk. "Are you and Talia...you know?"

I roll my eyes and wiggle away from him. "Don't be ridiculous," I say. "Do I seem like the kind to date princesses?"

"With the whole knight gig? Hell yeah," Shun replies. "Besides, you two act like it. It's in the way you two look at each other, like you can silently communicate or something."

"We've just been through a lot these last few days," I say. "That's all."

"Nah, it's not just that. You're comfortable around her in a way I've never seen you before. And she's comfortable around you."

"You've only ever seen her around me, Shun," I remind him.

"Comfortable isn't the right word...You two are very in sync."

"Okay, well can we please sync up a story to tell your wife and kids?" I sigh. "I'd rather not have Hannah and Mark run around telling everyone their aunt is a faerie."

"You're not *technically* a faerie, though, right?" Shun asks. "Is that even possible a thing?"

"I honestly have no idea."

"Mom likes Talia, so that's a plus. She never liked any of your boyfriends."

"Shunsuke!"

"Okay, okay. Sorry."

We decide that, for the time being, I'm Shun's cousin, Deidre, who's traveling cross-country with her roommate. Shun will tell his wife the truth in private, but that's the story we're going with for now. Just to be safe we hid the pictures of me that Mom has hanging around the house, so no one can notice any similarities.

When Amanda and the kids arrive, they're definitely taken aback by my appearance, but no one asks any questions. Well, Hannah asks if I'm a boy or a girl, but no one asks any real pressing questions.

We all join Dad on the back porch. I sit on the steps while Hannah and Mark play on a trampoline that must be new, and Shun sets up a game of horse shoes with Amanda. Talia and Mom decide to join in. Good thing iron doesn't affect Tal.

I watch them all for a while, marveling at what things change and what things stay the same. Shun still takes too long to use his turn when playing a game, but his aim is better. Mom still claps for everyone just for trying and actually hops up and down if they get a point, but I notice she has to squint before throwing.

The cold shock of a bottle of beer on my neck distracts me and I cringe.

"Ugh, really, Dad?" I wipe the condensation off my skin. "Is that necessary?"

"Sorry." He chuckles, handing me the beer and sitting next to me. "Couldn't resist." He leans back and looks behind me. "What's this?"

"Oh, that tat?" I contort myself to pull down the back of my tank top, revealing the cherry blossoms that spread across my shoulder blades like wings. Wispy foxes, lightly colored like they're done in water color, play and nap in the branches. One leaps off my right shoulder toward the river tattooed around my bicep. "That was for you, kinda. For where our family comes from, rather. The foxes are for that sanctuary in Miyagi that we went to."

Dad sits forward. "You remember that? You and Shun were so little."

"I was the cool kid at school for a few days because I got to hold a fox," I remind Dad. "I definitely remember that trip. Besides, it's one of the last ties I feel like I have to your family."

"And that's my fault," Dad mumbles, swirling his own bottle. "We talked to them a lot more once your grandparents' health started to fade. You missed out on that.... If you never spoke to me again, I would understand."

I roll my eyes and nudge him. "Please don't start again. At least not today." Maybe he can keep apologizing on a day when I'm not already emotionally exhausted, but not now. Now, I'd just like to be with my dad.

"No, I'm going to start," he continues. "Everything that's happened to you happened because of me."

"So, I got in shape, cut my hair, and got covered in ink. Big deal."

My dad studies me for a moment. He's never been as observant as Mom, but he's not oblivious either. "You've aged too much for that to be true. Not physically, but in more subtle ways. You have old eyes."

I take a long gulp of beer to avoid responding. "It doesn't matter now. I'm not a knight anymore."

"It does, though. Things follow you, DJ. They follow all of us..." He turns his gaze to Talia for a moment. "You don't want to tell us everything and I can completely understand that. Your mother and I don't deserve to be a part of your life, but if you won't turn to us, turn to her at least. She's good for you. I can tell."

I roll my eyes and get to my feet. "She's not *good for me*, Dad. I've known her for less than a week."

Dad shrugs and gets to his feet. "So? I fell in love with your mother after meeting her three times."

"And you would be okay with that? Me marrying a woman? Not that I'm marrying Talia, obviously."

Dad thinks it over as he checks the meat on the grill. "I don't see why not anymore, so long as you're happy and she's good for you."

"Okay, I'm cutting you off," I chuckle, getting to my feet as well. "No more beer. You don't sound like yourself."

Dad goes quiet as he places the hamburgers on a serving plate. "I'm myself. I just changed. It took time, I had to want it, and it was hard and painful, but I changed. People can change, DJ."

Heat immediately flairs up in my chest, "Are you saying—"

"No, I'm not saying anything of the sort, sweetheart. That's not something I think can be changed anymore. What can be changed is how we see the world, how we see the people in it, and how we want to move among them, but it's up to us as individuals." Dad gives me a sad smile. "I'm sorry you couldn't just beat it into me twenty years ago."

My anger fizzled out and is replaced with an ache in my heart because I know he's right. Even if I had stayed, I couldn't force Dad to change his mind. It was something he had to figure out on his own. I'd be lying if I said a large part of me wasn't still upset with him, but it's quieter than it once was. Now it's overshadowed by my anger at the universe and how little it lets me control and how unclear everything has to be. It makes me feel small and I hate it.

Hannah hops up the stairs and slips passed me. "Grandpa, is the food ready yet?"

Hearing Dad be called "Grandpa" is probably always going to freak me out.

"Yep." Dad gives her a big grin to hide all evidence of our conversation. "Go round everyone up, okay?"

"Okay." Hannah pauses to stare up at me. "I like your hair," she says. "It's really cool. I wish I could do my hair like that."

"But you've got such pretty curls," I tell her, kneeling down.

"That's why I can't make it cool like yours," my niece says with a pout.

"You know what, though? You could do even cooler things with your hair." I set my beer down to and gently stretch a few curls toward the back of Hanna's head. "If your mom braided the sides back like this, you would be the coolest almost-six-year-old ever. What do you think?"

Hannah feels the stretches of hair I'm holding back and beams. "I like it. I'll have Mommy do it during the fireworks." She lets her hair fall to her shoulders and jumps down the porch steps.

I stand and watch her run across the yard. Talia stands near the stairs and grins up at me. It's not the smug smile of before. It's something tender and kind. Something that knots my stomach and makes my heart race.

"What?" I snap, picking my beer back up.

"Nothing," she chuckles, coming up the stairs. "You're just a great aunt is all."

The rest of the family makes their way to the porch. Shun wiggles his eyebrows at me as he passes. "Yeah, DJ, you're such a great aunt."

I punch him in the arm.

Talia subtly casts the spell that lets me eat with the rest of my family and we dig in. It's the best meal I've had in years. The potato salad, home-grilled burgers, octopus-shaped sausages, sugar cookies, all the flavors of my childhood. All things I never thought I'd eat again with a family I never thought I'd see again. Every once and a while it feels like it might be too much, and Talia gives me a concerned look that I shrug off. Luckily, dessert distracts her, so I don't always have to dodge her glances anymore. Then, as the sun begins to set behind the mountain, Shun brings out sparklers to occupy the kids while we clean up, leaving Talia to supervise. Through the window, they dance and twirl, attempting to draw pictures and write messages that disappear before they can even really exist. I stare through the window above the sink. My skin prickles as my mother watches me.

Naturally, she denies it. "What? I can't look at you?"

"You can, but it's weird when you stare."

"You've been gone twenty years," she reminds me. "I have to stare. How else am I going to make up for all that time?"

She has a point, and I'm not about to deny her the chance to be close to me while I'm here, but I suspect she has other motives. Motives possibly put in her head by my brother.

"Amanda seems nice," I say. Maybe if I focus on my brother's love life, my family will leave my nonexistent one alone.

My mother beams and begins drying dishes. "Amanda's wonderful. She's been so great for Shun and she's a good mom. I hope you get to know her. She's your sister now, after all."

I guess she's right. I've never had a sister, though. I'll have to figure out how to have one when we get back from Triple Lake. *If* I come back this way, that is. The blue orb weighs my pocket down like an anchor, demanding attention. I don't even know what I'm supposed to do with it anymore.

Mom looks at her watch before I can think of anything. "We should head out if we want the good seats." She cranks the window open and calls, "Hey, you goof balls, come inside and get ready to go."

Given that Talia has my nephew dangling upside down from her shoulders and my niece wrapped around one ankle, "goof balls" sounds right. She lets him down, pries Hannah off her leg, and the three of them pick up the sparkler trash before coming inside.

I ignore Mom muttering "Talia would make a good aunt too" under her breath as she takes out the trash. Now that my family has accepted the fact that I'm bi, I guess that means they can jump right back into trying to manage my love life.

It's not as annoying as it used to be. Honestly, after the last twenty years, even pestering feels nice.

The park we attended every Fourth is a decent drive away—right at the gateway to the mountains—but it's worth the traffic and the lack of adequate parking. At least I've always thought so. Judging by the way my brother curses under his breath as we look for a spot, which Amanda slaps him for, he no longer feels the same. We still thankfully manage to find a decent spot to place our blankets and lawn chairs. The blue orb falls out of my shallow pocket when I plot down on the grass, instantly grabbing Hannah and Mark's attention. I snatch it up before either of them can reach for it.

"Can I see that?" Mark asks, holding out his hand. "I'll be extra careful. It looks cool."

Shun and everyone else gives me quizzical looks, begging for an answer, even if it isn't the entire truth.

I don't even want to think of one. I just want to get rid of this thing. "Talia, can I talk to you for a second?"

Dad scrambles out of his old Denver Broncos chair as Tal and I head down the path toward the creek. "Wait, where are you going? The fireworks are going to start any minute."

I pause to give him a reassuring smile. "We'll be right back. Promise."

The creases etched into his forehead and the frown he wears say that he doesn't believe me, but he lets Mom pull him back into his seat anyway. I look over my shoulder every few steps, and sure enough, he watches us the entire way until my family disappears behind the lush trees and tall grass that line the creek.

Once the chatter is as distant as the park itself, I figure it's safe enough to speak. "Tal, what do we do with this thing? I don't need it anymore, obviously, and I don't want to keep carrying it around."

Talia takes the blue orb and studies it in one hand while stroking her chin with the other. "Just destroy it. The magic will disintegrate since the spell wasn't properly activated."

She doesn't have to say anymore. I take the orb from her, walk to the water's edge, and hop from boulder to boulder until I'm in the center of the creek. Once there, I study the faint blue orb.

It was born out of so much pain and anger. The desire to just move on is one lie I can't tell myself anymore. Talia was right. I just wanted the hurt and resentment to go away, but this wouldn't have done it. It would have just made it so that I couldn't actually deal with it. It all would have been stuck behind that door in my mind from here until eternity.

I just wanted to run from it. I was afraid. Not anymore.

I wind up and hurl the orb as far down stream as possible. It soars through the night as a point of bright blue light and extinguishes against the face of a submerged rock. The muffled shatter it makes is the most satisfying sound I've ever heard. Streaks of neon blue dissolve in the water, and then I make my way back to the shore.

Up on the bank, Talia smiles and shakes her head. "Did you have to do so *much* to destroy it?"

"Uh, obviously," I say, taking a break on one of the slicker stones to get my balance. "This is a big deal. I just metaphorically rid myself of twenty years of pent-up resentment and hurt. This is a momentous occas—shit!"

My foot slips and I prepare to land with a face full of mud and pebbles, but Talia catches me.

She lets her hands linger on my shoulders as she chuckles. "A concussion doesn't strike me as a good way to end a momentous occasion."

"It would be very *me*, though," I reply, as Talia continues to touch me. I can't bring myself to pull away.

The first firework lights up the sky as she laughs again, giving way to an awestruck gasp. The emerald light makes Talia's eyes nearly glow and my heart race.

"I thought humans couldn't use magic," she whispers.

"They can't."

"Then what is this?"

A few more fireworks boom to life, but I can't tear my gaze away from the wonder on Talia's face. "No idea. Lots of gunpowder, chemicals, and other science stuff."

She looks back to me with a grin that freezes me where I stand. Even if I wanted to move, I couldn't. She has me completely trapped, regardless of the fact that the way she studies my expression terrifies me. "I've seen so much in the human world, thanks to you, DJ. I almost don't want it to end tomorrow."

"Lyle's still looking for you, though."

"That's why I said almost."

"Right. Duh."

Talia's slender hands slide up my neck, making me shiver before resting on either side of my face. "Say you'll stay with me, DJ."

Words catch in my throat. All the possible answers fight for first place and end up crowding my mind. I begin to tell Talia that I can't possibly stay. She takes my parted lips as a cue to bring her mouth down to mine, and I can't think of an excuse why she shouldn't. Her fingers trace my jaw and my knees shake. I have to take hold of her hips and pull her closer to steady myself. One finger grazes skin, just as brief and temping as her tongue against my bottom lip, gentle, slow, and patient.

She's nothing like Calista. Calista was always fast, hard, hungry. She wanted what she wanted and wasn't afraid to just take it so long as I was willing to give it. Nothing less and definitely nothing more.

Talia wants so much more. I can feel it in the way she traces my collarbone, then my shoulder, and slowly runs her other hand through my hair. Her kisses are curious, innocent, unsure of what to do with me but wanting to try. She's trying to know me.

Shit.

The world skids to a halt as I realize I'm still afraid after all.

Talia pulls away slightly before I can panic, and presses her forehead to mine. "I knew you were lying last night."

"Talia, we can't do this."

"Why? I want a real answer."

Before I can give it, nearby rustling startles us, and I push Talia away. Just because my family is okay with me kissing girls now doesn't mean the rest of the world is, and I'd rather not ruin Fourth of July with a fight,

Judging by our new guests, however, it might not be up to me.

Four men clad in black leather armor emerge from the underbrush armed with crystal blades, giving them away as members of the faerie courts. The Unseelie Court to be exact, judging by the black. Their leader is the only one who doesn't wear a helmet, probably to take advantage of the fact that I know him.

Willowy stature, long pine-green hair tied back, sharp onyx eyes, and a blade as dangerous as Lyle's. I'd know him anywhere. He's Queen Shaylee's champion, Dominic.

"I wish I could say it's nice to see you again, Daisy Jane," he says, "but unfortunately, by order of the Queen of the Unseelie Court, you're both under arrest."

Chapter Fourteen

I PLACE MYSELF between Talia and Dominic. "On what charges?"

"Treason," Dominic answers. "Apparently, you two have been making all the wrong friends." His gaze darts over my shoulder to Talia. "Then there's the matter of your lineage, Your Highness."

"A lineage she doesn't want anything to do with," I argue. "And *friend* is probably the last thing I'd call Lyle. Giant pain in the ass is a more apt description. Pretty sure you can relate."

Dominic ticks up an eyebrow. "So, you're not in fact looking for reinforcements?"

"Who the hell told you that's what we were doing?"

"Several sources."

"Your sources are shit."

"Then you won't have any issue having a little chat with Queen Shaylee about the whole thing, then?"

Oh, I still have an issue with it, all right. I don't trust Shaylee any farther than I could throw her. She's only been on the throne nine months. I highly doubt her backstabbing two-timing ways have changed that much.

I pry a heavy branch from a dying tree. "Tell Her Majesty whatever you want. Just leave us alone."

"You know faeries can't lie, Daisy Jane."

"Doesn't mean you bastards always tell the truth either."

Dominic glares. "So be it. I only need the princess anyhow."

"Come and get her, then."

Dominic launches at me and meets my impromptu weapon. It cracks with the force of the sword but, thankfully, stays in one piece when he pulls back for another strike. I nearly whack one of his followers in the head with the branch, but they're too fast. They're all too fast. I don't know if Talia could make it back to my family if she ran.

She takes a branch of her own, but her aimless swing does nothing to take out the two after her. One snatches the stick out of her hand and launches it into the creek. Meanwhile, Dominic has all but pushed me back into the water. I leap onto the nearest boulder, then another, all while his sword clashes against my meager defense. He steps on the stone I slipped on. I purposefully block low so he swings high. I drop to the creek bed and kick Dominic's legs out from under him. He goes down, and I scramble past him before he can gather himself out of the water. Another knight gets the log to the back of the head and drops like a ton of bricks.

I grab his sword just in time to deflect another one coming for me. He keeps me on the defense with his speed, which I use to my advantage. I let him back me into a tree, and when he aims to finish me off, I slip out of the way, resulting in his blade lodging itself in the bark. As he kneels to grab the dagger from his boot, I slice my sword through the small space where the plates of armor fit at his knee; he howls with pain.

I can't help but wince as I leave him there. They're just doing their job. I don't want to hurt them, but I can't let them take Talia. I can't.

When I realize she's no longer in sight, my heart seizes with panic. "Tal? Tal, answer me." I find her around the bend, standing just as proud as can be over the last knight crumpled on the ground.

I decide to grab her and run for the park before asking, "What the hell?"

"He overestimated how much a knife to my throat scared me," she answers. "I'm not dumb. They need me alive. They wouldn't kill me. So, I nailed him in the face with the back of my head. Then, when he was bent over, I hit him with a rock."

"That's...actually kind of metal, Talia."

She shrugs as if it's no big deal.

A few people watch us run through the park with quizzical looks, but most of them are still distracted by the fireworks overhead. It can't go on much longer, though. They're all going to notice the sword I swiped eventually. Shit. I should have left it behind. Too late now.

Shun's the first person from my family we run into. He scans the crowd with worry etched across his face. It turns to glee when he spots us coming toward him.

"Don't scare us like that," he says. "I really thought maybe you left us again. Plus, you're missing the show."

"We're about to miss a whole lot more of it," I reply, grabbing him by the arm and dragging him along with us. "We need to leave."

"What? Why?"

"Some people are after Talia and they found us."

My brother eyes the sword in my hand and his face pales. "You didn't think to mention that at any point today? My wife and kids are here, DJ."

"I know, I know. I'm sorry. I thought they were stuck all the way back in Iowa. I have no idea how the hell they got here." Or how Queen Shaylee figured out where we were going. Lyle, I can understand. His henchmen were taking Talia to him when I first met her. It wouldn't be a stretch for him to follow us.

Could she have the aunts?

No. They're fine. They've gotta be fine, for Talia's sake.

Hannah spots us through the crowd and her eyes light up. "You got a sword? Cool!"

The adults do a double take at the sight of us. Mom jumps to her feet.

"DJ, what on earth...? Why are you all wet?" She holds my face in her hands as she looks me over for any nicks or scratches, then does the same to Talia. Despite the situation, it's a reassuring sight.

"I don't have time to explain. We just gotta go." I yank the blanket out from under Hannah and Mark to fold it up. They roll off and giggle like it's a game. My chest tightens. What if I get them hurt? Maybe my original plan was the right one after all. There's no time to worry about that now.

Despite the confusion and worry, everyone hurries back to the cars. Amanda takes the kids and agrees to meet us back at Mom and Dad's place. Everyone's staying there tonight. I want my entire family where I can keep an eye on them.

As we drive back, staying on the road for a good half an hour before actually heading home, I explain the parts of our tale that I decided to leave out. Lyle, the queens, the aunts—I tell them everything.

Everything except how I wanted them to forget me.

Mom pulls her cardigan tighter around her shoulders as if the AC's up too high. "So, those men who came for you tonight...did you kill them?"

"No, Mom. I didn't."

"Are they going to hurt anyone at the park?"

"No. Faeries typically don't get involved with humans unless absolutely necessary. Besides, Dominic's a pretty good guy. He won't hurt anyone for no reason."

Talia scoffs.

"He is! I served with him. He helped overthrow Queen Mab. He's just doing what Queen Shaylee tells him to do. It's part of the job."

"So, what does that mean we're going to do now?" Dad asks as he pulls off the highway.

"Now, we're going to set up some charms around the house to keep you all safe. In the morning, Talia and I are going to Triple Lake to figure out our next move. I'll call you once we get it under control."

Mom reaches back for my hand from the passenger seat. "No. Absolutely not. We're not losing you again. You're staying here."

I hold her hand. "I can't. I've got to take care of Talia. I promise to stay in touch and come back as soon as I can. Really, I promise."

"I'll take them to Triple Lake myself, Mom," Shun chimes in. "It'll be okay."

Mom dabs at her eyes nonetheless.

Back at the house, Talia and I scope the place out first to make sure no one's been around. According to Talia, there are no signs of magic whatsoever. None of our pursuers have found us, and I'd really like to keep it that way.

Shun and Amanda get the kids ready for bed while Mom and Dad retreat to their room—a classic sign that they have a lot to talk about. Meanwhile, Talia and I walk the yard. She stops every few feet, kneels down, and places her hands in the grass. Every time, there's a small jolt of energy beneath my feet like a mini lightning strike. Once she's sure the area's secured, she takes an item from every family member to turn into a glamour of sort. It won't render them invisible, but a fae won't be able to recognize them if they come looking. It was apparently a very popular charm for avoiding disgruntled lovers back in the day.

Finally, right around midnight, we both drop onto the sofa. Talia massages her temple and groans.

"You gonna make it?" I ask.

"Hopefully." She sighs. "DJ, what happened? We were so close to the finish line."

"Welcome to Faerie."

She turns and gives me a tired smile. I notice the thin strip of dried blood along her neck. Maybe it's exhaustion, maybe that kiss is still messing with my head, but I can't help but reach out and run my thumb just below it. It must be from the knight she took out herself.

"I'm sorry, Tal. I'm not a very good bodyguard."

Talia places my hand against her cheek and closes her eyes. "You're doing your best. All this craziness wasn't supposed to happen." She opens her eyes just long enough to lean toward me.

"We can't do this, Tal," I whisper just as her mouth brushes against mine.

She leans back a bit, and her eyebrows pull together. "Why not?"

"It's just going to make things...complicated. And dangerous."

"More dangerous and complicated than they already are?" Talia chuckles.

"Love makes things complicated in a different way."

"Going straight to love, are we?"

My face burns, and I try to explain myself. "I just meant in a broad sense. Look at what happened with my family. Look what I had to do in the court to Amarantha and her family. Mab forced me to kill them because she knew we were close."

"Things don't have to be like that with us. It could be different. And you never finished telling me about her."

"You don't know that. And I might, one day. Just not now."

"No one knows until they try, DJ."

"That's what makes it complicated and dangerous."

Footsteps on the stairs end the conversation and send Talia and me to opposite ends of the couch. Even when I was pretending to be straight, there was no way I'd act like that in front of my family. It was just flat-out embarrassing.

Especially if it was my dad, and sure enough, he joins us in the living room and studies us both for a moment. "Everything okay?"

"Oh, you know," I say with a shrug. "As okay as it can be."

He takes a seat in the recliner and leans forward. "You two all set?"

Talia nods. "Everyone will be safe, even if Dominic and the others come looking for you. Though, once they realize we've moved on, I doubt they will."

Dad nods along. "And you two? What will you do after reaching Triple Lake?"

Talia and I look at each other. We hadn't gotten that far.

"Probably keep going," I finally answer. "We won't be able to stay if the entire Unseelie Court is after us too. Where that'll be, well, we'll figure that out when we meet up with the aunts and tell them what we know. Surely they know someplace else to go."

Dad frowns. "You won't come back here?"

I can't help but laugh. "Dad, an entire *court* is after us. I can't do that to you guys."

"Even after what we did to you?"

"You raised me better than that. Besides, we've got Amanda, Hannah, and Mark now. I've gotta look out for them too. They're family."

My dad pauses, then blinks back a few tears. "I don't think that was just our doing. You're much better than what we showed you."

"Of course, she is." Talia beams at me. "She's a faerie knight."

I squirm under the praise. "*Was* a faerie knight. And, given who I served, I don't think it counts for much."

"Who you are more than makes up for it." Dad gets to his feet and stretches. "All right, come give me a hug. All this faerie craziness has tired me out."

I oblige my father and let him hold me as long as he wants. He even kisses me on the cheek and I let him. That hasn't happened since I was a little kid. Teenagers are too cool for kisses from their parents, after all.

"I'm proud of you, DJ," he says, letting me go. "You did good."

I nod and take a deep breath, trying to keep back tears of my own. "Thanks, Dad."

"Don't take off tomorrow without saying goodbye."

"I won't."

As he heads upstairs, I pop downstairs in the den to check on Mom before I go to bed. Just like when I was a kid, she's cleaning to try to cope with the stress. Oddly enough, she's wiping the picture of me by the *butsudan*. She looks up at the sound of my footsteps and shows me the photo with a smile.

"When you make your way back here, we need to retake this picture. Maybe take some with the family."

"Won't that draw attention, though? I'd hate for a friend or somebody to start asking questions."

I also just don't like posing for pictures. I'll send her a selfie to print or something.

Mom puts it back in its place. "We'll think of something to tell everyone. I just want a better picture of you." She studies me for a moment. "You look more...you. More comfortable in your skin."

Good, because that's how I feel. I'm glad they're finally okay with that.

"I'll buy new clothes just for the occasion," I tease.

Mom takes it seriously. "Good. You look a bit raggedy. At least invest in a nice button-down. Or a dress. Or however you like to present yourself. Just do it well."

"Yes, Mom."

"I recognize that tone. It means you're going to shrug me off. Don't."

"I won't. Promise."

Mom rolls her eyes. Can't blame her for not believing me. She goes back to dusting. "I want a picture of you and Talia too."

"We're not a thing, Mom."

"Um-hm." That's her sign that she's shrugging *me* off. "I wasn't born yesterday." She raises a hand to stop me from arguing. "DJ...I probably don't have the right to say this but...don't let what we did stop you from loving people. If anything, accept more of it. You deserve it."

I can't argue, but I can't explain why she's wrong either. She just wouldn't understand.

"Yes, Mom."

She shoots me a dirty look, but it melts into a smile and she hugs me good night.

It's not until I discover Talia curled up in my old bed that I remember we never talked about who was sleeping where. Shun and his family took his old room and I'm not about to put Talia on the couch, so I guess that leaves me.

She stirs and pulls back the blankets as I quickly change into a pair of my mother's sweats. "There's room for you here."

"I can't, Tal."

"Please? What if someone breaks through the charms and comes through the window? You're supposed to protect me, remember?"

I know what she's doing. She isn't slick. Her plan is blatantly obvious. And yet I still slip into bed next to her and let her crawl into my arms.

"That's a bit much, don't you think?"

"Not if you want to fight off my bad dreams too."

"You have bad dreams?"

"No. Not with you here. That's the point."

In spite of the circumstances, in spite of my fear and hesitation, I find myself laughing. Love does crazy shit like that to you. That's one more reason I can't have any part in it. But, maybe, I can stop tomorrow.

Chapter Fifteen

THE WATERWORKS START up again the next morning as Tal, Shun, and I get ready to leave. It's early, so Amanda and the kids are still sleeping. I would have liked to say goodbye to them, but I don't trust myself not to blow it and tell them who I really am. After going so long without a family, it's killing me not to tell them how I actually fit into it. Maybe once this is all over, we'll figure out a way to do so.

Mom doesn't let me go until I promise five times to come home. I have to call her when we get to Triple Lake. She wants me to text her every day we're there too. When I try to explain that I probably won't be able to, she starts bawling again. I promise to at least try to send a smiley face, but she still sniffs and dabs at her eyes all the while. I hate making my mom cry. After this, it's never happening again.

Thankfully, Dad doesn't cry again. He hugs me tight and tells me again how proud he is of me. "And you take good care of Talia," he says. "You're a knight. You better continue to act like it."

"I'll be sure to return with the shield of my enemies and bring honor to our family and all that jazz," I assure him, slowly wiggling out of his arms. "See you as soon as I can." He and Mom wave at us until Shun drives us around the corner and onto the main road. With Triple Lake locked into the GPS, we're on our way. Nothing left to do for the next several hours except ride.

But, naturally, my brother can't let use enjoy that in peace.

"So, Talia, you got a boyfriend waiting for you back in Faerie?" he asks with a smug grin.

I punch him in the shoulder, but he just laughs.

"What? I'm just trying to make small talk." He chuckles.

Maybe we should just walk to Triple Lake, mountain roads be damned.

"I don't." Talia yawns. "I don't really fancy men enough."

Shun stares at me as he says, "You don't say?"

"Watch the road, buttface," I grumble.

"You have a girlfriend then?"

I turn up the radio.

"No girlfriend," Talia replies. "Things have been a bit hectic as of late."

Is it just me, or are her eyes boring into the back of my skull? I don't want to risk a glance in the rearview mirror to find out.

"What a pity." Shun sighs dramatically. "You're such a lovely girl. Anyone would be lucky to have you."

It's going to be a very long drive.

Shun spares me any more humiliation, for now, and decides to chat about how people and places have changed. The entire conversation is surreal and I'm not sure I like it much more than our previous one. Talia seems engrossed in it, though, so I let Shun keep talking.

About an hour into the ride, Shun dares to say, "So, tell me about Faerie. What's it like? What was it like being a knight?"

Talia and I exchange looks. She volunteers to go first and tells my brother all about her carefree days running around the northern Michigan forests as a wild child, eating fresh berries in the summer and fish caught by her aunts in the winter, all the magic they taught her, the campers she would watch, and the meteor showers over Lake Superior.

"That's incredible," Shun sighs wistfully. He nudges me. "How different was it being at court?" Damn. If Talia could have talked for two more hours, I would have been home free.

"Really different," I answer. "Parties every night, social rules and etiquette to follow, even if those rules did change from day to day."

"They didn't treat you any differently because you were a human?" Shun asks.

"No," I answer dryly. "Everyone was very kind to me."

"And the Queen of the Faeries? What was she like?"

I can still see Mab's gloating grin every time she rescued me from her servants or knights, despite her being the one to put me in those situations. Her praises, followed by scorn for things out of my control, ring in my ears. The glee in her eyes as she forced me to do terrible things.

"She's nothing like what you hear in stories," I answer.

My brother doesn't look satisfied with that, but he thankfully doesn't push the topic any further. "Something tells me I should make Amanda take the faerie paraphernalia out of the backyard," he says. "Hannah wanted it out there, but I don't think she should be trying to invite anything around the house."

"Do you live well within the city?" Talia asks.

"Sure do," Shun answers.

"Then she's fine. Away from civilization, it might be wise to make sure she wears iron on her person and keeps salt in her pockets. Faeries have a knack for finding people who search them out, especially children. Above all else, keep her away from faerie rings."

Shun's face pales a bit. "I'll keep that in mind. Thanks for the advice."

Talia smiles a bit, the sarcasm clearly going over her head.

Shun goes back to talking about anything and everything while Talia and I watch the mountains grow around us. The scenery never ceases to amaze me. The jagged slopes, the blanket of deep green, the clouds so big and defined that you think you might be able to touch them. God, I've missed this place.

About halfway there, we come out of a mountain pass and Talia lets out a sudden gasp.

"Stop the car," she exclaims, yanking on the back of my seat.

Shun obliges and pulls off at a dirt overlook. He hardly has the car in park before Talia leaps from the car and runs to the edge of the small hill overlooking the magnificent plain before us.

"Look at this. Just look at it," she calls back to us, spreading her arms toward the stretches of golden grassland that nearly reaches the horizon. The only sign that it ends are the mountains in the far distance. Mesas and smaller mountains dot the scenery, making the earth look enormous and empty. "It's so beautiful." Talia gives up on words and resorts to joyful shouts and cheers instead.

"She's weird." Shun chuckles. "Even for a faerie, I imagine."

"True." I sigh. "She is."

Talia runs back to the car. "Can I take a picture? Please?"

I hand her my phone, show her how to use the camera function, and she's off again.

Shun's face goes somber as she takes a million pictures from all sorts of odd angles and degrees. "I don't know what's going on between you two," he says quietly, "but please don't mess this up. I really do think Talia's good for you."

"The only way I can*not* mess things up is if there's nothing between me and Talia," I reply, sinking in my seat a bit.

"That's not true, DJ. After everything with our parents and everything you must have gone through over the years, you deserve someone who can make you happy the way Talia can."

"How do you know she makes me happy?"

My brother drums on the steering wheel for a moment as Talia begins taking pictures of the clouds and the nearby mountains. "It's in the way you look at each other. You're at peace with her. I've never known you to be at peace around much of anyone."

"I tried to be at peace with Mom and Dad and look how that turned out."

"They came around."

"After twenty years."

"That's not a fair comparison, DJ, and you know it," Shun snaps. "Why can't you just admit you like her?"

"You said you wanted her to stick around, right? There's your answer."

"DJ, you're being unreasonable."

"You know what's unreasonable," I hiss. "The fact that there are people who still know my full name running around the Faerie Realm, *including* Queen Titania."

My brother blinks at me. "I finally feel like we're getting somewhere, but I don't follow."

I lean against the back of the seat and fold my arms. If I finally open that door in the back of my mind, let it out little by little, maybe someone will finally see that I'm not crazy. I know what I'm doing.

"Names have power in the Faerie Realm. Don't ask me how it works. It's beyond me. All I know is that, when someone has your full name, they can control you if they want. They can force you to do things you don't want to do. One of the conditions of becoming a faerie knight is giving the queen your full name as a sign of complete submission.

"Normally, from what I understand, it's not a big deal. It's more symbolic than anything, but, unfortunately for me, I got to serve Queen Mab. She got quite a bit of mileage out of my name. Every chance she got, it was Daisy Jane Ann Suzuki, do this. Daisy Jane Ann Suzuki, do that. People heard her, so other people could use my name. Luckily, it was mainly for stupid shit, but still. A lot of those people are still around somewhere and they liked Mab. I didn't.

"Another person who didn't like Mab was Amarantha. She worked in the kitchen. She was young, by faerie standards, with one kid and a husband. I would hide out down there and help out when I got sick of being the queen's dancing monkey, so we became friends."

Amarantha's laughter the day she found me munching on a stolen pastry in the pantry rings in my ears and twists my heart.

"Now, Mab was not the most stable of individuals. She saw danger everywhere. Everyone was out to get her. Everyone was trying to take her crown. One day, she was *convinced* that Amarantha was trying to poison her since she had been in charge of the menu that day.

"I was in the kitchen at the time for lunch. Her husband, Oren, had brought stew and homemade bread for us, along with their son, Tamir. That was the first time I had met him."

That little boy's big brown eyes stare back at me in my mind. I remember the way the points of his ears stuck out just a bit too far from his head.

"Queen Mab stormed in raving about how Amarantha was conspiring against her. She was trying to take the crown for her own. She was talking with the queen's dead sister. The list went on until she finally ordered me—" My throat closes for a moment. "She ordered me to kill all three of them. I told her I wouldn't do it. That was the wrong answer."

I study my brother's face to see how much farther I should go with the story. He's somber and pale, but it doesn't look like he's going to be sick. I guess he can handle it.

"Shun, I've never felt anything like the pain that came when I refused an order from that woman." I instinctively hold my stomach, like that pain might come back. "My skin felt like it was on fire and turned red. I couldn't breathe. My intestines started trying to rip themselves apart. At least, that's what it felt like. I think I threw up at some point and there was blood, but I was so hazy that I can't remember. I just...I just needed it to stop and I..." I pinch myself to make sure I keep it together. "I did the one thing that would make it better. I followed orders."

Shun inhales a sharp breath. "Jesus, DJ."

I shake my head, hoping it'll stop him from saying the things I've heard a thousand times. I didn't have a choice. I was a victim too. It wasn't my fault. No one should have to make a choice like that. All true, but all like snowballs attempting to put out a fire when it comes to the weight of what I did that day.

"When Queen Titania took back over, she freed me from the court, but she needed my name. She has it. Everyone who witnessed the ceremony has it. There are people in the realm that can still use that name against me and some of them, the Mab supporters that escaped capture, very well might if I ever run into them. Anyone too close to me is as risk. I won't do that to anyone. Especially not to…"

Talia jogs back to the car, slightly winded from scampering around with my phone. I wouldn't be surprised if she used up what was left of my storage with how many she took.

"Thanks," she says, handing me the phone. She does a double take at my expression. "What's wrong?"

"Nothing," I answer, wiping my eyes. "Shun was just telling me about our grandparents who passed while I was gone."

"Oh, DJ. I'm so sorry."

I shrug it off. "It's okay. They lived full lives and had the family when they went. It's all right."

She puts a comforting hand on my shoulder from the back seat.

It takes Shun a minute to get the car back on the road. Not that I blame him, but I can't help but worry that his silence is going to make Talia ask questions. Still, I know it's a lot. I consider trying to give him a reassuring smile, but that'll probably just worry him more. What kind of freak smiles after revealing something like that?

Finally, with slow careful movement and one more final glance my way, Shun puts the car in drive. He doesn't say much more for the rest of the trip.

Another hour and a half and we finally, *finally* make it to Triple Lake. Shun offers to pull over so we can take a picture by the sign. When I refuse, he insists we have an early lunch at the diner next to the first of the three lakes in the chain. Part of me is in a hurry and just wants to get to wherever we're supposed to meet Talia's aunts, but most of me wants to stay with my brother for a little bit longer, so I cave, and we pull into the diner parking lot.

We get a seat by the window, which provides a great view of the lake and the tall grass surrounding it. It's long, thin, and not as impressive as I had thought it would be. Shun swears we drove through here as kids, but I really don't remember it. We must have never stopped.

With lunch eaten and all three of the tiny gift shops explored, Shun admits that he has no more excuses to hang around, so we walk him back to his car. Talia gives him a tight hug, tells him to take care, and walks toward the lake to give us some privacy.

Truth be told, I don't think I want my brother to let go of me ever again. I might not feel as at ease with a lot of people, but I feel more at peace than I have in years while he squeezes me so hard I can't breathe.

"You need that girl, Daisy Jane," he whispers. "Don't lose her because you're afraid."

"She could get hurt because of me. I can't go through something like that again."

"And keeping yourself cut off from people is hurting *you*. Besides, you could never see any of those people again. You can't live your life wrapped up in the fear of the unknown. You could miss some pretty magical stuff that way."

"I've about had my fill of magical stuff, to be honest."

Shun lets me go and musses my hair. "You're still such a brat. Go save the world or whatever it is faerie knights do. And make sure to text Mom and call me when you're ready to come back home. I never want to lose track of you again."

"I know," I call as I head toward Talia. "See you, big brother."

"And do something with that undercut," Shun shouts as he gets in the car. "It's getting shaggy. You look like a wild child."

And now he sounds like our father. My older brother is officially an adult.

Without Shun here to chat us up, an uneasy silence settles over Talia and me as we make our way to the trailhead that will lead us up to the other two lakes. Apparently, the asrai live in the last of the three lakes since it's so remote. Judging by the map we picked up at the diner, it's about an hour hike.

Talia breaks through my route planning. "Your family is really nice. And your parents are great cooks."

"Yeah," I reply. "I'm glad things are going well for them. Shun's family seems cool."

That silence creeps back in as we walk. I take the opportunity to study the smooth surface of the lake before we enter the dense cover the trees. At least Talia will have another beautiful place to live with her aunts when I'm gone. And she's still close to humanity, so she can sneak down and watch them anytime she wants, though with both Lyle and Queen Shaylee looking for her, that's probably not a very good idea. I'd rather not have to rescue her from the clutches of that psycho or that whack job. They both could be either or. Take your pick.

"Where will you go once all this is over, then?" Talia asks. "Michigan's an awfully long way to be away from your family, especially if you're trying to build your relationship again."

I have to think it over for a moment. "Maybe...but I can't draw attention to them either. I'm supposed to be a missing person. There's gotta be someone around here that would still recognize me, and I like working with Iver. I would like to start fixing things with them, though." I can't believe the next words that come from my mouth, but, "What do you think I should do?"

Talia slips her hands in her pockets—a curiously human move—and chews her bottom lip as she thinks it over. "I think you have to figure out what's more important to you first. Everything will fall into place after that. That's what my aunts always say."

For how simple it sounds, I guess it's good advice. The only problem is that I have no idea what the answer is. My family's important, but I don't want to leave Faerie either. I'm more a part of this place now, and even if I'm starting with nothing, it's where I want to start. I just have to figure out what exactly I want to start.

Piece of cake.

I wish.

Once we pass the small waterfall that spills from the second lake into the first, the air changes. It smells cleaner and fresher, which is saying something considering the altitude, and something about the sunlight in the trees looks brighter. I guess we're finally back in the Faerie Realm.

Ahead of us, a freshly cleared path veers off from the overgrown shabby one we've been following, which Talia takes without a word to me. We're back in her territory, so I guess she knows where she's going.

The second lake is even more beautiful than the first. The mountains tower around us and the nearby waterfall babbles without the competition of the nearby road. When the path follows the water's edge, Talia takes a moment to take in the view. She kneels to study the multicolored pebbles.

"I had been doubtful about this new home," she says softly, "but I have to admit this one is quite beautiful, even if it will never replace my lake."

"You'll be able to go home eventually," I say. "It might take a while, but Faerie nobility will find someone else to fight over one of these days. Who knows? Maybe you have another sister or cousin they can compete for?"

Talia gives a sad smile and gets to her feet. "I hope not. There are very few people I would wish this on."

"But there are people you would wish this on?" I ask. "That's surprising."

"The people after me, namely," she mutters.

Before we can get too far, the water bubbles near the shore, rising high enough to form the shape of a person. I reach for my sword, but Talia stops me and walks back to the water's edge.

The water falls away to reveal a bent-over old woman, her skin pruned, hair made of seaweed—lake weed?—and a gown and shawl made of muck. "You're early, child," she says in a gurgly voice. "Did something happen to the three sisters?"

"I pray not," Talia replies with a small bow. "We traveled through the Human Realm to save time."

The old woman nods and pulls her shawl tighter around her shoulders. "Yes, yes, they had mentioned you were half. Anyhow, the rest of your family lives on the banks of the last lake. Follow this path along the mountainside. It'll take you to the northern bank of the lake. Once they realize it's you, the asrai will make themselves known. If you reach the stones that look like an eagle at the most northern tip of the lake, make your way back to the Human Realm as fast as you can. It means something has gone terribly wrong."

"We thank you for your help," Talia said. "Is there anything we can do to repay you?"

"Your arrival is enough, young one." The old woman smiles as she sinks back into the water. Maybe because she's naturally malicious-looking but I can't help but be suspicious of the way she watches us leave.

Talia doesn't seem concerned, but as we continue on our way, I begin to eye the heights of the trees and the shadows cast by the exposed rock. With all the people after Talia, you'd think they would have sent someone to meet us instead of expecting us to come on our own. Or maybe the aunts just trusted me enough to handle it.

Nearby rustling makes me jump and for good reason.

Two humans, one I recognize as Lyle's crone, emerge from the bushes. Before they can raise their weapons, I grab Talia by the hand and we take off down the path. Talia tries to wrestle her bow and arrows from my backpack. No sooner does she have it out and loaded than an arrow grazes my shoulder. Talia returns fire. There's a startled cry and the *thump* of a body hitting the ground. Two goblins jump from the bushes, but don't last long, even though they both come straight for me. More swarm down the side of the mountain.

Running is the best option we've got.

I keep Talia in front of me as we bolt up the path beside the tumbling water. If we can literally keep the higher ground and reach her family, we might have a chance to make it.

Except as we come up over the hill, we stop dead in our tracks.

A line of knights block our path, their own bows armed. I jump in front of Talia as they let their arrows fly—

Right past us and into the swarm of goblins.

One of the knights shields both Talia and me, pulling us behind the line as most of Lyle's forces retreat, although some of the more reckless ones run straight into the knights' swords and knives. Before either of us can ask questions, we're yanked apart and I'm knocked to the ground with my arms wrenched behind my back and bound.

"What do you want, you bastards?" I demand, trying to pull free and find a face in the sea of black leather armor. "Don't hurt her."

"Get her up," says a familiar voice. A pair of hands hoist me to my feet to face the knight who found us during the fireworks. Dominic.

"We won't hurt either of you," he says. "Her Majesty wants you come in and answer for your treason alive."

Chapter Sixteen

AS MUCH AS I'd love to be a match for thousands of Unseelie soldiers, I'm not, so Talia and I get dragged away with relative ease and stowed away in a small cave on the east bank of the third lake. Judging by the way it's outfitted with crystal bars and locks, they've been waiting for us for quite a while.

Talia's nearly worn a hole in her shoes from pacing by the time someone useful shows up, not that it makes us any happier to see him. Dominic motions for the guards to stand down before entering our cell. Judging by his somber expression, he's not trying to mock the fact that we're unarmed. It seems more like a sign that he doesn't want to fight.

"Where's my family?" Talia demands, bristling like a cat. "If you've hurt any of them—"

"All of the asrai are perfectly safe, I assure you," Dominic says. "Including the three that call themselves your aunts."

The setting sun suddenly feels colder for some reason. "They're here?" I ask. "They weren't supposed to get here until tomorrow."

"They arrived early this morning," Dominic explains, leaning back against the bars. "They must have found a shortcut, much like your journey through the Human Realm."

"But they're okay? You haven't done anything to hurt them?" Talia reiterates.

"Absolutely not."

"Then I want to see them. All of them."

The knight shakes his head. "We can't let you. Not until we know for sure you're going to cooperate."

"I'll promise anything you want," Talia pleads. "Just let me see my family."

Dominic frowns. "I'd love to believe you, but you're half human with ample reason to lie."

I hate to admit it, but he's right.

Talia glares at him, her hands balled into fists. "I wouldn't lie at a time like this. I'm not like my mother, or your queen for that matter."

"Ouch," snickers a voice from a distance. "That's cold. Fair, but cold."

Queen Shaylee, ruler of the Unseelie Court, comes around the corner, clad in the same armor of her knights with the addition of a black cloak and a sword made of iron rather than crystal. She looks so much like Talia and, in turn, like Mab, that my heart catches in my throat for a second. She certainly has the former queen's devious smirk down. It looks like she turned her hair dark brown. Or is that her natural color and the chestnut shade she used to sport a glamour so that she'd look more like Mab?

"Your Majesty, I told you I would handle this." Dominic sighs. Judging by the tired expression that comes over his face, this sort of thing is nothing new.

"I got out of a meeting early," Shaylee replies, motioning for the guards to rest at ease again. "Besides, did you honestly think I could wait to meet my long-lost cousin? Especially after pretending to be her for fifty years?"

"You have a strange way of trying to reconnect with people," Talia grumbles.

Shaylee finally looks at her with an oblivious grin on her face. "I heard through the grapevine that your name is Talia. Is that right?"

Tal just glares at her.

The queen sighs and puts her hands on her hips. "Look, cuz, I don't like all of this any more than you do. If I had my way, I'd let you go free, but as long as Lyle's alive, I don't think it's going to happen."

"Just destroy him then," Talia scoffs. "He's amassed quite the following, sure, but it shouldn't be too hard for the Unseelie army."

Shaylee and Dominic exchange looks.

"You don't have all your forces, do you?" I ask.

Shaylee shakes her head. "Unfortunately, no. We had to act fast if we had any hope of snatching you before Lyle did, and even then, we almost failed. Lyle doesn't know how many men we have here, but he has us outnumbered, by quite a bit, until the rest of my soldiers and knights arrive. We're supposed to receive help from my mother, Queen Titania, but she hasn't sent word as to when."

Talia gives me a curious look.

"Queen Titania rules the Seelie Court now," I explain. "The two were split after being one court for nearly one hundred years."

"Knowledgeable human, aren't you?" Shaylee asks, raising an eyebrow. She studies me for a moment, then adds, "Haven't I seen you before?"

"That's Daisy Jane," Dominic chimes in. "The ex-knight I told you about."

"It's DJ, damn it, but yeah. I served Mab for a while before turning on her like the rest of you."

Shaylee scowls. "You make it sound like it was a bad thing. You should know what's at stake if Lyle gets Talia just as well as we do."

"What does it matter?" I snap back. "Talia has made it blatantly obvious that she doesn't want to be queen. Why can't everyone just let her and her family be?"

"Because, unfortunately, Lyle's right," Shaylee answers. "As Mab's actual daughter, Talia's technically in line for the Unseelie throne, and Lyle has made a pretty good job making sure people know it."

"So, I'll renounce the crown," Talia argues. "I'll officially pass it to you."

"That wouldn't be enough." Dominic argues. "Her Majesty could have bewitched you into handing over the throne. I guarantee you Lyle's rebellion, and probably plenty of others watching, would believe that's what happened, especially after how she helped overthrow Mab."

Shaylee rolls her eyes. "I did everyone a favor with that whole act, thank you very much."

Dominic raises an eyebrow in her direction. "There's a human family that would beg to differ."

"Would you please stop bringing up Jocelyn? I said I was sorry. Repeatedly."

"Sorry or not, you—"

"Okay," Talia snaps, trying to get them back on topic. "If I help you take down Lyle's rebellion *and then* renounce my right as heir, would you let all of us go? Would that be enough to convince everyone?"

Shaylee strokes her chin and looks to Dominic, who does the same. They look more like a comedy duo than a queen and her champion.

"Your mother wouldn't approve," Dominic says.

Shaylee smirks. "She doesn't have to know until it's all over. Hell, if I spin it right, she doesn't have to know at all."

"I hate deceiving Queen Titania." Dominic groans forlornly.

"The woman ditched me in the Appalachian Mountains for damn near fifty years. She'll live with a few white lies floating around." Shaylee turns her attention to Talia. "Which puts us in similar boats, as I've come to understand it..." She goes back to tapping her chin. "We could use your help taking down Lyle and making it clear that you've given up the throne."

"So, will you let us out of here?" Talia demands.

"Sort of. I'll have a few of my knights escort you to see your family while we draw up a plan. If you agree to it, you two and all the asrai go free. If not, well, use your imagination."

If Queen Shaylee expects us to use our imaginations the way she does, I'd really rather not.

The guards lead us out of the cave with the queen and Dominic close behind. Outside they split off, heading up one bank of the river while we're led down the other. As we climb a small hill overlooking the lake, homes begin to emerge from the boulders and trees. They're small, looking as if they only house three or four people comfortably. Wisps of smoke float up through the branches while warm windows glow against the fading twilight. I have to admit, this looks like a nice little community. Once we figure out what to do with Lyle, Talia will probably feel right at home.

We're led up to a house farthest up the hill and the guards announce our arrival with a heavy knock. Much to my surprise, it's Vervain. She glares daggers at the guard, but her eyes get wide and watery at the sight of me and Talia. With a delighted cry, she throws open the door and flings herself into her niece's arms. Eleadora and Juniper rush to see what all the commotion is about, only to throw their arms around Talia as well, knocking her to the ground.

"Oh, my dear child, we've been so worried," Vervain cries, wiggling out from under her sisters and lifting Talia to her feet so she can hug her again, only vertically this time. "When the queen's forces showed up only hours after we did, we feared the worst. With them and that git, Lyle, farther down the mountain, we had no way to get a message to you."

"I'm sorry we made you worry, auntie," Talia says, wiping the tears from her own eyes. "Things with DJ's family got a little complicated."

Finally, the aunts seem to remember that I'm here. While they don't knock me over, thankfully, they hug me just as tight. Eleadora even kisses both my cheeks.

"Thank you so much for bringing her to us," she says between kisses. "Even if you did hand her over to Queen Shaylee, we forgive you."

"Gee, thanks," I reply as Juniper pats me on the shoulder with a smile. Clearly, I did something right, seeing as that's the most emotion I've seen her emit yet.

"Come in, come in," Vervain says. "We were just sitting down to dinner. We'll introduce you to the rest of the family once you're settled. You've had a trying day, I imagine."

No joke.

Over a spread of grainy bread, fruit, and hot mulberry wine, Vervain and the others tell us about their journey cross-country. Judging by all the escapades they've gotten themselves into with leprechauns, truckers, banshees, and bus drivers, they've had quite the adventure themselves. I'm particularly curious about the story concerning the truckers, but they pass the torch on to us before I get the chance to ask. Maybe we'll come back to it later.

Talia takes the reins for most of the story. Her large exaggerated gestures and attempts to describe things in the Human Realm make it worth it. I can't help but squirm as she praises me and my efforts to protect her from everything. From the pool to large sudden noises the car made to real threats like Lyle and Dominic, apparently, I'm some sort of hero.

And apparently, the aunts think that means more than it actually does. They eye me with smug smirks as Talia praises my efforts to track her down in Iowa and my valiant sword work in that alley during the fireworks.

"It seems like you were worthy of our trust after all," Vervian says, helping herself to more wine.

"Good thing too," Eleadora adds with a wink. "Couldn't very well have our Talia pairing up with someone who couldn't take care of her, now could we?"

I choke on my wine. Beside me, Talia stiffens.

"It's not like that," I wheeze. "We're just friends."

"Of course you're not," Vervain argues. "That's simply not how these things are done. Well, obviously there are exceptions, but we see no reason why this case should be one. You've clearly proven that you care deeply for Talia—"

"I proved that I can still make friends and do my job," I snap back. "That's all."

"Nonsense," Eleadora snaps.

"Aunties." We all go still at Talia's sharp tone. "DJ has made the nature of our relationship perfectly clear numerous times. I'd like you to respect that, please."

She goes back to eating while Vervain glares daggers at me. While she's busy doing that, Juniper nudges Eleadora and holds out her hand. Eleadora rolls her eyes and hands her sister a gold coin with a pout.

Before I can demand to know what that was about, a hard knock comes at the door. The aunts jump to their feet and lower their heads as Queen Shaylee and Dominic let themselves in. Talia goes to stand, but I grab her hand so that she stays sitting. If she thinks we're going to bend under her will like that, she's got another thing coming. As far as I'm concerned, we have just as many cards as she does.

"Talia, DJ, can we speak to you outside for a moment?" Queen Shaylee asks. The way her hand rests on her sword tells us that it's not actually up for discussion, so we follow her and Dominic outside.

"We have a plan," Shaylee says, folding her arms. "You follow it and we'll forget we ever crossed paths. I might even work out some form of payment for the two of you, under the table of course."

"So, what do you have in mind?" I ask.

"Right now, Lyle has the numbers, but we have the higher ground, quite literally. The only reason we haven't destroyed him yet is that our forces have not arrived and, until he forced our hand today, he didn't seem to know that."

"So, hold off until the rest of your army gets here and Queen Titania's forces show up," I argue.

"We don't think we can," Dominic adds. "He saw what we were working with during our confrontation today. Odds are he's preparing for an attack, possibly as early as tomorrow."

"That's where you two come in," Her Majesty continues. "I need you two to infiltrate their camp and convince them to hold off on fighting us at least until the day after tomorrow. Tell Lyle that our forces have arrived, and he needs to regroup. Bonus points if you convince him to move farther down the mountain. The more high ground we have, the better."

"How am I supposed to do that?" Talia asks. "I've been running from him all this time. What could possibly lead him to believe that I've changed my mind?"

"Tell him Shaylee was ready to execute you," I chime in. "You see how she treats her people and know now that you're the true queen. You would protect your subjects from tyrants like her. Some variation of that should do the trick."

"Good idea," Shaylee says with a smirk in my direction. "I might have to offer you a position among my ranks when this is all over."

"I'll pass," I reply.

"So, we just need to convince him that I want to be queen and that your backup has arrived, so he needs to get more forces before attacking. Is that the general gist?" Talia asks.

"More or less," Dominic answers, "but it might be best if we practice a little bit before you go. One wrong line could get you both killed and us a whole lot of trouble."

"How are we supposed to communicate, though?" I ask. "It's not like you're carrying cell phones. I hardly get any service all the way out here anyway."

The Unseelie Queen snaps her fingers. "Bring Lyle to us. We wouldn't have to even worry about the forces if we could just get rid of him. As far as he's concerned, you're his queen. Once you convince him you're on his side, he'll follow you anywhere, so you lead him right into our territory. Feed him some poetic bullshit about how you have royal secrets to bestow upon him or whatever, and he'll be putty in your hand."

"Where should I bring him?"

"The waterfall between the highest and the middle lake. We'll have people ready and waiting for him at high noon to take him out and we can be done with this whole mess."

"What makes you think he'll believe me that easily?"

Both Shaylee and Dominic scoff.

"Trust us," Shaylee says. "Lyle is quite clever, but he turns into a total git when it comes to the crown. Mab had him wrapped around her finger."

"It was quite pathetic, really," Dominic adds.

"How exactly did he manage to escape again?" I ask.

Both the queen and her champion go quiet.

"Like I said," Shaylee repeats, "he can be quite clever when he wants to be."

"Um-hm," I mutter.

Shaylee looks back toward the small house that the aunts are sharing. "For now, rest up and brainstorm ideas. We'll be coming for you once we take care of our end to get our stories straight and send you on your way. You deserve a little time with your aunts before things get too crazy."

"Thank you, Your Majesty," Talia says.

Cringing, Shaylee says, "Please just call me Shaylee. As far as I'm concerned, we're family. Don't worry about formalities."

"Okay...Shaylee." Talia frowns as if the name has a strange taste to it.

The queen looks to me and says, "You might as well call me Shaylee, too, for the time being. When I get you to come work for me, I'll have you call me something else."

I shake my head and start back toward the house. "Not gonna happen," I call as Talia tags behind. "I'm done being a knight."

"Judging by the way you jumped in front of Princess Talia this afternoon, I beg to differ." Dominic chuckles.

I ignore him. I don't want to give him an explanation that would make him think there's something more going on between me and Talia, especially after how hard I've worked to avoid that.

"That reminds me," Talia says as we climb the tiny hill back to the house. "You need to think of a new form of payment since your family still remembers you."

"Don't worry about it just yet," I say. "We'll deal with it after we get this madness taken care of."

"Are you sure? You don't strike me as the type who likes to work for free."

"Who said I'm working for free? I'm just getting paid late," I argue. "And I almost feel like I should be offended by that statement."

Talia shrugs. "I don't mean anything by it. You just seem like the kind of person who wants what is owed to you is all."

"Doesn't everyone?"

Tal studies me for longer than what's comfortable, making my skin crawl. Maybe I shouldn't have said anything. "I suppose they do."

She leaves it at that, and I'm grateful since I don't have anything close to an answer for her. As she continues to scheme with Shaylee, her bright green eyes calculating and sharp as she attempts to fill a role she never wanted or dreamed she would be in, I realize that maybe I know what I want after all.

Too bad it's something I can't have.

Chapter Seventeen

IN THE EARLY hours of the morning, we bid the aunts goodbye. They weren't as warm toward me as when we first showed up, but I tried not to care. I'm more than holding up my side of the deal, and so long as they hold up theirs once this was done, it didn't really matter if they liked me or not.

Shaylee and Dominic go over our fabricated story as we do our best to look as if they've been rough with us. Talia put leaves in her hair and streaked her face and clothes with dirt. She even ripped her skirt a bit. I'm not thrilled with the way she tries to scrape up her arms and legs to make it look really convincing, but can't do much to stop her. Given that I do the same thing with my sword, I guess I can't complain too much.

Once we're sufficiently messed up, they send us on our way through the woods, running as if they truly had captured us. There's no way of telling how far out Lyle has people watching, so it's best to play it up as much as we can for as long as we can.

We get our answer just as the sky begins to lighten in the east. Three goblins leap from the brush, small swords ready to run us through if we try to continue down the path anymore.

"Halt," one screeches. "What business do you have here, Unseelie sympathizers?"

"We're not," Talia pants, out of breath and pretending to be panicked. "It's me, Princess Talia. We managed to escape Queen Shaylee's grasp, but only just. Please, if you don't take us in before she realizes—"

It doesn't take any more than that, though. The goblins drop to their knees and press their heads to the dirt, their swords abandoned.

"Your Highness," exclaims one of them. "Beg your pardon, but you don't look yourself. Please forgive such rudeness."

"You're forgiven, but we must hurry," Talia says, shifting uncomfortably under the praise. "Surely the Unseelie Queen knows we're gone by now."

"*You're* the Unseelie Queen, Your Highness," says a goblin as they get to their feet and lead us down the path. He leaves the others to guard the roads. "The wench that sits upon your throne is a filthy impostor. A Seelie pawn sent by the dreaded Queen of Light to control us." He seems to realize how he's rambling because he cuts himself off with a cackle. "But that's all for Master Lyle to explain. Come along."

Given how Titania used Shaylee to take the Unseelie Court from Mab, the goblin might actually be onto something there, but now's hardly the time to point that out.

The goblin leads us around the lake and up the banks of a western tributary. On either bank, small temporary huts stand between the trees. Goblins, trolls, giants, and boggles all pause as we pass, some watching with skepticism, others with subtle glee. A few of the braver souls even dare to cheer. We come to a stop outside the largest of the structures framed by two troll guards. They stand up a little taller and a bit friendlier at the sight of Talia.

The goblin gives us a little bow as he says, "Please wait here, Your Highness, while I fetch Master Lyle. Won't be but a moment." With that, he disappears within the mossy curtains.

We stand with the trolls in an awkward silence for a few moments, all of us avoiding eye contact with one another. Several people pass us by, stare, and whisper as they walk. I try not to pay them too much attention.

A sudden, "You idiot," makes us jump, even the trolls. It's followed by quick angry whispers I know must belong to Lyle. Another few moments pass. He bursts through the curtains, sword drawn as if he's ready to run us both through. I jump in front of Talia with my own blade at the ready, but it proves not to be worth it. Lyle just glares at us as if he's not sure he should attack or not.

"After all this time you've spent fighting me," he growls, "you honestly expect me to believe you'd come to me so quickly?"

"We needed to see Queen Shaylee's tyranny for ourselves," Talia says, reaching over my shoulder and making me lower my sword. I know it's to show we don't want to fight, but it makes me uneasy nonetheless. "She's as horrible as you said she is and she needs to be stopped."

"And you're the one to stop her?" Lyle asked, with narrowed eyes.

"With you to guide me, yes," Talia replies. "I am, after all, Queen Mab's daughter."

If our lives didn't depend on making him believe us, I'd probably throw up at those words.

Lyle studies us for a long time, then lowers his sword as well. "How am I supposed to trust you?" he demands. "You're half human. You could be lying to me the way Shaylee lied to your mother."

Damn it, he's right. I guess he's not as blind with devotion as we thought he was. Thankfully, Talia doesn't back down. "What do I need to do to prove it?" she demands, stepping out from behind me. "Just name it."

The knight looks from Talia to me several times, then motions to my sword. "Daisy Jane, give Princess Talia your sword."

I don't like where this is going, but I oblige.

"Now, Your Highness, if you're willing to prove that you want to become Queen of the Unseelie Realm, I need you to first prove you're willing to make the sacrifices to get there. Your dear friend is to be the first of those sacrifices."

My palms begin to sweat, and my stomach turns to an iceberg.

"Run her through."

Talia turns white as she looks down at the sword, then back at me. I'm sure I don't look much better. A small crowd gathers, giving us no way to form a plan or think this through. Our options are either Talia killing me here and now or both of us dying. She flinches as I turn to face her, and her eyes go wide with terror as I stand with my arms open. She backs away with a subtle shake of her head.

I know she can figure something out, though. I know she can.

"We have much to plan, Your Highness," Lyle says with a sneer. "I'd rather not have this take all day. Unless, of course, we need to work up to such an act of self-sacrifice."

I bite back a scoff. Self-sacrifice, my ass. I'm the only one getting sacrificed here.

"C'mon, Tal. You can do it," I mutter.

Talia lifts my sword with shaking hands and holds it close to her chest, a clear sign that she's never properly held one in her life. That could work to our advantage or make things worse for me. Judging by the way she aims it at the center of my chest, even if it doesn't kill me instantly, both death and recovery aren't going to be any fun.

"I'm sorry, DJ," Talia whispers. She takes a deep breath, then charges.

I hold her gaze. A few more racing steps and that blade's going through my chest. Talia screams as the sword—

"Stop!"

I take Lyle's words as a cue to slide out of Talia's way. She was close enough that the sword still manages to slice through my shirt as momentum carries her forward, leaving a shallow gash across my chest. The pain spreads, but at least it's not agonizing deathly pain. Talia drops the blade as if it catches on fire and brings her trembling hands to her ashen face. I'm careful not pay the throbbing pain any mind. I don't want to upset Talia any more than she already is, and I'll be damned if Lyle sees a single sign of weakness from me.

Lyle lowers his hands and approaches us with a proud smile on his face. "I wouldn't actually ask you to kill a skilled knight such as Daisy Jane," he says. "When the time comes to attack, we'll need her. I simply needed to test your resolve." Giving me a smug smirk, he adds, "And you have to admit that I owed you for our little scrap back in the farmhouse."

If I remember correctly, Talia was the one who knocked him over the head with a two-by-four, not me, but Heaven forbid his precious queen do anything wrong.

I take a deep breath to try to steady the shaking in my own hands. None of this is Talia's fault.

Lyle picks up the sword and hands it back to me, then motions to the structure behind him. "Come. We have much to discuss and little time to discuss it. And I'm sure Daisy Jane would like her wound attended to."

"It's just a scratch," I say with a shrug. "Really."

"I must admit, I always did admire that about you," he says as one of the trolls holds a mossy curtain open for us. "Your resilience as a human made up for your other…shortcomings."

I should save everyone the trouble and just kill Lyle tonight while he sleeps, the cheeky bastard.

Inside, the tent-like structure seems to go on forever. Shimmering drapes separate rooms, warm earthy scents I recognize from the Faerie Court fill the air, and elaborate chairs and sofas make it look more like a vacation spot than the headquarters of a military campaign.

Several faerie women in simple garb flit around the tent, making sure everything is in order. They come to attention at the sight of Lyle and us and come to hover nearby.

"Fetch Her Highness and her human friend something to wear," Lyle orders. Turning to us, he adds, "Once you're dressed, we'll see to breakfast and begin our campaign to take back to Unseelie Court." Thankfully he excuses us, further entering the depths of his makeshift keep.

The servants deliver our clothes with a basin of water and a cloth, then excuse themselves as well. With even their footsteps gone, Talia collapses on one of the sofas and chokes back a sob. I sit beside her and run a hand along her back.

"Hey, it's okay," I whisper. "It's all right."

"It's not, though," she cries. "I could have killed you."

"Nah, you wouldn't have," I lie. "I would have been hold up in bed for a few days, but I would have been fine. You're not exactly a master swordswoman. You couldn't have killed me with that thing if you really wanted to."

Talia glares at me through her fingers.

"I'm trying to make you feel better," I groan. "Would it help if I told you that you could definitely have killed me if you had your bow?"

"Not really." Talia sighs, wiping her eyes and getting back to her feet. "I'll just be glad when this is all over—and the Unseelie Court has its rightful queen." She glances around the room, eyeing a few of the darker corners. She gives me a stern look that, for now, I'm going to assume means we're not really alone, so we need to be careful about what we say. "Let's just get dressed and get on with it."

For Talia, the servants brought an elaborate black gown decorated with onyx and sharp chips of obsidian around the collar, wrists, and bottom hem. Definitely a Queen Mab Original, I'd bet. When I notice her struggling with the back clasp, I pause in my silent griping about the new bloodstain on my bra and help.

"Thanks." She sighs, letting her hair roll over her shoulders again. Studying herself in the mirror for a moment, she grumbles, "This dress is obnoxious. When I inherit my mother's kingdom, I hope I don't get her wardrobe with it."

Given that plunging neckline and the way it hugs her shape, I personally don't think it's all that bad, but I keep that opinion to myself. Talia turns and frowns at me, my chest in particular. Sure, I'm not as stacked as her, but that's just rude.

"We need to take care of that," she says, dipping the white rag in the water and wringing it out.

Oh, yeah. She nearly killed me. Duh.

She dabs at the wound she caused, wincing whenever I flinch. With it only faintly trickling blood now, she lays her hand over the wound to heal it. I really wish she had let me finish getting dressed before this.

Apparently she does too, because she attempts to make small talk as the warm tingle of magic knits my skin back together. "How come you don't like your name?"

I scoff and gesture to all five foot three of me, most of which is muscle, which easy to see in my current state of undress. "Do I really look like a Daisy Jane to you?"

The magic fades, and Talia wipes the blood from the faint pink scar that now sits where the gash was. "I think you look like you, and I think it's a nice name, honestly. It's very pretty."

"I'm not pretty," I remind her. "Strong, snarky, hotheaded, and I'll admit I have nice eyes, but I'm not pretty."

Talia picks up the leggings, tunic, and belt obviously intended for me and tosses them in my direction. "You're also sweet, generous, and considerate when you want to be. I think all those things could be considered pretty. Not to mention your smile, on the rare occasion I get to see it."

This is not a conversation I really want to have in my underwear, so I let it go for a moment and throw my clothes on. By the time I do, she's already waiting by the curtain Lyle went through earlier, so it looks like she gets to win this round.

The room next door is far less decorated and comfortable than the first. It's white with only a long polished wooden table surrounded by chairs with the rocky grass below us as a floor. It also includes Lyle and several other court faeries in black leather armor, which doesn't exactly help the atmosphere.

Lyle stands at attention with the others, clearly waiting for some sort of order from Talia. She fidgets under the attention and finally raises her hand to them.

"At ease, everyone," she says. "No need for such formalities. Let's just get to work, shall we?"

Lyle drops his shoulders and grins. "If we're doing away with formalities, Your Highness, might I just say that you look dazzling in your mother's attire. You are every bit her daughter, and every bit the queen our court deserves."

The others nod in agreement.

Yep, called it. It was one of Mab's dresses. Judging by the way Lyle openly studies every inch of her in it, that was done on purpose.

I'm definitely killing this bastard in his sleep tonight if I get the chance.

I take a seat on Talia's right, despite the offended glares of the other knights, while she and Lyle stand at the front of the table with a map of the Triple Lakes area spread out in front of them.

"Judging by what I've seen here, we're matched with Shaylee in terms of numbers," Talia lies effortlessly. "However, she has skill and the higher ground on her side. Most of her forces are knights and foot soldiers whereas most of ours seem to be simple Unseelie Court subjects and solitary fae that more closely aligned themselves with us when my mother was queen."

"That is correct, Your Highness," the knight next to me says. "Though we have considered enlisting some of the local folk in our efforts. Surely there's something they could want from the Unseelie Court."

"Like what?" I add. "And furthermore, where are they? Other than the asrai, we haven't seen any faeries in a while." I think back to the nisse. "Not to mention the fact there aren't any courts around here. None of the fae folk around here are going to want to fall under our banner if they think they're going to have to be subjects under Talia, no matter how great of a queen she's bound to be."

"Thank you, DJ," Talia replies with a grin. "And those are some excellent points."

Lyle glares at me over her shoulder, and I have to resist the urge to stick my tongue out at him like a child and silently chastise myself for it. Now isn't the time to get into a pissing contest with this putz, especially since I've already won.

I know that's not necessarily something to be proud of, but I've got to savor the little victories.

"Oh, they're here. I can assure you," another knight says. "They keep to the shadows. They're wary of us for some reason."

"My troop spoke to one," another knight chimes in. His expression goes grim. "It called us the Cursed Folk of the East. Said it didn't want us to bring our shadow into their lands. When I asked what shadow, it said it was too scared to speak the name and it was surprised we had escaped it this long. Then it bound off. It was a pretty nasty creature too. Made of bones and rot with the face of a dead deer. If that thing thought *we* were cursed, we're certainly not welcomed around here."

Talia folds her arms and studies the map in silence for a moment. "I suggest we investigate further. The fact of the matter is we need allies if we're going to take the Unseelie Court back from my cousin and I want to know what this curse is. If it's a misconception, we need to get rid of it if we want allies. If there really is something hanging over the Faerie Realm, I need to know what it is and where it came from.

"In the meantime, we make Shaylee think we have more forces than we really do. Send patrols, use glamours, get at least a few of the natives to help to create the illusion that we're well-manned."

If Lyle doesn't stop grinning like a proud mentor every time Talia says something he likes, I'm going to forgo killing him in his sleep and just kick his teeth in here and now.

"I had hoped you would say something of that nature, Your Highness," he says, setting a hand on her shoulder. "It sounds like the workings of a brilliant plan. Don't you think so, gentlemen?"

Everyone nods in various levels of agreement. Those who have additional ideas and strategies offer them up for the group to hear. Lyle seems taken aback by the way Talia listens to each of them in turn like—gasp—an actual leader.

I have to admit, if she ever wanted to become queen, with a few years of training and guidance from people with an actual clue, she might make a pretty good one.

By noon, we have a plan set in place. During the night, four of the knights will take small teams to make contact with the fae living in the region and try to figure out some sort of alliance, at least temporarily. They should be back the day after tomorrow, which works out perfectly for us. The rest will take teams to spook Shaylee and her knights, believing there are more people on Lyle's team than she thought.

His human renegades will be in on the action. The more races that seem to be on Lyle's side, the better. He has strict orders from Talia not to recruit anymore, though. Triple Lake is too small. Anyone who goes missing is bound to be hunted down.

Lyle, Talia, and I will be running a small scouting mission on our own. Nothing dangerous. Just some basic practice for Talia since she's never been in the field and has never used a sword before.

It won't be dangerous for us, at least. Lyle, however, will be walking right into Shaylee's hands. Getting himself captured after sending a good chunk of his men away from the camp sounds like the perfect way to lose a rebellion, if you ask me, no matter how small your opponent's army is.

Now we just have to keep the act up for about twelve hours or so and then get the hell out of Dodge, whether Shaylee wants us to stay and fight or not. She'll have her victory either way, so I'd rather choose not.

With a plan laid out, Lyle decides to move on to the next item on the list: presenting Talia as the True Queen of the Unseelie Court.

Wonderful.

While she's already in the proper attire, she has to sit through about an hour's worth of hair and makeup at the hands of the servants. After the glare I send them all, they don't dare try the same with me, but they do insist I at least get into a suit of armor. Truth be told, I have to admit how badass the Unseelie armor looks, so I change into it without any protest.

I'm to be presented as Talia's champion, which begs the question where Lyle sees himself fitting into this equation. I tuck that into the back of my mind for later. Given that he'll be finished before the day's out, maybe it won't matter.

Lyle goes ahead of us to speak to the masses gathered in front of the tent. Through the curtain we can hear him prattle on and on about the dawning of a new era for the entire Faerie Realm. Queen Mab might be gone, but her century of sacrifice will never be forgotten. The Unseelie Court will rise again to protect its own. Never again will the Seelie manipulate us from the shadows. Blah, blah, blah. God, I hate speeches.

"DJ, I don't know if I can do this," Talia whispers, looking as if she might be sick. "I'm just a half-human girl who's spent her entire life running around forests and lakes. I don't know how to lead people, and I certainly don't know how to lead a rebellion."

I slip my hand into hers, not even really meaning to. "Hey, you got this. You don't even have to actually lead the rebellion, remember?" I assure her, giving her a smile she apparently thinks is pretty. "If a wayward human like me can become a faerie knight and get you halfway across the country, you can do this. I know you can."

Talia meets my gaze for a moment, then leans over and kisses me. I do nothing to stop her.

Her lips meeting mine feels like a jolt of electricity to a battery that's long been dead. I could stand here and take her in forever, but just as I raise my free hand to her face, she pulls away suddenly and lets go of my hand.

"I'm sorry," she stutters, trying to hide the red in her cheeks with her hands. "You already made it clear this isn't what you wanted. I shouldn't have done that. It was selfish of me."

She's under all this pressure she never asked for, and *she's* the one worried about being selfish?

"No, Talia, I—"

"Behold," Lyle booms outside. "Your One True Queen of the Unseelie Court!"

As the crowds outside cheer, Talia drops her hands, squares her shoulders, takes a deep breath, and pulls back the curtain, letting in bright stream of midday light.

Even in that horrible black dress, she looks stunning. She might not know it or want it, but she looks like the queen she was born to be, and even if it's all a ruse that'll be over by tomorrow, I'm proud to call myself her champion.

As I follow her out into the light, surrounded by enemies, I try not to wallow in the fact that this is all I'll ever be to her. There are more pressing issues to tackle at the moment.

Like trying to just survive the day.

Chapter Eighteen

THE DAY PASSES as a sort of low-key party, which makes it go by faster. There's not really anything to do until the sun goes down, after all. I stay glued to Talia's side as she makes her rounds among Lyle's followers. They all dote on her, going on about how much she looks like her mother—the mother that left her to die in the forest, mind you. Quite a few of them praise Mab and what a great queen she was, how she brought so much freedom to the realm, and how they can't wait to have that freedom once again.

Freedom to torment other fae and abuse magic. I'm sure that'll be wonderful.

At least we don't have to put up with Lyle *too* much. There are plenty of gits giving him attention so that he stays pretty busy. I catch him staring at Talia from time to time, though, especially over lunch. During her first sword-fighting lessons in between, he leaves the lesson to me and several other knights and disappears for a while.

The kiss from earlier makes it difficult not to notice how close Talia and I get during the practice. Between showing her how to hold it properly, how to position her body, and how many times I help her get up off the ground, there's quite a lot of touching going on. What's worse is that I can't tell if anyone else notices. In normal circumstances, I wouldn't mind, but I'm worried it could make things more complicated in the long run.

Dinner gives us a good chance to put a little distance between us, especially since there are a few goblin children vying for spots by her while we eat. I have to admit, for as ugly as adult goblins are, their children can be pretty cute. They're kinda like pugs, so weird looking there's something charming about them.

By the time the meal's over, it's time to send off the fours knights looking for possible allies. The entire time we watch them prepare to leave, I'm sweating bullets, waiting for someone to figure out what's really going on. No one seems to, because the knights leave with promises of victory and returning to the cheers of their rebellious Unseelie comrades.

We repeat the same process when the scouts leave to mess with Shaylee's forces. It's not long before we head off alone with Lyle. As glad as I am that he bought the whole "extra sword practice and catch up" bullshit, I can't exactly say being alone with him in a dark isolated forest is my favorite place to be.

"Are you sure you don't need to rest?" he asks as we make our way away from the camp. "You've had a long couple of days, not to mention I heard you excelled quite a bit in your single afternoon of practice."

Kiss up. I love Tal, but she's terrible with a sword.

And I mean that I love her as a friend, obviously.

"I'm sure my mother wouldn't stop simply because she was tired," Talia replies. "Especially with a battle so close at hand."

"I would never put you in the middle of a battle," Lyle exclaims as if he was offended by the very notion. "Not when you're so inexperienced. For now, all you need to do is be seen. I'll handle the rest." He studies the stars above and sighs. "But you're right. Her Majesty never knew when to stop fighting. She was so strong and brilliant and selfless...not to mention beautiful."

Since I'm trailing behind the two of them, I take the opportunity to roll my eyes.

"I wish she had stopped every once and awhile," Lyle continues. "Maybe the Other World would not have worn her down so."

Talia twists her hands together for a moment before daring to ask, "What happened to her, exactly?"

The question makes me uneasy, but I suppose she has the right to know.

"She united the realm under one banner," Lyle explains, standing a little taller. "She took on the burden usually reserved for two queens and held up for over a hundred years. In the end, however, it proved to be too much. The constant strain of holding Faerie and the World Beyond together broke her down. It made her not herself. It pushed her past the point where even I could reach her, although I tried."

"Why make the courts into one?" Talia asked, engrossed in the story.

"That I could never fully understand," Lyle mused. "For a while, she cited humanity's growth. She said we would be stronger if we all bonded together. That way, we would endure, but several times, it didn't sound like she was talking about humanity at all. Something older. More dangerous. By then, however, she was so far gone, I imagine even she didn't know what she was talking about."

"Could it be tied to whatever makes us the Cursed Folk of the East?"

"It's possible. Our scouts will have to return with more information before we can be sure."

"Did you believe her? That there was *something* coming for the Faerie Realm?"

"I didn't know what to believe, other than that I needed to protect her. I heard tell that Shaylee kept quite a few of her belongings after she died to protect the Faerie Realm one final time, though. Maybe the explanation is in one of her journals somewhere. We'll have to look for them once we get back to court."

Talia gives him one of the fakest smiles I've ever seen. "I'd like that very much. I'd like to know her, even if I never got the chance to meet her."

Lyle comes to a stop and studies Talia in the moonlight. I don't like the look in his eye. Not one bit. "You look so much like her, you know." He sighs. "Except your hair. You got that from your human father, I imagine. It's beautiful, though."

So help me if he touches her...

Talia plays with her hair self-consciously. "I've always seen it as rather plain."

"It's not plain at all," Lyle replies softly. "Nothing about you is."

Am I just, like, not here anymore? Is that what's going on? And where the hell are Shaylee, Dominic, and everyone else? I glance at my phone and see that it's only eleven thirty. We've got about thirty minutes yet. Great.

"Tell me, Talia," Lyle continues, beginning down the path again, "Is there anyone particularly special in your life? A sweetheart back home near the court perhaps?"

"You're not trying to find me a fellow monarch so soon, are you?" Talia chuckles, sounding incredibly uncomfortable. "I don't even have the throne yet."

"It's something that simply crossed my mind," Lyle replies with a casual shrug that I don't believe for a second. "I would imagine a lovely girl such as yourself would have someone that worries about you and wishes to see you return home safe, other than your aunts of course."

"I'm afraid there isn't." Talia sighs. Then she gives me a look that makes me feel two feet tall. I study a nearby tree to avoid it.

"And Daisy Jane?"

"A friend. More like an associate, really."

Ouch. It's not like I don't deserve it, though, with the way I've pushed her away.

"What a pity," Lyle mutters. He looks to me—for affirmation or an argument, I can't tell—and I do my best to ignore him.

We walk in an awkward silence for a while and come to a nice clearing that would work well enough for sparring practice, which Lyle seems to know since he stops.

"This looks like it will work well enough," he says, turning to face Talia. "But before we begin, there's something that belonged to your mother that I would like to give you."

Talia and I give each other confused looks as he digs in his pocket and pulls out a surprisingly simple ring. I'm assuming it's faerie-made, judging by the fact that it seems to be constructed from a ring of thorns, and I'm sure Mab wore some plain jewelry from time to time, but something doesn't feel right.

"This was my mother's?" Talia asks, studying the ring intently.

"It wasn't exactly her favorite," Lyle says. "But it was the only thing I could snatch before escaping the court."

Talia takes it and studies it for what feels too long. It's not as if I can say too much to protest it. I don't want to make Lyle suspicious, but I can't help but feel like something about this situation is very wrong.

"Want me to hang on to it?" I suggest. "It'll just get busted while you're practicing. That or one of those thorns will stab you."

"Maybe I could just try it on," Talia muses, rolling it over in her hands gingerly. "It belonged to my mother, after all."

"So?" I argue. "Put it on after you spar."

Lyle snaps his head toward me. "This isn't any of your concern, Daisy Jane."

"You're the one that named me her champion," I remind him. "You made it my concern."

"Let her have this one connection with her mother."

"She can have it after she practices sword fighting. It's not safe."

"Who said she'd be sword fighting with it on?" Lyle sneers.

I turn just in time to see Talia slip it onto her finger.

"Tal, don't!"

As the words leave my mouth, her face goes blank and her eyes glassy. She drops to the ground like my stomach, but I manage to catch her before she can hit her head. While her eyes stay open, they're unfocused and her mouth is slack. She's not unconscious, but she's not here either.

"Talia! Tal, c'mon. What's wrong?" I beg, turning her to face me. I spot the ring on her finger and try to pry it off, only to jump back as it burns my hand. A closer inspection shows beads of blood across my fingertip.

The damn thing's cursed.

Cold crystal against my neck makes me freeze before I can stand and rip Lyle apart.

"Did you honestly think I was that stupid?" he demands. "Did you really think I would believe that Her Highness would just waltz back to me after one night with that traitorous bitch? Shaylee's losing her edge. You, unfortunately, never had one."

"What did you do to Talia, you bastard?" I hiss.

"I just made her a bit more agreeable is all." He snickers. "She just needs a little persuasion to see the way things really are, and she's definitely not going to get that with your annoying voice bouncing around her head." With a sigh, he adds, "Your Highness, do get up off the ground. Lying like that isn't very becoming of you."

Talia sits up and gets to her feet as if I'm not even there. Once up, she stops as if she's waiting for her next command.

Lyle says, "Good girl," and the way he talks down to her, like she's some sort of pet, makes me sick.

"I meant what I said earlier," he continues, distracting me from all the different ways I could kill him. "I do still need you. You're going to be my delivery girl. When I remove this sword from your neck, you're going to run to Shaylee as fast as you can and tell her to move her forces back to the southern face of the mountain, giving us the higher ground. There they will stay until we are ready to attack and obliterate them."

"And why the hell should I do that?" I snarl.

"Your Highness, come take this dagger from me. I think it would look rather fetching against your neck."

My body turns to ice as Talia does as she's told. "Wait, wait, wait, stop!"

Lyle holds up a hand, causing Talia to pause.

"Are you crazy?" I shout. "You need her."

"All I need her for is the crown, really," Lyle explains. "Which she can pass on to me easily enough. She's the last of her line, after all, and in cases like that, it's customary for the throne to go to the queen's champion." He sneers down at me. "Unless that champion is the one that turns around and stabs the potential queen in the back. With you being, well, you, it would be an easy enough story to weave, I'd imagine. In a way, you are killing her, what with the way you failed to protect her and all. You couldn't even stop her from putting on a silly ring."

The fact that he's right is like a punch to the gut.

"I'd hate to have it come to that, though," he continues. "Talia is quite lovely. She looks so much like her mother, after all. I really would like to keep her, but it's entirely up to you. Run and tell Shaylee what she needs to do, or kill your dear friend. It's up to you."

I study Talia in the moonlight. She doesn't look like herself. I already miss the light in her eyes and her smile something terrible. I can't let Lyle snuff that out of the world. Not when I can bide my time and figure out another plan with Shaylee's help.

"Fine." I sigh. "Let me up so I can do what you need me to do."

Lyle removes the sword. "I knew you'd come around. Now, run along."

I glance Talia's way one final time as I get to my feet. Lyle shoos me deeper into the forest. Before this is all over, I sincerely hope I get to break one or both of those hands.

"Don't worry about Her Highness," he says. "I'll be sure to take good care of her. Unless, of course, Shaylee's men aren't where they're supposed to be tomorrow night for us to attack that next morning. Then I can't really promise you anything."

I give him one final glower and take off farther down the path as fast as my legs will carry me. The entire time, I'm cursing myself in my head.

Stupid, stupid, stupid. How could we have fallen for that? Could Shaylee have set us up? With Talia out of the way, there's no one to actually challenge her for the crown, even with Lyle's rebellion. Even if the Unseelie Court wins, what do we do to get Talia back? How to we break her curse? Shaylee better have some goddamn answers. I'm not above knocking heads together to find them. That's what I should have been doing from the beginning.

Even the uphill climb beside the waterfall doesn't slow me down. The burn in my muscles and my labored breath just pushes me harder. It's nothing compared to the idea that I could get Talia killed.

I've let this get too far.

A sword from nowhere brings me back to reality as I reach the top. Of course, it results in my tumbling back down half the hill, but hey, at least it brought my wits back to me.

I dig my heels and hang on to a nearby tree for dear life, reaching for a knife in my boot as I go. No sooner am I ready to hurl it at my assailant than he shows himself.

"DJ? Is that you?"

I know that voice. It owes me a raise.

"Iver?" I call in disbelief. "What the hell are you doing here?"

"I could ask you the same question," he says, sheathing his sword. "Where's Talia?" Apparently, the look on my face clues him in that she's nowhere good. He offers me his hand and pulls me up the rest of the hill. "Tell me everything. Leave nothing out."

Now if I only knew where to start.

Chapter Nineteen

IVER LISTENS AS we make our way back to Shaylee as fast as we can. He doesn't seem particularly surprised by Talia's identity, nor by my parents' newfound acceptance of me—though I gloss over that part, seeing as he'd gloat about it. He apparently doesn't have any ideas about what we should do either, which raises even higher the obvious question of what he's doing here.

"Dominic and I go back long before Shaylee was queen," he explains as we slow to a walk at nearing the asrai settlement. "And if it means keeping the courts separate and at peace, I'll gladly offer up my sword to both him and the newest queen."

"And you rag on me for quitting being a knight," I grumble.

"You're different," he says. "As much as you claim to hate it, being a knight is a part of you. You just need the right banner to fight under."

I roll my eyes and let it go. We have much bigger things to worry about.

The soldiers standing guard allow us to pass and give us directions to Shaylee's whereabouts. Turns out her people have a camp strikingly similar to Lyle's, except they're sandwiched in the tiny valley that runs up between two mountain peaks instead of either side of the lake. Judging by the glowing fires and distant chatter, Lyle really does outnumber us and reinforcements are still a day out.

Wonderful.

Two more soldiers grant us entrance to a simple white tent jam-packed with tables, maps, and people huddled in groups, discussing a million things I don't care about right now. Shaylee stands near the back with Dominic at her side and several other knights, their expressions grim and exhaustion written across their faces. Dominic glances our direction. A giant grin spreads across his face at the sight of Iver and he welcomes him into the circle with open arms.

"My friend." He laughs, patting my boss on the back. "I feared you would arrive after all the action had passed."

"I wouldn't dream of it," Iver replies, returning the gestures. "I could never show my face in either court again if I missed this. By the way, I found a stray on my way here. She brings news that you and Her Majesty need to hear immediately."

When Dominic realizes I'm the stray in question and that I'm very much not with Talia, his face pales. When Shaylee realizes the same thing, her expression turns stormy. She looks so much like Mab in that moment that I almost hightail it out of the tent.

Those around her go quiet as I explain what happened and how Lyle saw right through us. I guess he wasn't as blind with devotion as we thought. The silence extends to the rest of the tent as I tell everyone how he wants Shaylee to move her forces to the opposite slope of the mountain, giving him the advantage and practically guaranteed victory.

"And you actually think I'd be willing to do that?" Shaylee scoffs.

"Of course not," I reply. "I'm not stupid, but we have to do something to save Talia."

"Why?" Shaylee demands. "Let him kill her and crown himself king. Then, once my backup arrives, we'll obliterate him and the rest of his following. We'll be killing two birds with one stone, so to speak."

My blood runs cold and yet still manages to boil behind my eyes, tinting my vision red. "We're not abandoning Talia."

"*You* don't have to," Shaylee reminds me. "You could walk right out of here and figure out some suicidal rescue mission if you wanted to. Knock yourself out."

"But she's your cousin," I argue. "She didn't want to be roped into any of this insanity any more than you did."

Shaylee places her hands on the table and leans over toward me with narrowed eyes. "When Dominic found me, I was a starving wild child. From what I've heard, Talia was living quite the charmed life with her adoptive aunts before she so foolishly poked her nose in the Human Realm. I don't feel sorry for her."

"But she's still family."

"Family doesn't mean anything in Faerie. You should know that."

"Then you're just as bad as Mab—"

My head snaps to the side as my cheek erupts in sharp pain. The room goes dead silent. Even the noise from the camp seems muted. Shaylee leans farther in as I turn to face her again. Half-human magic really must be stunted, because if she was fully fae, I'm sure that look would turn me to stone.

"Say something like that again," she hisses, her hand shaking as she points at me, "and I'll have you executed for heresy. No prison. No trial. I'll just cut your throat where you stand. Do you understand me, Daisy Jane?"

My answer is a glare, daring her to threaten me again.

"If I may, Your Majesty," Dominic pipes up.

"You may, Dominic," Shaylee growls, "but do so *very* carefully."

"While we *could* go ahead and let Lyle kill Talia and attack the day after tomorrow, I think saving Talia would be better in the long run."

"Yes," Shaylee scoffs, "having the legitimate heir running around would do *wonders* for my reign."

I thought that was the plan. Talia gives up the crown after the battle and Shaylee lets us go. What had she been planning behind our backs from the beginning?

"But she doesn't *want* to be the legitimate heir," Dominic reminds her. "If she reveals that Lyle cursed her, it will disenfranchise the entire rebellion. It'll make it all about him, not restoring the proper heir to the Unseelie throne. Not to mention, once Talia formally gives it to you, none of Lyle's followers will have grounds to rebel against you again. Even if they want to, how on earth would they scrape together the support, not to mention the know-how of actually running the court?"

Shaylee taps her foot while he speaks, then paces the length of the table for a while. Once he's done, she studies him for a silent moment and demands, "Why are you defending her? She's Mab's *daughter*."

"So? All the more reason that having her give up the title will work to our advantage. Besides, you were her daughter too not too long ago."

"Watch it, Dominic," Shaylee growls.

"All I'm saying is that DJ has a point. Talia is family and, in addition to her strategic value, maybe her relation to you should count for something...even if isn't particularly *fae* to do so."

"I am fae," Shaylee barks.

"You're human too, just like Talia," Dominic replies sharply. "You'd do well to remember it."

The entire tent holds its breath, waiting to see what will happen next.

Shaylee turns to face her knights, making everyone flinch. "Get me someone who can reach my mother and her troops in the next six hours and bring them to me."

A few of her men shout, "Yes, ma'am," and bolt out of the room.

The queen turns back to Dominic, Iver, and me. To Dominic, she says, "Just so you know, I hate you." He just smirks in reply. To Iver and me, she orders, "For now, you two are in charge of getting everyone to move. We're moving to the other side of the mountain tonight. Anyone who isn't ready gets left behind to be trampled by Lyle's men."

Iver stands up, salutes Shaylee, then turns on his heel to leave. I go to follow him, but Shaylee calls after me.

"I meant what I said, DJ. If I hear you've been saying anything comparing me to Mab, I'll hunt you down and kill you myself."

"Roger that," I mumble.

"And one more thing: I'll save my cousin from Lyle, but I won't lift a finger to protect her from my mother. If Queen Titania says she dies, it's on you to save her. If she can take Mab out to get what she wants, I can promise she'll crush you. Keep that in mind."

"Will do, Your Majesty," I say.

With that, we take our leave.

Once we're out of hearing distance of the tent, Iver pulls me aside, just within the brush surrounding the camp. "What the hell has gotten into you?"

"What do you mean?" I demand.

"You were supposed to drop Talia off, receive payment from her aunts, and leave. Now you're defending her from the Faerie Courts?"

"Talia's a good person," I argue. "She doesn't deserve to be in the middle of this, and she sure as hell doesn't deserve to die because the Faerie Courts can't keep track of their whack jobs. As soon as she's safe, I'm gone."

Iver smirks as he looks me over. "No you're not. You're too in love with her."

"I am not," I bark. "Jesus, will everyone get off my case? What is it with you people?" I don't actually want an answer, so I storm off to try to accomplish the job Shaylee told us to do.

Too bad Iver's going to give me one anyway. "The Hidden Folk are quite gifted at deception," he explains, trailing behind me. "True love is by far the hardest thing to hide and, well, you're no faerie, DJ."

"Oh, God, don't make me hurl," I scoff. "People like me don't get true love."

"People like you?" Iver repeats with a raised eyebrow. "Care to explain?"

I walk a little faster to put some space between us. "People who hide. People who keep everything locked up safe and sound for everyone's safety. People who are afraid of hurting and of hurting others."

From the corner of my eye, I notice Iver shake his head. "You can change, you know."

"But is this really the time?"

"I suppose not. We have a job to do, but you'd do well to keep it in mind."

"Noted. Now, let's go."

Thankfully, Iver lets the topic go and focuses on getting everyone around the lake to move. Shaylee's forces are encouraged to spread the news and get packing while the asrai are given a choice. They can either come with us over the mountain and settle in the valley beyond our camp, or they can take off and go wherever they think they'll be safest.

Talia's aunts refuse to do either.

"We're staying with you," Vervain declares with folded arms. "We're not leaving your side again until our Talia is safe."

"You can't stay with me. I'll be in the middle of a battle," I remind them. "And how do you think Talia would react if one of you got hurt? She'd kill me."

"You're lucky *we* don't kill you for getting her into this mess," Eleadora snaps, stomping her foot. "You were supposed to protect her."

Juniper glares at me from behind her sisters.

"I know that and I'm sorry," I say. "But I'll get her back. I promise."

"And if you do, how do you plan on freeing her from Lyle's spell? You've told us yourself that you don't love her," Vervain scoffs.

"She told me the same thing," Iver interjects.

"What does that have to do with anything?" I demand.

"The ring you described," Eleadora explains. "It's a very old kind of faerie curse. It puts the wearer under the command of whoever gave it to them. Only someone that truly loves that person can break the spell. I've no doubt that it did once belong to Mab, the old witch. She probably enslaved countless poor souls that wandered too far from home. If no one around you truly knows you, no one can truly love you. And it's not like anyone can get to know you when you're a mindless pawn."

That's why Lyle was asking Talia if she had anybody. With both courts trying to kill her and the only people who really know her being her aunts, there are only three people in the world that could stop him and none of them are capable of storming a rebel force to get to her.

"Can't I just bring her back here once we win? You three can break the curse, can't you?"

"If Lyle gives her permission to leave his side," Vervain argues. "Which I doubt he will, even if you kill him."

"I've heard of servants dying like that," Eleadora adds. "Their masters forget to tell them to eat or sleep, so they waste away. It's one of the reasons the curse fell out of use. It's rather cumbersome."

Damn it. It looks like I'll have to drag one of them along with me anyway.

I let out a long sigh and massage my temple as I think it over. "One of you can come. I can't protect all three of you. Whoever comes has to listen to me, got it? No going rogue."

Both Vervain and Eleadora look to Juniper, who nods and steps out from behind them. When I think about it, I suppose she's the obvious choice. Talia did mention that Juniper was the one who taught her all those kickass archery skills. At least this way, we can cover each other's backs.

"Are you sure?" I ask her. "This isn't going to be easy."

Juniper nods again, then pauses. She holds up her hand, signaling for me to wait, then rushes back in the small house the three aunts are staying with. A moment later, she emerges with her bow and arrows, covered from head to toe in the leather attire I first saw them in when the three of them broke into my apartment.

"Are you sure Her Majesty will approve?" Iver asks skeptically.

"She already said she doesn't care if I go on a crazy suicide mission to save Talia," I remind him. "If the two of us can focus on that, leaving the actual battle to Shaylee, I'd say we're doing her a favor."

Iver doesn't look any more convinced, but doesn't argue.

"We still refuse to go as far as the next valley," Vervain says. "There's no doubt there will be wounded to attend to. We'll put ourselves to use among them."

"Not a bad idea," I reply. "You'll be closer to the action, but no one can really complain about you being there."

"Exactly," Vervain says. "Now, if you excuse us, the sun is coming up. We need to prepare like our sister."

I hadn't even noticed, but they're right. Faint pinks, reds, and oranges line the eastern mountain peaks. We need to get a move on.

The sisters say a tearful goodbye to Juniper and allow us to part ways. Iver and I make sure to alert the few people that haven't heard that the camp's moving, then circle back to Shaylee's tent. She, Dominic, and several others stand around one of the tables, poring over maps and discussing plans in urgent hushed voices. When she sees us enter, she leaves Dominic in charge and excuses herself.

"What's one of Talia's aunts doing here?" she demands.

"She's here to help me get Talia back," I explain. "She's going to break the spell Lyle has her under." When Shaylee continues to study Juniper with doubt, I add, "That also helps our case, proving she was bewitched and whatnot."

"Fine," Shaylee finally concludes. "But I can't be held responsible for her."

Juniper shrugs.

"Do we have a plan in place, Your Majesty?" Iver asks.

"We've sent messengers to meet my mother and her troops," Shaylee explains. "Once they hear the news, I expect they can make it here by midday at the earliest, but we can't be sure. We're going to have to be able to stall just in case, so only half our forces are moving over the mountain and down the opposite slope. The rest will be hiding up along the tree line of the summit. There's still enough cover there that they should be able to lie low until Lyle's men cross over. Once they do and the battle starts, they attack from behind. It's not a guaranteed win, but it'll definitely keep them busy and confused for a while."

"Once Lyle realizes what happened, he could kill Talia," I argue.

"Then you better haul ass and get to her as fast as you can," Shaylee snaps. "I'm hoping you and her aunt here can be in and out before that happens and the Seelie forces arrive. Your idea of keeping her alive really would help us out in the long run, but we can improvise if she dies."

It's less time than I had hoped to work with, but I'll have to make it work. Since Juniper is coming, we might still have a chance. We don't have any choice but to try.

"Get what you have packed up," Shaylee orders, turning back to her tent. "We'll rest once we're moved. I don't want to see you or anyone else so much as sit before then."

"Yes, Your Majesty," I grumble.

She gives me a dirty look before disappearing within the tent.

"Could you *not* get on the Unseelie Queen's nerves, please?" Iver sighs.

"What? She started it."

"Her Majesty didn't start anything. This is much bigger than her."

"Doesn't mean she has to be a coldhearted, manipulative bitch."

Iver pats me on the shoulder and shakes his head. "Go help Juniper pack her things. I need to wait to speak to Dominic. Meet me back here in an hour."

"Can do," I say. "Oh, and Iver?" He pauses. "You owe me a raise."

He chuckles and slips his hands into his pockets. "Damn. I had so hoped that mending your relationship with your parents would soften your need for such a material reward."

"Hell, no. Mended relationship or not, I got bills, dude."

My boss shakes his head and continues along his way. "And yet you think true love is out of your reach."

"Don't change the subject," I argue.

"It's a subject you need to reckon with, DJ."

"Who's to say this isn't going to mess me up worse than my parents did the first time?"

Iver shrugs. "No one really can, but you'll never get your answer until you open yourself up to the possibility."

"The only possibility I'm opening myself up to is kicking your ass if you think you're getting out of giving me that raise."

The elf laughs as he lets himself back into Shaylee's tent. I can tell by the tone that he's not laughing at me, nor is he gloating for having tricked me into reuniting me with my family. It sounds like he's genuinely happy for me. I'd almost rather he'd just laugh at me. That I know how to handle.

Chapter Twenty

BY HIGH NOON, Shaylee's army is in position on the western face of the mountain. It's quieter over here and I can't say for sure exactly why. I feel like the impending battle has something to do with it. The world always felt quieter before battles back when I was still a knight. The waiting was always worse than the actual fighting, if you ask me. At least when you're fighting, there's constant movement and thought. When you're waiting, there's hardly any movement and the thought does you little good.

What feels like hours but is probably only twenty minutes later, the first signs of Lyle's forces come over the pass. They're more heavily armored than I expected, but even from here, I can tell a lot of it is ill-fitting, worn, or just falling apart. It's all leather armor, no doubt stolen from piles of discarded clothes or homemade. The goblins, trolls, giants, and even misguided humans make up for it with their swords, enormous cleavers, and arrows, made of both metal and crystal.

Lyle rides out in front of his ragtag army atop a black horse, the only one with well-suited armor and the impression of someone who knows what they're doing in battle. When Talia catches up to him, my heart sinks.

They've outfitted her with the black armor of the Unseelie Court, no different than what Shaylee's side is wearing. The suit belonged to Mab, no doubt, along with the simple silver crown that winds around her helmet. Mab didn't wear that part of the uniform very often, but when she did, everyone knew that she was trying to make a statement.

Much like Lyle is doing now.

"Shaylee, this is your final chance," he booms with his voice magnified by magic. "Hand over the crown you stole from the rightful queen, or feel the wrath of those you've wronged."

"Come and get it, you bastard," Shaylee shouts back, ever the tactful one. From where Juniper and I are hiding just beyond the clearing,

Shaylee looks every bit the queen she tries to be. Perfect black armor, a gray horse in similar trappings, and a knight holding the Unseelie banner behind her. I don't know her relationship with Queen Titania, but I'm sure Her Majesty would be proud. "When we cut you down, we'll show all of Faerie how deep your deception runs. You couldn't even get the princess to support you willingly. You had to bewitch her."

"Silence! Enough of your treachery," Lyle cries back. He draws his sword as the sign to charge and his army roars to life in response.

Shaylee does likewise, charging forward on a horse on her own, and the battle begins like a clash of thunder. The sounds of blades on blades, of bodies trampled and flesh torn never gets less jarring. The sound of gunshots, however, adds a new level of terror to the sight.

Jesus. Lyle's human recruits brought guns. Faerie armor can slow the sharpest blade if it's designed right, but the craftsmanship and protective spells were never intended to stop bullets. I can feel a cold sweat break over my body. We're not just outnumbered, we're outgunned. I've never heard of faeries healing from bullet wounds. What sort of slow, burning death must that be?

I hold tight to my hilt and take a few deep breaths.

We have to stick to the plan. They can't have that much ammo. We'll be okay.

Beside me, Juniper pales and I worry for a moment that she's going to be sick, but she shakes it off and draws her bow in preparation. She's the sign that will tell the rest of Shaylee's knights to swoop down from the surrounding forests. All we have to do is keep an eye on Talia and Lyle and wait for them to be far enough apart that we can get to Tal in the chaos before he can. Judging by the way he charges to the head of his men and aims straight for Shaylee, leaving Talia behind, it shouldn't take long.

He leaves a protective ring of trolls and giants in his stead. The fact that the supposed true queen isn't actually fighting should signal to them that something isn't right. Lyle probably spun some bullshit about her being out of practice or too precious to risk at the front lines and they all ate it up.

When Lyle and Shaylee's blades clash, easily a football field's length away from Talia, if not more, Juniper taps the tip of her arrow, setting it ablaze with neon green flames and a trailing cloud of matching smoke. I cover my mouth and nose as she pulls it back against the bowstring and lets it fly.

As it reaches the zenith of the battle, the fighting below pauses. The second it begins to fall, the other half of the Unseelie forces emerge from behind, sending Lyle's army into a panic.

That's our cue to move.

Lyle's going to have to choose between trying to end Shaylee or going back to defend Talia. Either way, we need to get to her before the reinforcements do or Lyle does. With a reassuring nod to one another, we move.

Between my blade and Juniper's bow, those who stand in our way don't seem to know what hits them until it's too late. Those who don't see us coming anyway. The ones that have a chance to prepare are stronger than I expected.

Goblins swing their swords with startling accuracy. Since when are trolls fast? They all get a few decent swings and even manage to put some rather deep slashes into my armor. A few of them I only manage to wound before moving deeper into the fray. I guess Lyle trained them better than I thought.

As I raise my sword against a particularly talented goblin, a gunshot rings out and my right side erupts in pain. The goblin tries to take advantage of my moment of weakness, but leaves his left flank wide open. I slice through the space where his shoulder and chest plate meet. The wound won't kill him, but having a sword run right through your shoulder like that will definitely slow you down.

Juniper already has the bastard who shot me down for the count. She pries an arrow from his neck as I turn, then rushes to my side, pulling my hand away from my ribs.

"It's just a graze," I assure her. "I'm okay." Surprisingly enough, I don't have to lie about how bad it is. The bullet sliced through the leather and there's definitely blood, but not enough to worry, even if it does sting like a bitch.

For now, Juniper accepts my words and we go back to hacking our way through Lyle's forces. I can't help but notice how the Unseelie soldiers are starting to outnumber the rebels. Given that they're fighting the trolls and giants to get to Talia, I don't count that as a good thing.

Sure, they distract the creatures, giving us a few less obstacles, but that means we have to fight past them too. Judging by the way one tries to take my head off, I think it's safe to say they either didn't get Shaylee's message about making sure Talia lives or Shaylee didn't give it to them at all.

That's going to make for an interesting conversation when this is over.

I feel a twinge of guilt as Juniper and I take a few of Shaylee's soldiers down, only with injuries, mind you. I fought alongside these knights years ago in the name of a queen none of us truly wanted to protect. I want to give them the benefit of the doubt and believe their attacking Talia is Shaylee's doing.

With a giant's back turned, we take advantage of the opening he leaves and tumble into the safe space they've created around Talia. There's only a hundred feet between us and her as she stands beside her horse with her sword drawn. Her eyes look sharp, but not in that she's awake.

She looks ready for blood.

She looks nothing like my Talia.

When she attacks both me and Juniper, I know that, at least right now, she isn't.

"Tal, it's me," I shout as our swords clash. She just glares at me and attacks again, this time low and fast. "Tal, come on, you gotta wake up. Juniper, do something."

Talia's aunt tries to come up behind her, keeping her weapon low, but Talia realizes she's there and attacks. Juniper nearly gets herself impaled before weaving out of the way, but still makes no move to defend herself.

The Unseelie knights cheer as a giant begins to fall backward, right on top of us.

"Talia, please," Juniper says softly, heedless of the body tumbling toward us. "Please, my sweet girl. It's me. Don't you know I—"

The sudden shadow tells her it's time to move. We all take off running, even Talia.

I lose my footing as the earth trembles and stumble to the ground. Juniper wasn't so lucky. She lies pinned and dazed beneath the giant's arm, struggling to breathe and free herself from the weight. Talia came out the best out of all of us. She's still on her feet. When she sees that her aunt is trapped and closer than me, she seizes her chance. The Unseelie knights flood the space, but they're still too far and there are still enough rebels to slow them down. They won't stop Talia in time.

And if they stop her, they'll no doubt kill her.

"Juniper, come on. Wake up," I scream, getting to my feet. "Talia, don't!"

Juniper's eyes flutter open and turn to frozen terror at the sight of her beloved niece raising a sword above her chest.

"Talia, please," I shout.

Nothing.

Goddamn it, I'm never going to hear the end of this.

"Talia, I love you!"

Talia freezes. I hold my breath. She stands in suspended animation, like a robot rusted in place. From where I kneel, I can see the thorned ring crumble to the ground. When she finally moves, she brings the sword to her side and holds her head in her other hand, bent over like she might be sick. As she slowly stands up straight again, she looks around with her eyes wide with panic. I can explain everything easy enough after this is all over. For now, all I need is some sign that she's truly my Talia again.

It comes when she tosses the sword aside, kneels and begins to pry her aunt out from under the giant. "DJ, don't just stand there," she shouts. "Help me."

I run over and together we pull Juniper free. She's shaky and leans heavily on her niece once she's on her feet, but it looks like she's going to be okay. Tears well in her eyes as she kisses Talia on the cheek repeatedly.

"My precious girl," she cries, kissing her niece one last time. "I knew you were still in there. I'm so sorry I failed you."

"You didn't, auntie," Talia says, looking around frantically for a way out. "DJ, what do we do? We need to get out of here."

Did she not really hear me? I might be able to wiggle out of this after all.

There's more important things to tackle right now, though.

With Juniper wounded, getting out of this battle is going to be quite the feat, especially with the Unseelie and rebel forces alike closing in around us. I stand between Talia and Juniper and what feels like all of the Faerie Realm. If nothing else, I'm going down fighting.

My sword clashes with a goblin's just as a horn sounds from the summit of the mountain. Both sides stop and look up, some in horror, others with relief.

Regardless of reaction, what looks to be the entire Seelie Court storms down the mountainside. They're an endless wave of green, like spring come to drive out winter once and for all.

The goblin drops her sword, lifts her hands in surrender, and runs. This was clearly more than she signed up for. Judging by how many others on her side decide to hightail it and run, most of them have similar sentiments.

Got an army with nerves of pure steel there, Lyle.

They've got the right idea, though. The Seelie Court won't be any happier to see Talia than the Unseelie court was. Being in between them would be a good place not to be right now.

"Head for the trees," I order Talia, coming back to help her carry Juniper. "We need to lie low until they clean up this mess, find Vervain and Eleadora, and get out of here."

Juniper nods in agreement and does her best to walk on her own.

A few rebel stragglers put up a fight, screaming at me about how the true queen must rise again, but it's nothing I can't handle in mere moments. It's the Seelie soldiers I'm more worried about. Luckily, we avoid them and slip into the brush.

"Okay, now we need to get behind Unseelie lines," I pant, gingerly feeling my bullet wound. It's not bleeding any worse and I don't feel too light-headed, but between our attempt to run and the need to carry Juniper, my side is killing me. "Vervain and Eleadora are tending the wounded. We need to get there before this is over. I'd bet what's left in my bank account that Shaylee's going to put them under arrest once she realizes we're not hanging around."

"Do you really think she's that terrible?" Talia huffs, resting against a tree for a moment.

Both Juniper and I look at her like she might still have the curse on her.

"Okay, so maybe she is," Talia concludes with a shrug. She peeks out beyond the tree line for a moment. "Do you think we have a moment?"

"Like, half of one," I say, standing upright again.

"Good." Talia takes my face in her hands. "That's all I need."

If my heart was racing before, it's beating at light speed with Talia's lips against mine. This time I don't stop her. I wrap my arms around her hips and hold her tight, savoring the deep warmth and strength of her touch as she kisses me harder.

She wants me. All of me. Just like I want her.

For once, the idea brings comfort instead of worry.

"You were going to just pretend you never said you loved me, weren't you?" Talia chuckles, pressing her forehead to mine.

If there wasn't a battle going on, I could lose myself in those blue eyes forever.

"Well, obviously," I reply.

"Why? I've been telling you how I feel for days."

"How you *think* you feel," I correct. "This whole thing is crazy. We've known each other for what, two weeks? If my parents can throw me out after a lifetime, what's stopping you? If you haven't noticed, I can be a lot. There's plenty not to love about me. And so long as my name's floating around out there, you're in danger."

"That's what this is really about, isn't it?"

"They're both pretty decent things for this to be about. There's too much I don't know."

"So, you can feel fear after all."

"Don't rub it in."

Talia laughs again and kisses me on the forehead. "We'll finish this conversation when we're not running for our lives. It just didn't feel right leaving a broken spell without a kiss."

I resist the urge to roll my eyes, mainly at myself because I can't disagree with her.

As we help Juniper through the rocky terrain and try our best to stay hidden, I attempt to ignore the smug look on the asrai's face. Finally, with the suspense killing me, I acknowledge it.

"What?" I demand.

"We told you so," Juniper snickers.

"I think I liked you better when you didn't talk," I grumble.

Beyond the trees on the battlefield, things start to get quiet. At least I think they are. The deer path we've found to use veers away, shielding us from view more. But it wouldn't get *that* much quieter, would it?

"We need to hurry," I say, lowering my voice with a new fear of being found. "It sounds like we don't have much time—Ugh!" Something sharp lodges itself in my left shoulder and I tumble forward, getting a face full of rocks and leaves.

"DJ!"

"I'm all right," I gasp, feeling the hilt of a dagger in my back as I scramble to my feet. There's no way I'm going to be able to pull it out myself, but we clearly have company. Guess I'm fighting right-handed. "Take Juniper and keep—"

A jet-black figure bolts from the underbrush and nearly runs me through with a crystal blade before I can block it. "You're not going anywhere," Lyle snarls.

I almost didn't realize it was him. His armor's slick with blood and he's lost his helmet. Blood trickles from a nasty gash where his right eye should be and the rest of his face is black and blue. His once white-blond hair is now matted with dirt and blood. Rage practically radiates off him. That must be the only thing keeping him going.

"You stole my queen," he hisses. "You ruined my uprising. You destroyed these courts. You obliterated any chance of us protecting ourselves from what Mab feared." He swings again at my practically useless arm. "Now, I'm going to obliterate you."

Chapter Twenty-One

LYLE MIGHT BE a hot mess, but he's still in better shape than me. For starters, he can at least use both his arms. I can make a fist with my left hand and that's pretty much it. Then there's the fact that he's clearly using his dominate hand. I can barely keep up with his attacks since I've always been slower with my right hand. He even manages to nick me a few times. It's pure dumb luck that he hasn't run me through yet.

My left shoulder screams as I hoist myself up onto a nearby boulder. It's hard to focus on Lyle past the white flashes that the pain causes. My right arm trembles under his blows, even with the higher ground.

"I should have killed you in that farmhouse," Lyle snarls. "We would have won, and things would be as they should be."

"You can't seriously believe things were better under Mab," I wheeze. "She was unhinged, Lyle. Dangerous, sadistic."

"It wasn't her fault."

"It was, though. She made the choice to join the courts and made everyone pay for it," I reply. "Even people like me who had nothing to do with it."

"She saved you from your mistress' service, you ungrateful bitch," Lyle snarls.

"Yeah," I scoff. I wince as my wrist turns too far as Lyle tries to break my hold. "Killing innocent people, turning a blind eye to torture, ripping apart families, what a *great* setup that was."

"You don't understand," Lyle snarls. "None of you understand. After I sent you back to Shaylee, the scouts returned. They found another creature that knew who we are. There's something dark coming for Faerie, Seelie and Unseelie alike. Her Majesty wouldn't even tell *me*, but Talia...she can save us. She's Her Majesty's daughter. She has to."

The burning in my shoulder threatens to make me black out, but I use it nonetheless. It's that or give Lyle the chance to cut my throat.

"Talia doesn't have to be or do anything she doesn't want to." I don't mean to scream, but the look of shock on Lyle's face is satisfying.

The look of rage that follows, not so much.

My words make Lyle attack with even more ferocity that I can't keep up with.

"She will be what she was meant to be," he screeches, a blow accenting every word. Each one opens a wider window for him.

The next is posed for my chest.

I'm not fast enough to block it.

Suddenly, everything around me looks sharper and moves slower.

I'm going to die here. I won't get to make new memories with my family. I'll never get to watch my niece and nephew grow up. I'll never really explain to Talia why I pushed her away. It's over.

A cry startles me out of my thoughts.

Talia comes, seemingly out of nowhere, and knocks Lyle to the ground while Juniper does her best to drag me higher up the boulders. When had they come back from above?

I'm too stunned as Talia takes on Lyle to even begin to ask. Juniper yanking the dagger from my back wakes me up, followed by a chain of colorful profanities as she places her hands over the wound in an urgent attempt to heal it.

Talia scrambles to her feet, Lyle's sword now in her hands, leaving him with only a second dagger. "I am done," she shouts, "having everyone tell me who I'm supposed to be. Especially you." She takes a few swings at him, nicking his right cheekbone. He returns the favor with a small gash to her collarbone that startles her for a moment.

"You don't understand, princess," Lyle pleads, backing away. "Once this is all over, you'll see. I promise. You'll understand who you truly are and what you could become."

"I will decide who I am and what I become," Talia snarls back, attacking again. Maybe I spoke too soon of her not being a master swordsman, because she certainly has Lyle on the defense.

He's unwilling to give up, however. He pushes back with his dagger, making up for his lack of range with speed. "I don't want to hurt you any more than I wanted to bewitch you, Your Highness," he barks. "Don't force my hand."

"The only one forcing you to do anything is yourself," Talia snaps. She ducks, and Lyle misses her face by a centimeter. In a single swing, she brings the sword down on his wrist.

The dagger falls to the ground, along with his hand.

Lyle screeches in pain, cradling his bloody wrist. Talia jabs her blade to his throat, stopping short of slicing through the skin.

"The sooner you learn that, the sooner I show you mercy," Talia says, her voice soft and dangerous. Her voice gives me chills that churn my stomach.

I know Talia. I love her, but now I can see that she's every inch an heir to the Unseelie Throne that Shaylee is. She's as dangerous as her mother before her.

"That human bitch and those damn asrai have corrupted you," Lyle cries. "The Unseelie Court are your people, not them. We need you! When the Fomorians come, we will need your guidance like we needed your mother's before yours."

"Who are the Fomorians?" Talia demands.

"Our most ancient enemies, lost to us, cast out to the eons of time. They must have been the ones your mother feared. If you help me, if you destroy Shaylee and return to the Unseelie Court, we can relearn our past. We can defend our court, our people. You just have to—"

An arrow to his good eye cuts off his instruction.

How close it came to Talia's head nearly makes me faint, if the blood loss and pain weren't already about to. Juniper and I scramble down the rocks to defend Talia from our newest threat. As we stand before her, sword and bow ready, Shaylee makes herself known on the ledge above us, along with the blend of Unseelie and Seelie knights at her side.

"Unless you want to be next," she calls, a bow in her hand already posed with a new arrow, "stand down."

We do as we're told, letting out a breath we had collectively been holding. Apparently, it had been the only thing still keeping Talia together, because she crumples to her knees and throws up what little had been in her stomach.

"I'm sorry, DJ," she mutters when I kneel down to hold back her hair. "I didn't mean to cut his hand off like that. I didn't want to hurt him at all, but he was going to kill you."

I hold back a chuckle at the absurdity of it all. She just saved my life, wasn't even the one to do Lyle in, and yet she's apologizing to me? She might be Mab's daughter all right, but she's definitely still my Talia.

The queen and her followers approach, still armed and ready for a fight, a clear sign that this isn't over.

"Get up," Shaylee orders. "By the order of Queen Titania of the Seelie Court, you're all under arrest for treason against the Faerie Courts."

"This wasn't part of the deal," I growl as a knight yanks me to my feet and roughly ties my hands behind my back, heedless of the way my shoulder still throbs in pain. Two others do the same to Talia and Juniper. "You were supposed to let Talia denounce the throne in front of everyone and let us go."

"That was before my mother decided to weigh in on the plan," Shaylee explains, studying Lyle's body. As she looks back at Talia, I can't help but wonder if that arrow had really been meant for him or if she had missed her real target. "Thank the gods we don't have to drag this hysterical wack-job back with us. That wouldn't be a fun trial."

"Did you have to shoot him in the eye?" Dominic asks with a sigh. "You already cut the one out before he managed to get away."

"The bastard took one of mine, remember?"

"That doesn't mean you take both of his."

"It does when you're queen."

Dominic rolls his eyes, but doesn't argue.

Shaylee turns back to us and barks at her knights, "Don't just stand there. Take them to my mother already." Snapping her fingers at the empty-handed ones, she adds, "Grab the body. We don't want to leave it out here."

Talia keeps her gaze down as they pick up Lyle, including his severed hand. Since the men carrying him walk ahead of us, she keeps her focus on the path the entire march back to the camp. Maybe that's for the best. This way she doesn't see all the bodies strewn across the field, and there are quite a few. They're mostly goblin, troll, and giant bodies, but their blood is as red as ours and their bodies break and tear as easily as anyone else's.

A stony silence covers the living rebels as we're marched in front of them and Lyle's body is tossed among the growing piles of the dead. The message is painfully clear: your leader was nothing; your cause was nothing; your queen is a sham.

It must have sunk in already, because we're marched away from the captives and the dead and into the Unseelie camp. We don't stop until we reach the tent Shaylee was using the day before.

Inside, the first thing that grabs our attention are Eleadora and Vervain. They sit on the ground with their arms bound like ours, but their eyes light up at the sight of their sister and niece.

"You're alive," Eleadora exclaims. A stern look from one of the knights keeps her from getting to her feet.

"We were so worried." Vervain sighs. "Is it over? Are you alright?"

"As alright as we can be," I answer. "And I certainly hope it's over."

Dominic gently escorts Juniper over to the others and eases her down beside Vervain, then comes to stand beside us again. With a subtle nod, he draws our attention forward.

Before us, standing eerily still, is Titania, Queen of the Seelie Court. With her arms folded, she studies us, bright green eyes calculating. Her pine-colored leather armor is still smeared with blood, but there's not a single hair out of place in her intricately woven waterfall of grass-like braids. When her gaze darts to me in particular, I flinch.

"Daisy Jane Suzuki," she says. "It's been a while. I'm disappointed that you used your newfound freedom to go around starting trouble."

"And I'm disappointed I'm still getting into your power struggles," I argue.

"You should learn to quit when you're ahead."

"I've come to realize that, thanks."

The aunts all tense up at my tone, but the Seelie Queen just smirks and turns to Talia.

"And you must be Talia. My daughter has told me loads about you already." Titania lifts her niece's face. "You truly are one of us. If only my sister could have seen you."

"Given what everyone's been saying about my mother," Talia says quietly, "I think it's better that she didn't."

"You're probably right," Titania replies. "Especially given her state. She would have killed you, no doubt. She tried to kill Shaylee on several occasions and we all know what a disaster that would have been."

Shaylee winces, but I'm the only one who notices.

"Which brings us to the question that's been weighing on my mind for days now," Titania says, drawing a dagger from her hip. "Why, when you could just as easily go behind our backs and start a second rebellion, should I let you live?"

Talia opens her mouth to speak, but Titania raises a hand to silence her.

"Take some time and think it over," the queen says. "There's some more pressing matters I need to tend to. You're more of a loose end—no offense." As she walks past us, she instructs Shaylee, "Stick them somewhere they won't cause trouble. I want to give them both the chance to think of a proper defense. I'll be back to deal with them in an hour, regardless of the outcome."

"Why wait?" Talia asks, making both queens pause. "I pose a threat. Why not kill me right here and now and save yourself the trouble?"

Titania pauses for a moment, looks to Shaylee, then back to Talia. "Simply put, I am your aunt. I'd like to think I can be something close to the woman your mother should have been, if given the chance," she explains. Turning to leave once more, she says, "Do yourself and us a favor and think of a good defense. Don't make us be like her."

Chapter Twenty-Two

IT'S BACK TO the holding cell in the cave for us. With the guards' backs turned, Talia helps me take off my armor and goes about finishing the healing of my shoulder and right side.

"You don't have to do that yet," I say, noticing how her hands shake.

"It's not like I can let you bleed out," she replies. The gentle warmth of magic spreads across my back and down my left arm, numbing the remaining throbbing pain.

"I'm not going to bleed out," I scoff. "Juniper fixed me up pretty good. I'd be all right for a while."

"I want to, though," Talia says. "It gives me something else to think about."

"We need to think about what we're going to say to Queen Titania," I remind her.

Talia stays silent as she massages my shoulder for a time. As the magic fades and her hand drops to my side, she says, "I'm just going to tell her the truth. I don't know what else I could say. Even if I wanted to be, I couldn't be queen. I wouldn't know how. Both my aunt and my cousin are ruthless, but they at least know what they're doing."

"Are you sure?" I ask. "I could help you think of something else if you want." The magic fades from my side, and Talia wraps her arms around my waist, pulling me back against her.

"I just need you to be here," she mutters, holding me tighter. With a small chuckle, she adds, "And maybe explain to me why you've been so reluctant to tell me what was worrying you."

I sigh and slump back against Talia. "It's like I told you. I figured you'd reject me like my parents. You still could. You still don't know me very well, and I'm not exactly the most likeable person. It just feels easier to avoid the whole thing."

"I know you plenty well. I know what you're made of, and that's what really counts. All the details will work themselves out later. Besides, you don't seem too concerned about rejecting me," Talia points out.

"Well, yeah. You're you. You're sweet, curious, optimistic, caring—"

"And you're brave, selfless, resourceful—"

"I've done terrible things, Tal," I argue. My stomach tightens at the thought of that door at the back of my mind. It's not overflowing anymore, but it's certainly not empty. I doubt it ever will be. "My friends are the tip of the iceberg."

Talia holds me tighter and rests her head on my shoulder. "I know who you are now, and that's who I love. You don't have to tell me who you've been if you don't want to."

My heart jumps into my throat when she says she loves me. As she kisses my neck, it all but breaks through my ribs.

I crane around to meet her eyes. "Are you drunk again?"

"Just on you," she replies, leaning in to kiss me again.

Footsteps scuff against the rock floor a good distance away. Talia lets me go and gets to her feet, pulling me along with her.

Lo and behold, it's Shaylee. I brace myself against her typical flippant, deceitfully friendly attitude, but I can't find a trace of it. She stands with her arms folded as she studies us through the crystal bars and wears a somber but still calculating expression on her face.

"Time for the trial already?" I ask.

"Oh, there won't be a trial," Shaylee explains. "My mother's just going to ask you what your intentions are from here. If she believes them and likes them, you get to live. If not—well, you're both smart. You can figure it out."

"So, what do you want then?" I sigh.

Shaylee's gaze shifts to Talia. "I just wanted to talk, now that I know you don't want my position. Other than my mother, you're the only family I have."

"How do you know?" Talia asks, brow scrunched in confusion. "You didn't seem to believe me before."

Shaylee scoffs. "You threw up when I killed Lyle. If one death has that effect on you, you're not Faerie Queen material, cousin. Be grateful for that and use it to your advantage."

"Were you the one that killed my mother, then?" Talia demands.

Shaylee shakes her head. "That was Queen Titania. I was preoccupied at the time with Lyle, as fate would have it. Why? Are you looking for revenge?"

"She abandoned me. Why would I go looking to avenge her? I just...wanted to know more about her."

Shaylee nods. "I understand. I wanted to know who Titania was before Dominic came for me, even though she abandoned me too."

"And what do you think of her now?"

Shaylee paces for a moment as she thinks the question over. "I'll have to get back to you on that. I'm still not too sure. She made me Queen of the Unseelie Court, which is a pretty sweet gig when no one's trying to kill me, so I can't complain that much, but she still abandoned me and only took me back in when she needed someone to overthrow *your* mother. You see my conundrum?"

"I do indeed," Talia replies. "You knew Mab, though, correct? What was she really like?"

Shaylee tenses. "Unhinged. Cruel. Sad. Lonely. Afraid. Sadistic and masochistic in equal parts. Trust me, you don't want me to go on much more."

Talia droops at each word but doesn't ask for any more explanation than that.

"Consider yourself lucky that you never met her. If my mother pardons you, get as far from the Faerie Courts as you can get and stay away."

"I thought being queen was a sweet gig," I point out.

"The gig, yeah. The rest of the Faerie Courts is a different story. Trust me."

For once, I know for a fact she's telling the truth. I can verify her story.

"Did Mab ever mention the Fomorians? Do you know who they are?" Talia asks.

Shaylee's brow knits together, and she looks off to the ceiling for a moment. "It rings a bell, but not a particularly loud one... Mab might have mentioned them once or twice when she was ranting and raving, but she went on about a lot of things that can't do any real harm. They've been gone for millennia."

"But could they come back?"

Footsteps come our way, making our guards stand up taller and the conversation come to an end. Even Shaylee tries to look more alert and aware when her mother and a group of knights come around the corner.

"Shaylee? You're already here?" Titania asks, her dainty eyebrows raised in surprise. "I wondered where you ran off to."

"Just thought I'd shoot the breeze with my cousin for a moment," Shaylee replies, stepping aside. I can't help but notice that her usual upbeat farce is back, but it's probably best not to call her out on it.

Apparently not seeing anything out of the ordinary in her daughter's behavior, Titania turns to Talia and me instead. "Your hour's up. Why shouldn't I kill you? And your knight here for good measure?"

"It's simple, really," Talia says, folding her hands in front of her and standing up taller. "From what I've seen, the Faerie Courts are a terrible place to live. They're full of deceit, backstabbing, and a great deal of pettiness, I imagine. I'm actually quite grateful to my cousin for ruling in my stead because I certainly wouldn't want to deal with that terrible place."

I hold my breath and frantically look between Talia and the two queens, waiting for them to get offended by her words. It's not like faeries to take insults like that lying down, but neither of them seems to care. I don't know if that's reason to be more worried or at ease.

"I had a great life with my aunts," Talia continues. "I did what I wanted, where and when I wanted to do it with no one to judge me or decide there were more important issues to take care of. Not that any of that seems to stop you two, but it's nice to do what I please without the risk of waking up dead as a result. Why would I give that up for the insanity you deal with on a daily basis? Rebellions, unrest, crazy loyalists with unfounded conspiracy theories? No, thank you. Besides, everything would fall apart with me at the reins. It really is in the best interest of the realm if you two stay in control."

The room stands frozen for what feels like forever.

When the silence breaks, it's with the most unlikely noise: Queen Titania's laughter.

Her giggles quickly turn to a boom as she throws her head back to laugh.

Yep. All these women are definitely related.

"Well, one thing's for certain." Titania sighs, wiping a tear from her eye. "You're definitely a Faerie Queen by blood, even if you don't want the title."

My stomach flips at the possible implication.

"She's made it clear she doesn't want to be, though," I remind her.

"Relax, Daisy Jane," Titania says as she takes the keys from one of our guards. "I believe her. There's not the slightest bit of desire for either of our courts in this girl." With one hand on the handle, she locks eyes with Talia and adds, "But mark my words, if I hear word that you've returned to either the Unseelie or Seelie Courts, I'll see it as a sign that you've changed your mind. I'll have you executed. The both of you. Do we understand each other?"

"Perfectly, Aunt Titania."

Both Shaylee and I inhale sharply at the words, but the Seelie Queen just smirks.

"I like the sound of that," she says, turning to leave. "It's almost a shame I have to banish you. Though you might want to stay a bit more formal when you address the two courts together."

"You mean I still have to do that?" Talia groans.

"Of course," Titania says as everyone, including the two of us, follow along. "Can't have it in anyone's mind to go looking for you again, now can we?"

"I was hoping you'd just slip me out the back or something and tell them all I'm dead," Talia mutters.

I open my mouth to speak, but there's no point to it. I'm just going to have to accept that this is how she is, even if she does fear public speaking more than death itself.

A clear night sky greets us as we leave the cave. It's strange to see the same stars in the same place they've always been after a battle like the one we've just witnessed. That was another thing that always felt strange after fighting, the way nothing else seemed to change other than the state of our lives.

With the paths lit with torches, Titania leads us back to the battlefield. The dead have been cleared away and there are fewer rebels than I remember. I don't want to think about why. Titania and Shaylee break off when we reach a small mound being used as a makeshift platform. Talia silently pleads with her aunt and cousin to let her just leave, but Titania shakes her head and nods toward the mount. With a quiet moan, Talia takes me by the hand and ascends her platform with me close behind.

"Um, hi," she says with a timid wave. Out of the corner of my eye, I spot Shaylee slapping her forehead and shaking her head. "You know who I am. Only hours ago, you thought I was going to be your queen, and by blood right, I should be. It's true that I am Mab's daughter, the only one as far as we know."

She looks to Titania for confirmation on how badly she's blowing it, but her aunt just smiles and nods.

"I was never raised to be a queen, though. I was just raised to be me, which really isn't a lot. Trust me. It's not enough to lead, protect, or guide an entire court, no matter what Lyle told you. He knew it, which is why he had to bewitch me to get me to support his cause."

A stir spreads over the rebels and knights alike. Apparently, this wasn't common knowledge.

"I know Queen Titania and Queen Shaylee's methods of gaining control weren't exactly...orthodox, but I do believe they're what's best for the realm, if you would give them a chance." Talia clears her throat and stands up a little taller and adds, "That's why I'm formally giving up my right to the throne of the Unseelie Court and my position in line for it. I hope that, if not now, then one day you can come to understand why I'm doing this." She fidgets for a moment, then gives an awkward bow. "Thank you, and I'm sorry."

She hops down off the mound as quickly as possible and dashes to Titania's side.

"There," she mutters. "I made my statement. I renounced the crown. Can we please go now? I'm sure my other aunts are nearly sick with worry by now."

Titania nods and steps aside. "I'll have one of my men escort you to them. Our forces will be out of this valley by morning. After that, you're free to do whatever you like for the rest of your life, so long as it's not within the borders of the courts."

"I understand," Talia says, "and thank you."

As we make our way into the night, Shaylee calls after us, "Hey, cuz." We both pause. Shaylee looks uncertain for a moment, then says, "You're free now. Take advantage of it, for the both of us." With that, she gives a quick wave, then turns to speak with Dominic as if she hadn't said anything at all, hopefully for the last time.

The knight walks with us all the way back over the mountain, to the small house where the aunts are staying, and only then leaves us with a bow. By then, unfortunately, the eastern sky is turning the slightest shade of pink.

No sooner is he gone than the door flies open, and the aunts tumble out of the house along with several asrai I have yet to meet. The commotion they cause in tackling us both causes all the other nearby houses to come alive and even more asrai to join the impromptu party.

"My dear sweet girl," Vervain cries as she crushes me in her arm. "I knew you weren't being honest with us or yourself. Juniper told us everything."

I spy the quietest of Talia's aunts through the growing crowd, and she gives me an encouraging smile and a wink. I need to thank her later.

"Now, I know you two are exhausted and there are still all of Talia's other aunties to meet, but there's the matter of your payment for bringing our Talia here," Vervain says, finally letting me go.

That's right. I had actually forgotten about all of that. And now that I have Talia, I'm not completely sure what I could possibly want.

Well, that's not completely true.

"Vervain, do you know how to lift the spell that binds my name?" I meet Talia's gaze, and she gives me a curious look. "If I'm going to keep protecting Talia, I don't want a single soul to be able to use it against me."

Vervain strokes her chin for a moment, then beckons Eleadora and Juniper over to her. "That is quite the request, Daisy Jane." She joins hands with her sisters. "If your name cannot be bound, you can't swear allegiance to either court. You'll be cut off from the protections they provide, regardless of the dangers that may be on our horizon."

"If they don't want Talia, I don't want them," I argue. "We'll be okay."

Talia puts a hand on my shoulder and kisses me on the cheek.

Vervain takes my right hand while Juniper takes my left. Eleadora stands between them.

Juniper has the honor of saying the words of the incantation. "Daisy Jane Ann Suzuki, we free your name from the Realm of Faerie and gift it to the wind. No whisper, no word shall bind you until gales no longer stir the seas and breezes no longer shake the leaves of the Earth's trees."

Slowly, the warm hum of magic spreads up my arms and onto the rest of my body, making me feel lighter than I've felt in forever. It's like the curse is a weight being lifted off my shoulders.

Though I have to admit, once it all fades away, nothing feels all that different.

"How am I supposed to know if it worked?" I ask as the aunts drop my hands.

Eleadora points to me and orders, "Daisy Jane Ann Suzuki, fetch me a lily pad from the lake."

I flinch, waiting for the signature wave of pain that comes with refusing to obey an order, but it never comes. There's nothing but the cool mountain breeze.

"You know, Eleadora, I think you can get it for yourself."

"Daisy Jane Ann Suzuki, cut a lock of my niece's hair," Vervain demands.

"Absolutely not,"

With every new silly request, I laugh a little harder as I refuse. It's like I'm high on this newfound freedom I would have taken for granted twenty years ago. My name is as much mine now as it was before I came to the Faerie Realm all those years ago. It can no longer be tugged or pulled at like some sort of weapon. It's just me. It's just who I am, just like any other human.

Who knew something as simple as owning our name makes us what we are?

The aunts join in the laughter, congratulating themselves for a job well done, but I'm distracted from the celebration as Talia cups my face in her hands and brings me close. "Daisy Jane Ann Suzuki, kiss me."

"You don't need to command me to do that," I whisper, closing the space between us. "I'll do so more than willingly."

The other asrai around us cheer and holler in celebration of any number of things: the danger being gone, finally getting to properly meet their niece, the fact that their niece has someone to love. Faeries will celebrate anything. It's one thing I can genuinely say I love about them.

Juniper pats me on the back and gives me a proud smile. "Well done, DJ."

"I was just doing my job," I insist, hooking one arm around Talia's waist. "No thanks needed."

"I'm not talking about that," Juniper says. "You opened yourself to healing, you let Talia love you. That's far harder than any job could ever be." She pulls me into a hug as well. Suddenly, I realize I have two families to adjust to, one in the Human Realm, one in Faerie.

"For that," she whispers, "well done."

Chapter Twenty-Three

THE NEXT TWENTY-FOUR hours pass in a blurring blend of rest and celebration. The aunts let us take time to sleep off the battle in one of the small houses while they go about with preparations that they refuse to let us help with. Talia wakes up a few times from nightmares but falls back asleep quickly once she curls up in my arms. I can't say I mind the setup.

At some point—I didn't get up to check the time—I tell her about Amarantha. I tell her everything I told my brother and then some about the dark place I had to crawl up from after that. She understands a bit more now, but still refuses to let go of me, both figuratively and literally. She's not the least bit scared of who I've had to be because of her mother, making her ten times more courageous than I am even now.

We don't properly get up until dusk. When we do, we're greeted by a giant party outside by the lake. Orbs of light dot the trees, tables full of food and drink span what seems to be the entire settlement, and reedy music already fills the air.

Asrai know how to party just as well as any other faeries I've met, including how long to go. The sun's first rays poke over the mountains as we decide to crash yet again. This time, however, I use what little is left of my phone battery to call Shun and ask him to pick us up the next day. I'm not sure where we're going next, especially if Talia's coming with me, but we both think it would be best if we spend some time with my family, a few weeks at least.

The aunts aren't surprised. Nor are they all that torn up at the idea of losing their niece for a while, so long as we spend some time with them up at Blue Fish Point next. It sounds nice, especially since I've never spent time in the Upper Peninsula of Michigan. Maybe Juniper and Talia can teach me some of their badass archery skills.

After that, I have no idea what we're supposed to do. I guess, for now, we'll just have to take it one day at a time.

The following morning, we say our goodbyes and head back down to Triple Lake. It's as quiet as when we first arrive with no sign of change or upset. Judging by the small talk we eavesdrop on over breakfast at the little diner by the lake, no one's noticed anything out of the ordinary over the last few days.

Our waitress recognizes us from when we first arrived and asks how our hike was. We feed her some vague comments about how beautiful the mountains are, how well the national park takes care of the trails, and so on. As she shakes her head and pours me another cup of coffee, she mentions how dangerous it is for two young girls to be out and about on their own. Talia and I exchange a look as she heads back toward the kitchen.

After that, we head out to the lake to wait for Shun. I haven't bothered to check what day it is, but I'm assuming it's in the middle of the week because there isn't a soul in sight. Every once in a while, someone will stop to get gas, but the trails and lakeside are pretty much abandoned. There's nothing but the chilly mountain breeze, the lap of the lake, and the shifting shadows from the giant puffy clouds from above.

Not that I'm complaining.

"Have you thought any more on where you want to go after we spend time with our families?" Talia asks, sitting beside me as I stretch out on the bank of the lake.

"Not really," I sigh in response. "I thought I'd go back to working at Iver's club, maybe enroll in some college classes, but if we're going to be on the move for the foreseeable future, that might not be the best idea."

"Guess you got that raise for nothing," Talia teases, poking me in the ribs.

"Eh, I wouldn't say it was for nothing," I reply, catching her hand and placing a kiss on the back. "It certainly made things more complicated, though. Now I've got my feet firmly planted in both Faerie and the Human Realm, probably more so than before."

"That might prove to be a good thing," Talia says. "Especially if Lyle turns out to be right."

"You actually think he was *right* about something?" I exclaim, opening my eyes and studying Talia's expression. Please tell me she hasn't been bewitched again.

"My mother was clearly afraid of something coming for Faerie, probably these Fomorian creatures. Who's to say they were wrong but went about protecting the realm the wrong way?"

"Uh, the fact that Mab was batshit insane?" I suggest.

"Not at first," Talia argues. "If all the accounts I've collected are true, Mab was perfectly in her right mind when she first took over the two courts. It was her role tying the world and the Other World together that wore down her mind. Both Lyle and Shaylee can agree on that, and they have very conflicting images of my mother."

"So, what are you suggesting?" I ask, propping myself up on my elbows, "We go Fomorian hunting? See if there is really something lurking, waiting to attack the Faerie Realm?"

A heart-stopping grin spreads across Talia's face. "I hadn't thought to call it Fomorian hunting, but that's exactly what I want to do. Besides, that way we get to see what the realm's like in the rest of the country and possibly get the courts a few allies."

"And we would want to do that...why? Both courts want to kill you."

"Making friends for them sounds like a good way to help them get over that, don't you think?" Talia says. "Besides, even if I don't really want to visit the court, it would be nice to be on better terms with my aunt and cousin."

I think it over for a moment. Talia's plan sounds like a good way to get into a lot of trouble, but I think it's pretty well established that trouble's not something I'm good at avoiding anyhow. And I can't blame her for wanting to be closer to Titania and Shaylee. Her aunts are great and clearly will always come first, but the queens are family too.

Talia leans forward, setting one hand on my other side so that she leans over me. "Monster hunting sounds like the perfect job for a strong faerie knight such as yourself, doesn't it?"

My heart hammers in my chest thanks to the way she looks at me through her lashes. With a smirk of my own, I tuck a lock of her hair behind her ear.

"I suppose someone has to protect the last faerie princess that the realm knows of. Especially if she plans on running around the Human Realm."

"My thoughts exactly." Talia chuckles, closing the space between us.

A shiver runs through my body like the chilly breezes coming down the mountains, yet her kiss is like a flame after a day spent in the bitter cold. As she leans into me, I wonder how long it'll take before I'm on fire.

"Someone could see us," I whisper between kisses.

"So, I'll bewitch them to forget," Talia mutters against my mouth. "Or I'll turn them into a frog."

I can't help but laugh, ruining the moment. "Very romantic."

"You can pick what I turn them into then," Talia replies, sneaking in a few more kisses. "Better?"

Before I can answer, my phone rings. It's Shun.

"Hey, sis. I'm about half an hour out. You two ready to go?"

"Yeah. We'll wait at that gas station for *you—*"

I flinch and wiggle away from Talia as she kisses my neck.

"You okay?" Shun asks.

"I just tripped is all," I answer. "See you in a bit." As I hang up, I give Talia a dirty look, but she just giggles as if she's done nothing wrong. "Why do you always have to do that?"

"It's not my fault you have such an obvious weak spot," she teases. "What did your brother say?"

"We've got about thirty minutes until he gets here."

"Hmm, I wonder what we could possibly do for thirty minutes," Talia says, inching closer.

"Me too," I reply.

I think I'm already getting used to this.

Thirty minutes later when Shun shows up, he flips out a bit when he spots that Talia and I are holding hands. "I freaking knew it," he exclaims as we get into the car. "You're sure a terrible liar, DJ."

"I am not," I argue as he makes a U-turn to get back on the road. "Mom and Dad thought I was straight until the day I actually opened my mouth. I'm a terrific liar."

My brother scoffs. "Our parents didn't realize I almost failed freshman English until I was a senior. They're not hard to dupe. Literally everyone else at Red Well High knew you were bi."

"They did not."

"Did too. Want me to call them up?"

We bicker a bit more, much to Talia's amusement, and then we give him an edited version of what happened in the last few days. He seems to buy it well enough and is excited for our plan to stay around for a few weeks. We end the story with our plan to go see the aunts in Blue Fish Point. Newly rebuilt relationship or not, there are just some things my family doesn't need to know, mostly for their sake. If Talia, and by extent, Lyle and Mab, were right, there's something coming for Faerie. I don't want my family involved.

Talia and I won't be so lucky, but as long as we stick together, we'll be okay. We've got something resembling a plan that we've got time to work out, plus we've got each other.

Besides, I know now that I'm a faerie knight. Always have been, probably always will be. And if I'm brave enough to face love, I'm brave enough to face anything.

About the Author

Tay grew up reading too many fairy tales and watching too many movies, which is probably why she writes fantasy now. When she's not at her day job or writing, she can be found taking spontaneous drives to new places and drinking way too much coffee. Her first book, *Portraits of a Faerie Queen*, is available from NineStar Press.

Email: author.tay.laroi@gmail.com

Facebook: www.facebook.com/taylaroi

Twitter: @TayLaroi

Website: www.taylaroi.wordpress.com

Other books by this author

The Faerie Court Chronicles

Portraits of a Faerie Queen

"Smile Like You Mean It" within *Into the Mystic, Volume One*

Also Available from NineStar Press

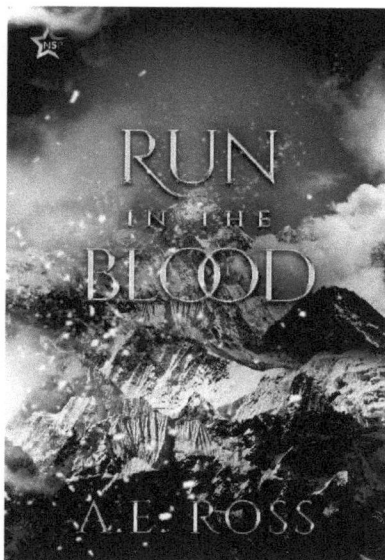

Connect with NineStar Press

www.ninestarpress.com

www.facebook.com/ninestarpress

www.facebook.com/groups/NineStarNiche

www.twitter.com/ninestarpress

www.tumblr.com/blog/ninestarpress

Lightning Source UK Ltd.
Milton Keynes UK
UKHW011445061221
395184UK00001B/85